> ## "How fair is it to use sex to get me on your side?"

Elise bristled at Dylan. "How dare you? I never *use* sex! I kiss someone when I have strong feelings for that person—" She stopped, realizing she'd been trapped.

Dylan smiled smugly. "So you do like me a little, eh, Doc?" he concluded. "In fact, even if I were the best-looking, sexiest guy in the world, you wouldn't let me get anywhere near you—you wouldn't let me kiss you like I just did—unless you genuinely liked me as a person."

Elise glared at him, speechless.

"What's the matter, Doc? Is the truth hard to swallow? Are you ready to cry uncle?"

"Just because you have a few good qualities doesn't make up for everything you've done to hurt me and lots of other women, McAllister!" stormed Elise, infuriated by the cocky grin on Dylan's face.

"So what are you going to do tomorrow, Doc, to try to make me miserable enough to confess and forsake my evil-lawyer ways?" he demanded, laughing. "I've already given an enema to a horse, nearly broken my back lifting a fat poodle and stood helplessly by while you emasculated a great male specimen of a dog. What else could you possibly do to me?"

Dear Reader,

Have you ever faced a New Year's Eve without a date? If you have, you'll understand why Elise and her friend Dana decide the best way to get a date is to *buy* a guy! But with the studly "New Year's Bachelors," these two women get more than they bargained for!

We hope you didn't miss the companion novel to this one, last month's *Dana and the Calendar Man* by Lisa Bingham. If you did, and want to catch up on Dana's adventures, you can order books from our distribution center:

Harlequin Distribution Center
3010 Walden Avenue
Depew, NY 14043

Happy Reading,

Debra Matteucci
Senior Editor and Editorial Coordinator
Harlequin
300 E. 42nd St.
New York, NY 10017

Emily Dalton

ELISE & THE HOTSHOT LAWYER

Harlequin Books

TORONTO • NEW YORK • LONDON
AMSTERDAM • PARIS • SYDNEY • HAMBURG
STOCKHOLM • ATHENS • TOKYO • MILAN
MADRID • WARSAW • BUDAPEST • AUCKLAND

Dedicated to Scott Barden, Doctor of Veterinary Medicine, and his wife, Cindy, Animal Health Technician, at the Colborne Street Pet Hospital in Orillia, Ontario, Canada.

Thanks for answering all my vet questions, guys! And thanks for making my tour of Scotland twice as nice because I met and made friends with you. God Bless.

ISBN 0-373-16666-4

ELISE & THE HOTSHOT LAWYER

Copyright © 1997 by Danice Jo Allen.

Printed in U.S.A.

Chapter One

Dylan McAllister was the curse of all women trying to keep body and soul together after a divorce. So, in Elise's hard-learned opinion, he had no business standing on the stage at a charity-sponsored Celebrity Bachelor Auction, looking for all the world as if he considered himself God's gift to women.

How dare he? she fumed as she clasped her hands tightly together to keep them from trembling. After all he'd put her through…!

But the rest of the roomful of eager women apparently didn't share Elise's unfavorable opinion of Salt Lake's hottest attorney-at-law. The moment he'd strutted onto the raised platform behind the emcee's podium, gasps, giggles and excited whispers had rolled over the crowd like a giant tidal wave. Obviously none of these women had been mentally and financially pulverized by McAllister's brilliant command of the law.

In a painful divorce hearing, he was definitely the wrong man to have on the opposing side. But if you were a woman, he was always on the opposing side, because in divorce court he only represented men. The buzz in the circles of divorced women comparing war stories was that McAllister—a divorced man himself—believed the male sex historically got a bum rap in court, and he was out to change history. If Elise's crippling settlement was any indication, he was doing exactly that.

"Five hundred dollars!" shouted a petite blonde in blue sequins…and the bidding had begun.

"Did I hear right?" asked Elise's friend Dana, throwing her a keen look. "Did they just introduce that store-window stud as Dylan McAllister, your ex-husband's lawyer?"

"Yes," Elise rasped, her throat gone suddenly dry and tight. "It's McAllister, all right. But I'm surprised to see him walking instead of slithering. He's unique—a snake with feet."

"I can't believe that gorgeous hunk of a man is the same guy who raked you over the coals last spring," Dana murmured wryly. "I pictured him with horns and a pointed goatee."

"He's gorgeous, all right," Elise agreed with a sigh. "But killer looks just give men like him an extra edge in their chosen profession."

Yes, Dylan McAllister had looked just as good in the harsh fluorescent glare of the courtroom as he did now in the mellow, more flattering lights of the hotel's large ballroom. And since she and Dana had front-row seats at a small round table not three feet from the stage, Elise could see Counselor McAllister quite clearly.

He was approximately six feet two inches of lean, muscular male, from his squared, tailored shoulders in a Wall Street wonder of a jacket, all the way down his slim, razor-pleated slacks to his Gucci loafers with mandatory tassel. He had dark hair swept back from his forehead, wicked eyebrows, almond-shaped eyes as blue as a high-mountain lake, chiseled cheekbones and a mouth to die for....

Wasted. All wasted on a hotshot lawyer bent on revenge against the opposite sex...probably the result of his own disastrous foray into divorce court. Where was the justice?

"Seven hundred fifty dollars!" screeched a voluptuous brunette.

The amounts of money belted out by starry-eyed females when McAllister appeared onstage had begun several hundred dollars above the usual starting bid. If they only knew he was a piranha disguised as a prince!

"You ought to buy him, Elise," advised Dana with a speculative glint in her eye.

"What for? He's already cost me enough money," Elise replied grimly. "Besides, Dottie made it quite clear that she was bequeathing us each a thousand dollars to spend for pleasure and amusement. She said we were not to use it for paying bills or for anything similarly aggravating. In case you hadn't noticed, Dylan McAllister aggravates the heck out of me."

"The point is," Dana explained patiently, "this would be a great opportunity for you to aggravate *him.* You know the deal—you donate your money to the Make a Wish Foundation to fund a terminally ill child's fantasy-come-true, and in return you get up to a week's worth of servitude from your favorite bachelor."

"But the idea is to take advantage of his specific expertise," Elise argued doubtfully. "What would I do with McAllister for a week? Boiling him in oil would only take a few minutes. I'm glad you got *your* man, Dana. Maybe by showing up with Sean O'Malley at your aunts' annual birthday ball at the retirement center, they'll quit lining you up with every Tom, Dick and Harry that comes their way. But a fireman moonlighting as a calendar model isn't exactly the type of guy I've always pictured you with."

"You're right, Elise, he's not my type. But the aunts don't know that. All he has to do is look good and look smitten. I'm even willing to pay the guy extra to convince my aunts that he and I are an item. Eliminating the problem of finding stray men on my doorstep every other week is worth any amount of money. Besides, this is my chance to finally interview the elusive Sean O'Malley."

"Sounds like a plan," agreed Elise.

"Your money can buy you the same kind of peace of mind, Elise. Buy McAllister and teach him a lesson. Show him how hard he's made your life since he took you to the cleaners. This is your golden opportunity!"

"Nine hundred dollars!" screamed the blonde in sequins, obviously trying to outbid the busty brunette.

"You know I'm right," Dana said with an I-dare-ya smile and a nudge of her elbow. "But if you don't get into the bidding soon, someone else is going to walk off with the prize."

Elise looked at her friend's expectant face. Dana was a beautiful woman—smart, ambitious and funny—but she'd never married. Elise only wished *she'd* shown the same restraint. They'd been getting together every December 31 for several years, having lunch, then separating for New Year's Eve celebrations with their current significant others. This year neither of them had a date…much less a significant other.

Elise would never forget the fun four years she'd shared living quarters with Dana while they'd both attended the University of Utah. Coming together quite coincidentally, they'd answered an ad specifically aimed at female college students. Offering spacious rooms in a charming bungalow in the Avenues, the ad also promised a housemother thrown in to cook and clean.

It had sounded perfect to Elise, and that's the way it turned out. A bond was forged between her and Dana that would last a lifetime. Even Dottie, their housemother, grew as dear to Elise as an aunt or a foster mother. Then Dottie surprised and saddened them by dying just before Christmas, disabusing them of the notion that she was as immortal as the Wasatch Mountains that surrounded the Great Salt Lake Valley.

She'd surprised them again by leaving her favorite dorm daughters one thousand dollars each…with conditions. The conditions were to spend the money entirely on themselves and for something that would give them pleasure. In short, mad money. Elise didn't have a clue how she was going to spend her share of the loot. She had so many practical things she could spend it on, it was tempting to ignore Dottie's conditions and hope she'd understand.

After discovering that neither of them had dates for the evening, Dana had slapped the tickets to the Celebrity Bachelor Auction on the table in front of them as they ate a catered lunch at her downtown apartment. Dottie had purchased the tickets weeks ago as a Christmas present for the girls—a typical Dottie ploy to spice up their dull lives.

"Dottie wouldn't want us to sit around and sulk," Dana had said emphatically. "It'll be a kick just watching the auction, but if we get a hankering for one of the bachelors, we could use Dottie's money to pay for him. That way, we'd be honoring Dottie's wishes and putting the money toward a worthwhile cause at the same time!"

Her argument was persuasive and seemed to strike a responsive chord in Elise. Two hours and four department stores later, they returned to Dana's apartment and decked themselves out in black silk, chiffon and beads. Then, dressed in new duds that sparkled like the star-studded sky above them and bubbling over with nervous excitement, they'd headed for the auction.

Elise had never expected Dylan McAllister to be one of the bachelors up for bid. And now Dana—her best friend in the whole world—was urging her to throw good money after bad, so to speak, and calling that courtroom Blackbeard a "prize."

He was a prize, all right, she thought to herself. A prize prima donna.

"Twelve hundred dollars!" bellowed a new bidder in the back, apparently caught up in the frenzy of the moment. The crowd responded to the three-hundred-dollar jump in bidding with a collective ooh! The emcee's gavel hovered over the podium.

"I pity the poor woman who gets him," said Elise, watching the "prize" turn a perfect swivel in the middle of the stage, managing to pull off with aplomb what made some of the men look self-conscious or even a little effeminate. But not Dylan McAllister.

No-siree-bob. He worked the crowd like royalty, holding his head like a king and mesmerizing the masses with a small tilt of a smug smile. And he dripped masculinity like summer rain off a hot tin roof.

Elise took it all in stride, offsetting her unwelcome stirrings of attraction with an anger that had been festering since last spring. She'd almost lost her veterinary practice because of this man. What would have been a simple and essentially amicable divorce was complicated by her husband's sudden reversal of attitude after he'd met Dylan McAllister.

Ted hadn't worked more than three months total in the two years they were married, yet he'd walked away with half of Elise's assets—assets that were far from liquid. She couldn't even afford hired help at the clinic anymore, not till she paid off her loan at the bank…the loan she'd had to take out in order to give her ex-husband what amounted to half equity in her veterinary business.

But she would have left things alone, gone home without taking Dana up on her daring suggestion, if Dylan McAllister hadn't done the unthinkable, the unpardonable. As he skirted the edge of the stage, flashing sexy glances over the adoring crowd, McAllister's eyes locked with Elise's. Her heart started beating like crazy, and an invisible finger traced a ticklish path up her spine. He'd remember her. She knew he'd remember her and there would be a stunned look on his face, an embarrassed acknowledgment of guilt written all over those arresting features.

Their gazes held for a long moment, but there was no trace of guilt on his face…or of recognition, either. Elise's temper flared like a dry twig put to flame.

After all he'd done to her, he didn't even remember her! Perhaps mistaking the kindling of fury in her eyes for a flirtatious gleam, he had the nerve to upgrade his smug smile to an all-out grin...then he winked.

The wink was the last straw. For divorced women everywhere—heck, just for the principle of it—Elise had no choice but to serve Dylan McAllister his summons to the court of comeuppance!

She pushed her chair back with a cringe-making scrape of wood against wood and sprang to her feet. Her eyes ablaze, her dark, shoulder-length hair flung back with an impatient hand, she faced the emcee. "Two thousand dollars," she said in a voice of ominous calm.

There were three beats of silence as the crowd absorbed the shock of such an unexpected, and unbeatable, bid. Then, slamming her borrowed auctioneer's gavel against the podium, the emcee smiled broadly and shouted, "Sold!"

THERE WAS A RECEPTION planned for after the auction, a chance for the bachelors to meet the women entitled to order them around from nine to five for however many days they'd agreed to make themselves available, but Dylan wasn't staying for it. He had other plans—namely a date. A cool-looking, Hitchcock-type blonde, but with a much warmer disposition, was waiting for him at Nino's.

He'd done his duty by drumming up a couple thousand bucks for the Make a Wish Foundation—and he was very glad he had—but the rest of the night was his. He'd been working hard lately and he wanted to start the new year on a slightly more relaxed note.

Backstage, amid the murmurs of bachelors coming and going, he politely shouldered his way through the crowd to the coatrack. As he searched for his coat among the thirty or so hanging in a neat row, he couldn't help but think for the umpteenth time that he wouldn't have to work so hard if his ex-wife didn't require a king's ransom worth of alimony to "make ends meet" each month.

Hell, he'd seen the diamonds dripping off her fingers when they'd accidentally run into each other a week ago. She didn't look as though she'd been reduced to cutting coupons or shopping for bargains at MacFrugals. In fact, it looked as if she was enjoying her alimony as well as some other poor schnook's hard-earned money, too. He knew she didn't work for a living.

Dylan forced thoughts of his ex-wife to the dustiest corner of his mind and concentrated on the evening ahead. He found his coat and shrugged into it. Buttoning up against the teen-degree weather outside, he noticed Sally Decker, the auction coordinator, headed his way. He sighed. She'd probably try to talk him into staying for the reception, and he had no intention of capitulating.

Giving in under pressure was not his style. He didn't do it in the courtroom, he didn't do in the world outside the legal chambers he frequented and tonight...well, tonight was a closed case. He'd be a fool to keep a good-looking blonde like Carol waiting too long at the bar at a hot spot like Nino's.

"Mr. McAllister, you aren't leaving, are you?"

"I have to, Sally," he told her, smiling apologetically at the young woman. "I'm expected elsewhere, and it's impolite to keep a lady waiting, you know."

Sally's brow wrinkled with concern. "But I thought you understood that it was customary to stick around to meet the woman you've been auctioned off to."

"No one told me it was mandatory." He let that point sink in, sure he'd be able to avoid the dreaded sentence of an awkward hour of cocktail chitchat by mentioning this technicality. "Is it?"

"Well, no, but—"

"She'll be seeing plenty of me in the next few days, so I don't think she'll be miffed if I skip the reception. In fact, I'm sure she'll understand. After all, it is New Year's Eve."

Sally looked doubtful. "I *hope* she understands."

Dylan smiled reassuringly and tugged on a pair of leather gloves he'd pulled from his pocket. "If she's a reasonable woman, she will." Privately he didn't think such a woman existed—at least not for the long haul. Reason always seemed to be the first thing to disappear into thin air when disagreements arose between couples. He was a cynic, he knew. But how could he be otherwise in his line of work? Seventy-five percent of his workload was divorce cases.

"If you really won't stay, then I'd better give you the name and phone number of the woman who bought you. You'll have to make arrangements about where to report for duty on January 2."

Dylan glanced, frowning, at his watch, then folded his arms across his chest and waited while Sally wrote the information down on a sheet of paper pinned to her clipboard. While he waited, he thought about the woman who had made the surprising two-thousand-dollar bid, which was so much higher than the preceding offers for his services.

The stage lights glaring in his eyes, and the contrasting darkness as he'd tried to look past them, had made it impossible to see the audience clearly. But the woman who bought him had been seated in the front, and he'd managed to make eye contact with her. Her black dress had melted into the shadows, keeping her curves—or the lack of them—a secret. A fuzzy oval of a face, a halo of dark hair and eyes that flashed in the shadows were all he could really distinguish.

His brow furrowed as he thought about those eyes and that look she'd given him. At first he had assumed she was flirting with him, but the grim way she'd stated her bid didn't jibe with the usual coy approach of a woman on the prowl. Perhaps she'd bought him because she had a legitimate need for his legal expertise, and not because she liked what she saw as he'd paraded up and down the stage like a peacock. They'd told him to camp it up, and even though he'd felt damn foolish doing it, he had. Anything to line the pockets of his favorite charity.

Dylan grimaced. He was sure that many of the women who took part in the auction were hoping for a romance to develop from close association with their chosen bachelor over the next week, and maybe some of them would get it. But Dylan intended to stick to the rules. Even if his buyer was a looker— which he tended to think she was, judging solely by his first hazy impression of her—he was only going to put his professional expertise at her disposal, or whatever other service he could render as an able-bodied male, but nothing of an intimate nature.

Even his little sister, Beth, who had died of leukemia when she was just ten, wouldn't expect him to prostitute himself in the name of a children's charity.

Taking a week off work was sacrifice enough at this point in his busy career, though he had to admit he didn't think the duties he'd be assigned would be too arduous. The woman probably just wanted him to advise her on a civil suit or the writing up of a will. Things he could do in his sleep. Lord help her if she needed divorce advice....

"Here you go," said Sally, handing Dylan the paper and giving him a reproachful pout that was a half grin. "It's a shame you can't stay."

Dylan repeated his apologetic smile, then looked down at the paper. The name Elise Allen sounded vaguely familiar.... He glanced at the phone number and said, "This isn't a local number. Where does she live?"

"I don't know for sure, but I think that's a number in Alpine. I have a friend who used to live there."

Dylan had a client who used to live there, too, but he couldn't remember the guy's name. Alpine was a small town about a half hour's drive south of Salt Lake. The setting was rural, a bedroom community nestled in the mouth of a canyon and surrounded by farmland and horse ranches. He frowned, suddenly realizing that he'd have to drive out there every morning and drive back to his apartment in the city every evening at rush hour.

In good weather that wasn't too great a hassle, especially when you considered that you were doing it for a good cause. But if one of Salt Lake's famous snowstorms hit the valley in the next week, trying to get around the notoriously icy point of the mountain as you drove north into the city would be more than a hassle. It would be downright treacherous. He might even have to find lodgings overnight in Alpine.

Dylan suddenly remembered the time, stashed the paper in his pocket, said goodbye to Sally and headed for the door. Outside, under the canopy of the Red Lion Hotel—where the auction was taking place—the uniformed doorman clapped his gloved hands together against the cold.

"I need a taxi," Dylan told him, noticing there weren't any waiting at the curb.

"It'll take a while, sir," replied the doorman. "There's a big do at Symphony Hall tonight, and it's just getting out."

Dylan gave a huff of exasperation, his breath visible in the chill air. He always used taxis in town; it was easier than trying to park, and there were usually plenty of cabs around. But apparently not tonight.

Just then, a cab pulled up to the curb, and Dylan was in the midst of thanking his lucky stars when the doorman interrupted. "There's a lady ahead of you, sir. She's waiting inside."

As the doorman went inside the hotel lobby to fetch the lady, Dylan got an idea. He headed for the cab, opened the back door and slid across the plastic-covered seat.

"Where to?" asked the driver, flipping on his meter.

"I'm waiting for another passenger," Dylan told him.

"All right, fella, but the meter's running," the cabbie warned him.

Dylan tapped his fingers against his knee while he waited for his traveling companion to show up. If she balked at the notion of sharing a cab with a stranger, he'd have to try out some of that stage charm he'd used inside.

The door opened and the doorman's head appeared. "Sir," he began diffidently, "I thought you understood—"

Dylan smiled. "Don't worry, I'm not trying to steal the cab. I just want to share...if the lady is willing."

The doorman straightened and seemed to turn and defer to the woman. Dylan craned his neck to see the mystery woman, but with such meager light coming from the open door, he could only make out the faint outline of a slim female shape. And having to hold his head at such a disadvantaged angle, he only saw her from the neck down. She was dressed in a dark coat that fell to midcalf, and below the hem was a pair of trim legs, neat ankles and spiky high heels. Such obvious attributes in a woman always stirred Dylan's interest.

"The lady is a little peeved by the whimsy of fate," came a wry, feminine voice out of the darkness. "But she is still willing to share the cab...with Mr. McAllister."

Now Dylan was more than interested; he was intrigued and even a little aroused...by the sexy pitch of her voice, as well as her words. Dylan watched with pure male curiosity as the woman bent her head and angled her body "just so" to preserve her modesty while climbing into the vehicle. Despite her efforts, her long coat separated in the front, and a good deal of leg was revealed.

By the time he'd wrenched his gaze away from smooth calves and shapely knees, Dylan caught only a glimpse of the woman's profile behind a cloud of dark, shoulder-length hair before she shut the door and the light went out.

"Where to?" asked the driver.

Dylan turned to the woman, squinting in the dark to try to see her. "You first, Ms...? I'm afraid you have an advantage over me. You know me, but I don't know you."

"Oh, you know me, all right," said the woman dryly, "but you seem to have a very short memory." Then she leaned forward and directed the cabbie to go to the Eagle's Gate Apartments.

Dylan leaned back, bent his right leg and pulled it slightly up on the seat. Turned sideways, he was now in a position where he could stare as much as he pleased. The streetlights cast flickers of illumination into the interior of the cab, but she looked straight ahead, denying his eagerness to see her face and remember where he'd seen her before.

"When did I meet you?"

"The first or the last time?"

He shrugged, smiled, enjoyed the game. "The last time."

"About twenty minutes ago."

He gave an uncertain chuckle. "At the auction? But twenty minutes ago I was up on the—" Then it hit him. "Ah," he said. "You're the woman who made that generous bid of two thousand dollars. You have to forgive me for not recognizing you right away. The lights were in my eyes on the stage, and in this dark cab a guy would be lucky to recognize his own mother. Your name is Elise...right?"

"Yes. Elise Allen."

Now she turned. In the sporadic glow of the streetlights he could see her eyes trained on his, could feel them boring into him as if she expected some kind of reaction.

"Let me guess," he began in a beleaguered tone. "I'm supposed to know that name."

She turned to face forward again and didn't reply. He felt her silent rebuke. He pushed on, attempting to be conciliatory. "I'm sorry I don't remember you, and I'm sorry I didn't stick around for the reception, but—" Then it occurred to him that she hadn't stuck around, either. "Did you run out on me for the same reason I ran out on you? Do you have a date?"

She gave a rueful chuckle. He liked the sound of her laughter as much as he liked the faint scent of her slightly spicy perfume. Shalimar? he wondered. "Actually, after I pick up my car at my friend's apartment, I have to drive all the way home to Alpine tonight. By now George is sure to be missing me, and if he thinks I've abandoned him, he ransacks my underwear drawer, drinks all the Dr Pepper in the fridge and erases the programming in my VCR that keeps the digital time." She sighed. "I hate it when it flashes twelve o'clock over and over again."

Dylan was appalled. "Are you talking about your husband?"

"No, George is boarding at my house for a week. My neighbor, Jan, is keeping him company, but even with supervision he gets into mischief."

"Why don't you throw him out?"

"He's a chimp."

"A *chump?*"

She laughed. "No. A chimpan*zee.*"

"*What?*"

"Normally I wouldn't be so worried—I mean, after all, I can refold my underwear, buy the chimp more of his favorite pop and figure out *again* how to program the VCR clock—but I had a break-in last week and I wouldn't want Jan or George involved in anything dangerous. I have a security system, but I had to turn it off. It's not that I have anything especially valuable, mind you, but sometimes people get it into their heads to steal an animal for some awful prank."

"Okay, I'll bite," said Dylan, wondering where all this was leading. "Why did you have to turn off your security system?"

"It's activated by certain sounds, one of which is breaking glass…like a window being smashed. My parrot, Geraldo, has learned to imitate the sound of glass breaking."

"You're kidding."

"I wish I were. I've had the police at my house three times in the past month."

Dylan had to state the obvious. "It sounds like you live in a zoo."

"Close. I run a veterinary clinic."

This information seemed to stir a distant memory but offered nothing solid enough to help him remember where he'd met this woman before. "So, you're a vet," he mused aloud, wondering how he could have ever had anything to do with a vet. He didn't have a pet. Pets were like kids, requiring constant attention, and he was seldom home. He wouldn't mind a pet…or even a kid, for that matter. He liked kids; he just didn't like the idea of marriage.

"Yes…a vet without a security system," she continued. "I was saving up for a new parrot-proof model, but tonight I blew my whole nest egg on you."

"Why?" he asked, somehow knowing he wouldn't like the answer. A premonitory chill inched up his spine.

She turned toward him again. A flash of light revealed a deadpan expression on her face. "Because of what we used to mean to each other," she said.

Dylan swallowed hard. She was an old lover? How could that be? He'd remember this one, if not for her legs and sexy voice, at least for her menagerie of patients. But if they'd been an item, and he'd forgotten her, she'd be furious.... A scene from the movie *Fatal Attraction* flashed through his mind: the image of a bunny bubbling in a pot on the back burner.

Dylan was no longer intrigued or amused, and he sure as hell wasn't aroused. Deathly serious, he said, "You'd better tell me who you are, Elise."

The cab pulled in in front of the Eagle's Gate Apartments. The driver, who had undoubtedly been listening to their conversation the whole time, didn't interrupt the tension by asking for his fare. He simply sat there, his head cocked to the side, his ear none too subtly trained in their direction.

The mystery woman, Elise Allen, was bathed in light now from the bright entryway of the posh highrise apartment complex. Just as he'd expected, she was a looker, all right. She had dark hair with mahogany highlights that fell to her shoulders in soft waves. Her eyes were a clear, true green. She had lovely lips, a model-straight nose and a fair complexion with—if he wasn't mistaken—a faint sprinkling of freckles over the ridges of her cheekbones. And somehow she managed to look cool as a cucumber and mad as hell at the same time.

"I'm one of your victims, Dylan McAllister," she said evenly.

The cabbie gave a betraying shake of the head, then sat stone-still, listening again.

Dylan recognized a situation that definitely required the kid-glove treatment. Soothingly, tactfully, he began, "If you and I were once...er...involved, Elise, and I've somehow managed to forget our relationship—"

"Don't be ridiculous, McAllister. You and I were never—and could never be—'involved,'" she said scornfully. "I guess I'm just going to have to spell it out for you."

"Please do," he said earnestly.

"You were my husband's lawyer in our divorce last March. Ted Muldare. He's probably living quite comfortably on the money I had to beg, borrow and steal to get him out of my life permanently. Remember now?"

He remembered, all right. But that casually dressed woman, with her hair pulled back in a ponytail and an angry expression plastered on her face throughout the divorce proceedings, only remotely resembled the glamorous female sitting beside him now in the cab. By his reckoning, she didn't look as though she'd been suffering because of the divorce settlement....

Dylan sighed. He would have much preferred Elise Allen to have been an ex-lover. Trapped inside a small enclosure with a woman scorned was bound to be better than facing off with a woman deprived of funds. Nothing used to make his wife behave more irrationally than charge-card withdrawal.

He asked, "Did you buy me with revenge in mind?"

"I'm not out for revenge, McAllister, but I do plan to help you see that you're waging an unfair war against women in the divorce courts. In my case you gleefully manipulated the laws so that my husband, who never lifted a finger to help me, got half of everything I worked hard for."

"Sounds like revenge to me, but I'll take it like a man," he said with a desperate attempt at humor. "So tell me, Elise, what sort of torture have you got planned for me for the next week?" He raised a brow. "Does it involve chains and whips, etcetera?"

"You should be so lucky," she told him, her green eyes gleaming. "No, I've got something far worse in mind." Her smile was devious. "You're going to be my veterinary assistant."

Dylan considered this for a moment, then said, "That doesn't sound so bad."

Elise's smile broadened, became more devilish. More alluring...damn it. "We'll see," she said, her voice rich with promise.

Chapter Two

Dylan took great pleasure in the fact that as crowded lanes of traffic crawled at a snail's pace into the city, he was driving in the opposite direction. It had snowed the night before, coating the valley floor in a fresh blanket of white and dumping in the mountains another foot of the stuff skiers live for.

This morning, though, the roads were plowed and easy to navigate. He just hoped the weather would hold up for the return trip home.

Dylan popped in a Miami Sound Machine CD, then settled back in the seat of his BMW with a satisfied smile. Thank goodness he still made enough money after alimony payments to enjoy some of life's little pleasures...which was a hell of a lot more than his brother Craig had gotten after *his* divorce. Sure, he'd bought the car used and he had to watch for sale ads to buy the name-brand clothes he enjoyed wearing, but a guy had to cut corners somewhere.

As for Elise Allen, despite her attempts to intimidate him, he wasn't the least bit worried about the next few days. If anything, he'd be bored stiff. But the up side was that he'd catch up on his rest and be raring to go when he got back to the office. Business was booming these days. So many divorces…so little time!

Off the freeway now and nearing Alpine, Dylan enjoyed the view of Mount Timpanogos, the "princess" mountain, which loomed over the tiny town. There was a tragic legend about the mountain—a star-crossed love story, of course—and the majestic peaks of Timpanogos were said to resemble the figure of an Indian princess laid out for burial.

He couldn't remember the details of the story, but that didn't matter, because he wasn't the sentimental type anyway. And for the life of him, he'd never been able to make out the shape of an Indian princess in the terrain of such a roughly serrated mountaintop. Women's curves were soft, not hard as rocks. Although, he admitted to himself ruefully, sometimes their hearts resembled cold granite.

Alpine was a charming little town. Even without the directions Elise had given him, it would have been hard to lose his way. Her house was on Main Street, a block down from City Hall, with its quaint bell tower and adjoining fire station, and opposite the folksy-looking grocery store and a large sign in front of a half-erected building announcing the arrival of a new dentist to the area.

Dylan parked his car at the curb and walked toward Elise's house. It was big and old—turn-of-the-century, he guessed—but in great shape. It was one of those half-and-half buildings—half two-story with a steep gable, and half single-story where the formal areas and the kitchen were usually located. It was a combination of wood, mottled brick and stucco painted a warm tan color, and had a huge wraparound porch.

The yard was large and deep, dotted with towering fir and cottonwood trees. Dylan stuffed his hands in the pockets of his long black wool coat and followed the curving sidewalk to the wooden steps leading to the front door. He noted that the walk had been shoveled as clean as a whistle. He grinned, picturing the chimp hard at work flinging snow over his hairy shoulders. Dylan couldn't really picture Elise, as he'd last seen her in black hose and high heels, wielding a shovel.

He rang the doorbell and waited. And waited. He rang the bell again, and this time he heard what he could only describe as unusual noises on the other side of the thick paneled door. *Monkey* noises, Dylan finally pinpointed. But there was also a soft series of grunts that seemed to be separate from the monkey noises.

Suddenly Dylan heard a scrape, like a chain being slid from a latch, and the door opened. Expecting to see Elise standing in the midst of a menagerie, his gaze dropped about two and a half feet to the solemn face of a chimp. The chimp was dressed in a yellow child-sized sweatshirt and a pair of jeans. Standing beside the chimp, making a sound like a quiet and continuous belly laugh, was a pig. A small black pig...without clothes, thank goodness. If Elise dressed up all the animals, he'd have to wonder about her.

"Hi, George," said Dylan, feeling sheepish as he addressed the animal. "Rattled any cages lately?"

The chimp bared his teeth in an unpleasant smile, hooted and did a little dance. He seemed agitated.

"Great," said Dylan under his breath. "Just what I need...an ape with an attitude. Where's Elise?"

"There you are, McAllister! You're late!"

Dylan looked up to see Elise walking quickly toward them, dressed in a white lab coat over a blue sweatshirt and jeans and pulling off a pair of rubber gloves. He noted the similarity in clothing between Elise and the ape and couldn't help saying, "You and George shop at the same outlet store?"

Elise stopped in front of him and raised a brow. "Very funny, McAllister. I just hope you've still got a sense of humor by the end of the day. I know for sure you're going to wish you'd worn something more appropriate for the kind of work you're going to be doing." While she slid her gaze in a disapproving manner over his open coat, with a nice sweater and slacks underneath, he slid his approving gaze over her.

He liked her better in a short black dress, but even in surgical white, she was still a looker. She had her hair pulled back in a ponytail, the way she'd worn it at the divorce hearing, but today he noticed how the severe hairdo showed off her long, slim neck and high cheekbones. Just as he'd suspected two nights ago in the cab, she had a charming sprinkle of freckles.

He grinned and cocked his head in the direction of the pig, still grunting quietly as it stood at Elise's feet and stared up at her. "Am I going to be mucking out the pigsty?"

"You've got a lot to learn, McAllister," Elise said dryly, "especially about animals. Rowena isn't just—"

"Rowena?" Dylan repeated, astonished. "You named that little porker *Rowena?*"

"She's not a porker," said Elise, stooping to pat the pig on the head. "I'll have you know, Rowena is quite svelte…for a pig. And as I was about to say, she's not just any old pig, raised to supply you with bacon for your brunch. Rowena is an exotic breed of animal, a miniature potbellied pig from Asia. She's highly intelligent and very affectionate."

"And she sleeps indoors like a pampered poodle, right?"

"Yes, she sleeps inside. And she uses a litter box, too, like a cat."

"No pigsties to clean, then…so what *do* I do, Doctor?" Dylan spread his hands wide and knew he looked and sounded like a first-class smart aleck. But he was determined that this female wasn't going to get under his skin or teach him a damn thing while he was under her roof. He was going to do his bit and get out.

Elise straightened, regarding him with patent dislike. "Since you couldn't haul your carcass out of the sack this morning and arrive at the agreed upon hour, McAllister, I don't have time to familiarize you with procedures, so just do as I ask, okay? I have a waiting room full of people and sick and injured animals to take care of."

Dylan looked around. "Where's your office?"

"Follow me," she said, then reached past him to relatch the front door. He was disappointed when he didn't catch a whiff of that great perfume she'd worn New Year's Eve. She took the chimp's hand and marched through a spacious dining room furnished in antiques, breezed through an old-fashioned kitchen and down a narrow hallway. The pig nearly tripped him up as both of them scrambled after her. Finally they stepped from the hallway into a small room.

If Dylan weren't so used to cloaking his true feelings in the courtroom, he'd have stood there with his chin on his chest. Except for a door that opened to the outside, the room was lined with chairs. In every chair was a person, and on every person's lap—or in their arms, or at their feet on a leash—were animals. Dogs, cats, a lizard in a glass box and a gerbil in a cage. As he entered the room, the animals reacted in various ways...hissing, meowing, growling, etc. Dylan had no idea if they were reacting to him or the chimp and the pig or the combination of all three. They weren't exactly the dream team.

"Save the slack jaw for the end of the day, Mc-Allister," Elise whispered sarcastically, then walked to the far side of the room, turned and faced her patients. She smiled, and Dylan noticed that the tension in the room lessened noticeably. The humans even smiled back.

"I'm sorry things are so crazy today, folks," said Elise, "but I'll get to each of your pets as soon as possible."

There were eager murmurs of approval. A few eyes turned Dylan's way and stared curiously.

"As you know," Elise continued, "I've been without an assistant since the divorce—"

Lord, thought Dylan, *I hope she doesn't finger me as the culprit who put her in this fix.* He wondered if there were still vigilante hangings in rural parts of the state....

"But Mr. McAllister here is going to be helping me out for the next few days. Long enough, I hope, to catch up with everything after the two days I took off for the New Year."

Now everyone turned to look at Dylan. Most of them scanned his city clothes and looked dubious.

"Don't worry," said Elise, chuckling softly. "Once I get Mr. McAllister into a lab jacket, he'll do just fine."

As he took off his coat, rolled up his sweater sleeves and shrugged into a lab jacket, Dylan was sure he'd do just fine, too. After all, how hard could it be to doctor domesticated animals?

He followed Elise into the adjoining room, where she examined and treated the animals, and was impressed with how clean and organized it was. Elise instructed him to wash his hands and handed him a pair of rubber gloves. She observed him narrowly as he pulled them on.

"You seem awfully calm and sure of yourself, McAllister," she commented.

"Why shouldn't I be calm?"

"This isn't a courtroom," she reminded him. "All that legal mumbo jumbo you use to manipulate the law to suit your purposes won't do you a bit of good here, Counselor."

He smiled blandly. "I'm ready for whatever you throw my way, Doc," he assured her.

Elise shrugged and moved to the door. She called into the waiting room, "Thanks for watching George for me, Mrs. Spencer. If he pets the kitten too hard, just scold him. He understands very well. Now, Amber, why don't you bring in Fluffy?"

Dylan leaned against the counter and watched a little girl about seven or eight enter the room carrying a large taffy-colored cat. The cat was panting and had a nervous look in her eyes.

"How's she doing, honey?" Elise asked gently.

"She's awful scared," said Amber, her own eyes wide with anxiety.

"I'll give her something to calm her. In fact, she'll probably go right to sleep," said Elise. "Can you lift her up onto the table? Mr. McAllister will help you hold her still while I give her the shot."

"What's wrong with the cat?" asked Dylan, pushing off from the counter and sauntering over.

The little girl looked up at Dylan and said, "She's been shot."

"Shot? Then why isn't she bleeding?"

"She was shot by a BB gun, McAllister," Elise explained, filling a syringe with a clear liquid. "We get a bunch of these the first few days after Christmas. Parents buy their kids BB guns, then don't teach them what or whom they shouldn't shoot. The BBs usually embed quite deeply but are almost always puncture wounds that don't bleed. Sometimes it's best just to leave them in the animal, other times it's a good idea to take them out. BB wounds can occasionally become infected."

"Can it kill the animal?" he asked.

Elise gave him a look that clearly showed her annoyance. When he stared back at her, all innocence, she inclined her head toward the little girl. Dylan felt like a dunce. He realized that he'd been insensitive toward Amber's feelings. He was doubly sure he'd said the wrong thing when Amber looked up at him and said, "She'll be all right, won't she, mister?"

As Dylan gazed down at the little girl and really looked at her for the first time, his heart gave a curious lurch. She reminded him of his little sister, Beth. It wasn't just her dark hair and big blue eyes; it was the way she seemed to be appealing for comfort—and from him, of all people. He hadn't comforted a child since…well, since Beth died.

Self-consciously at first, then with a more natural feeling, he reached over and stroked the girl's hair. "I'm sure your cat will be fine, Amber," he said, smiling. "Dr. Allen is the best vet this side of the Mississippi."

Miraculously his words seemed to reassure Amber, and she managed a small, nervous smile. But when Dylan glanced at Elise, she was staring at him as if he'd just grown another nose. He was sure the good doctor had him totally pegged as a blackguard and distrusted any little act of kindness he might perform.

They got the cat on the table, and after a bit of scuffling, with the cat's nails making a tap-dancing sound on the stainless-steel surface, the tranquilizer took effect and the cat dozed off.

"Why don't you go back to the waiting room and sit with your mom, Amber," Elise gently suggested. "Fluffy's asleep now and won't even feel it when I take the BB out."

Amber nodded solemnly and, with one last caress for her cat, walked out and shut the door behind her.

"Hold the cat, McAllister," said Elise, extracting a dangerous-looking instrument from a sterile surgical pack.

"I thought it was asleep and wouldn't feel a thing," said Dylan, nevertheless placing his hands on the cat's inert body.

"I numbed the area around the wound to make sure it doesn't feel anything, but since I only gave it a mild sedative, it could twitch or even wake up. So just do as I ask, okay?"

"Okay, Doc, you're the boss...for a week, anyway."

Elise gave him one last, sharp look before she began to probe for the BB, which was embedded in the cat's shoulder. Dylan watched with interest. He couldn't help himself; he was impressed. She was a skillful surgeon, and judging by what he'd seen so far of her rapport with the pets and their owners, she had an excellent bedside manner, too.

Now, why did that thought evoke erotic images?

Suddenly Elise surprised him by saying, without looking up from her delicate task, "You're awfully good at getting results, aren't you? Even when you have to use unsubstantiated facts." She shook her head. "Once a lawyer, always a lawyer."

"What are you talking about?"

"You told Amber I was the best vet this side of the Mississippi."

He smiled. "Well, aren't you?"

"I'm good, but I don't know if I'm *that* good."

"If you're good at something, why be shy about it?"

She glanced up at him. "I guess you're talking from experience. You're awfully good at what *you* do, aren't you, McAllister? I'm living proof of that."

Her persistence in believing him so totally in the wrong was getting to Dylan. He frowned. "Well, I have to admit you could use a regular assistant, but I find it hard to believe that the settlement left you so strapped that you can't hire help."

"Qualified help is too expensive, and amateur help isn't worth having."

"I'm an amateur, and you paid through the nose for me."

She glanced up at him and smiled archly. "Oh, I'll get my nickel's worth out of you."

Dylan doubted it. He wasn't working too hard so

far. Then suddenly the cat woke up, yowled loudly and jumped off the table before Dylan could even react. Luckily Elise had already extracted the BB, but it took Dylan ten minutes of coaxing, and two scratched knuckles, to get Fluffy off the top of the medicine chest.

Five hours and sixteen animals later, the inside of Dylan's ulcer-prone stomach felt as if it had been sandpapered. He was hungry, he was cranky, his back and shoulders ached and so did his feet. He'd assisted with distemper shots, boil lancings and stool samples, and had forced more pills down the throats of cats and dogs than he cared to count.

He'd also had his fill of sponging off the examining table with strong-smelling disinfectant, the scent of which still clung to his fingers despite the rubber gloves he'd worn and repeated hand-washings. It also made his scratched knuckles sting like the dickens. He was exhausted and he was in dire need of a breath of fresh air.

As he and Elise walked into the waiting room, where no one but the chimp and the pig awaited them, Elise looked no worse for the wear. But she, apparently, couldn't say the same for him. She eyed his sweater, snagged several times by flailing and grabbing claws and covered with cat hair, and at his slacks, which were splattered here and there with spots of varied colors Dylan had no desire to identify.

"I told you you'd regret wearing Eddie Bauer casuals to work in a vet clinic."

"I wish you'd told me as much on the phone," he groused.

She shrugged and smiled, but looked totally unrepentant. "Wash up and I'll get us some lunch," she said. "Come on. I'll show you where the bathroom is."

"She calls it lunch," Dylan grumbled under his breath, stalking behind her with the other members of the dream team. "And it's past two o'clock."

Elise directed Dylan to a small bathroom on the main floor, and after he'd combed his hair, brushed off his sweater, dabbed at the spots on his pants and washed his hands with the demented determination of Lady Macbeth in Shakespeare's tragic play, he returned to the kitchen. The delicious smell as he entered the room made his salivary glands kick into overdrive.

Seeming to sense his imminent collapse from starvation, Elise set a large, steaming bowl of homemade vegetable soup in front of him, slices of bread slathered with butter, a tall glass of milk and a substantial piece of apple pie. Sitting at a table by a bow window, Dylan ate hungrily, minding his manners but unable to force himself to pause between bites for the smallest conversational exchange.

When he was halfway through the piece of pie, his body seemed to finally signal that death by emaciation had been avoided, and he was able to sit back in his chair and notice his surroundings.

Elise was sitting at the opposite end of the table, sipping something steaming from a mug and…damn it…looking smug. George was in a high chair, neatly picking up and eating apple pieces off the tray and sipping on a can of Dr Pepper. Dylan thought he might be imagining it, but the chimp seemed to glower at him as he chewed…or maybe that was just one of George's habitual apelike expressions. Rowena was rooting her way through a dish of some kind of pellet food.

Dylan made an observation. "You're all vegetarians, aren't you?"

Elise raised a brow. "In good conscience, how could I possibly eat meat?" She smiled demurely. "Some of my best friends are animals."

"Obviously," drawled Dylan, returning to his pie. But he was distracted by movements he noticed out of the corner of his eye. He looked up, and his suspicions were confirmed when he scratched the bridge of his nose and George exactly imitated the motion.

"That monkey is imitating me!" said Dylan, throwing the chimp an accusing look and getting a toothy, taunting smile in return.

Elise laughed. "You know what they say about imitation...." she offered.

"I don't consider being mimicked by a chimp a form of flattery," Dylan objected, ever so slightly raising his voice. But George apparently objected to Dylan's tone, because he thumbed his nose at him and hooted loudly.

"Is that the only hand gesture he knows?" asked Dylan suspiciously.

"It's one I wish he hadn't learned from the children of his trainer," said Elise, seeming to try not to smile too broadly. "But he does actually know some bona fide sign language."

"He does?"

"Yes, although while he's staying with me, he doesn't get to use much of it. I only know the basics...'please,' 'thank you' and 'I love you.'"

Dylan narrowed his eyes at the chimp. "Can he answer yes or no to a question?"

"If he understands the question."

"Ask him if he likes me," suggested Dylan.

"I think we both know the answer to that already, McAllister," said Elise. "I've noticed his antipathy toward you right from the beginning." She shrugged, obviously not overly concerned. "Maybe he considers you a threat, kind of like a new male primate trying to insinuate himself into the tribe, so to speak."

"Well, tell him he's got nothing to worry about," said Dylan emphatically. "Like him, I'm only a temporary inmate at the Allen Asylum. At the strike of five, I'm out of here."

"I wonder..." Elise said casually, reaching over and lifting the edge of the kitchen curtain to look outside. "It's been snowing since eleven, and there's already ten inches out there. I caught the weather-cast on the radio while you were in the bathroom, and it's supposed to keep this up all day."

Elise watched as the blood drained out of Dylan McAllister's face. She couldn't help it; she enjoyed every gradation of color as he turned from a skier's tan to as white as a mime.

"God," he groaned. "We were so busy back there, I never once looked outside. I'll never get home tonight if this keeps up."

"I'm sure you're right," Elise replied, taking another sip of tea and peering at McAllister over the rim of her cup. She loved watching him squirm. She was enjoying this teach-a-lawyer-a-lesson scheme more than she ever imagined she would. Now that he'd worked as hard as she did—only to give half of it away to pay off her loan—McAllister couldn't even escape for a few hours of recuperation. He'd be forced to think about his evil deed all night long....

"I don't suppose Alpine has a Hilton?" asked McAllister in a resigned voice.

Elise rested her warm cup in the palm of her hand. "Not even a Motel 6."

"What about a bed and breakfast?"

Elise cocked her head toward George, who was rubbing the back of his neck…just as McAllister was doing. "To make ends meet, *I* occasionally take in boarders."

"Even a primate *without* hair on his back?"

Elise felt an unexpected shiver as an image of a shirtless McAllister flashed through her mind. She tried to ignore the hormone surge and answered glibly, "As long as the primate in question is well-behaved."

"Well, I think I can promise to behave at least as well as George. I'll leave the VCR alone, and I don't drink pop…so your Dr Pepper is safe. And here's the deal—" McAllister threw her a teasing leer "—I'll stay out of your drawers if you'll stay out of mine."

Elise felt herself blushing. "Cute, McAllister. But just to be extra safe, I'm putting you in the *attic* bedroom."

He shrugged, and she took another sip of tea before dropping the bomb. "And you'll have to share a bathroom with George."

McAllister's blue eyes narrowed, and he clenched his jaw till a muscle ticked in his cheek. "The hell I will," he said, then caught George mugging an exaggerated version of his own angry expression and getting even angrier.

"Don't worry, McAllister," said Elise with what she hoped was infuriating nonchalance. "George wasn't raised in a barn. He's been potty trained since he was a year old. He *does* tend to leave a little extra hair in the sink when he washes up, but unlike the *evolved* male, he actually enjoys cleaning up after himself. There is one thing he does that's a bit annoying, though—he sucks on the toothpaste tube."

"Is it too much to ask that I have my *own* tube?" growled McAllister.

"Not at all," said Elise. "The grocery store across the street is open till nine. You'll have time after our next shift to pick up whatever you need."

McAllister groaned.

"Don't forget to get a toothbrush while you're at it, then hide it in your room tonight."

"Don't tell me…George?"

"Yes. After I caught him scrubbing the bathroom fixtures with mine, I bought another and keep it hidden between brushings."

"Dare I ask where George sleeps at night? I'm picky about roommates."

Elise wondered about that, but tactfully refrained from voicing her doubts. "He sleeps in the spare bedroom next to mine in a large playpen with a barred wooden lid that locks with a key. As you know, George opens doors, and I don't want him pulling a Wee Willie Winkie and roaming the streets of Alpine in his jammies. I don't want him loose in the house, either."

By McAllister's expression, Elise was sure he completely shared her sentiments on this subject. Too bad he didn't share her sentiments about fair divorce settlements for both sexes. He was a brilliant lawyer— if only an adequate vet's assistant—and if he employed his considerable skill to make sure fairness was the order of the day, both parties in a divorce would get what they deserved instead of what their crafty lawyers managed to finagle.

Elise used to think McAllister's campaign to win cases for the male sex, disregarding just deserts, was because he'd been taken to the cleaners himself. But the BMW he drove and the expensive clothes he wore made her doubt that being alimony poor was the underlying reason for his strong bias. There had to be something else that made him so prejudiced.

He was staring morosely out the window at what was fast becoming a virtual whiteout...and she stared at him. Dana had been right about the incongruity between his fabulous looks and his ruthless courtroom behavior. With those striking blue eyes, that thick dark hair and all the other physical assets too numerous to list at the moment, he looked like every little girl's fairy-tale prince come to life. He should be rescuing damsels in distress instead of condemning them to a dungeon of debt!

Thinking of little girls made Elise remember the way McAllister had handled the situation with Amber. It proved he had a heart somewhere inside that tinman's chest. Then she couldn't help herself; she found herself wondering if his chest was as smooth as he claimed his back was....

"Is that your next appointment?" said McAllister tiredly, jerking Elise away from her wayward daydream.

She looked out the window and saw her neighbor's son, Justin, plowing through the snow toward her side door. He was carrying a covered bird cage.

"No," she answered briskly and took her empty cup to the sink. "My next appointment isn't till three-thirty. Justin's bringing back Geraldo."

McAllister dragged his hand over his face and ended by rubbing his jaw. "I'd forgotten about the bird. Where's he been?"

"Justin took him to Show-and-Tell at the school," she answered, going down the hall to open the door for the child. After a brief conversation with Justin, she returned to the kitchen with the parrot, hung his cage on a chain that was suspended from the ceiling near the window, then removed the cover.

"Hi, pretty boy," Elise crooned to the parrot. "Did you have fun at school?"

Geraldo poked his head and paced up and down the bar. "This is your brain," he answered, then made a sizzling sound like something frying in a skillet. "And this is your brain on drugs."

"Oh," said Elise, laughing. "It must have been antidrugs day at school."

"Just say no! Just say no!" the parrot squawked.

"He learns by frequent repetition," Elise explained to McAllister.

"Great, another mimic," McAllister returned, his chin resting on his hand as he leaned on the table. George had assumed the exact same pose.

McAllister's voice caught the bird's attention, and Geraldo cocked his head to the side and stared at him.

"We have a visitor, Geraldo," said Elise. "You've heard me mention him before…. This is McAllister."

"Aawwk! Aawwk!" the parrot screamed, flapping his wings. "McAllister! McAllister! McAllister's a *sssssnake!*"

"Frequent repetition, eh? You taught him to say that," accused McAllister unnecessarily, because they both knew she had.

Elise smiled. "I plead guilty, Counselor."

To Elise's utter surprise, McAllister smiled back. "I object," he said ruefully.

She raised a brow. "Objection overruled."

Chapter Three

By the time Elise's three-thirty appointment rolled around, Dylan was feeling a little less like a bear with a sore ear and more like a human. But in a veterinary clinic, he wasn't sure which was better. At any rate his stomach was full, he'd been off his aching feet for an hour and he was reconciled to going back to the salt mines for the second shift.

The fact that Elise put George into his pen for an afternoon nap helped lift Dylan's mood, too. At least he wouldn't have to put up with that hairy mimic "aping" everything he did for the rest of the day.

He decided that he kind of liked Rowena. Her quiet, continuous grunting was the only noise she made, and after a while Dylan got to thinking it was a soothing sound...like a bubbling brook. And when she nuzzled her snout against his leg as he sat at the table drinking coffee, he gave her head an experimental stroke and was pleasantly surprised to discover that her hair was soft.

"She likes you," Elise observed dryly.

"That amazes you, I suppose," Dylan returned, still stroking Rowena's head.

Elise shrugged and smiled sweetly. "Well, pigs are *supposed* to be smart."

As Elise cleared the dishes, Dylan couldn't help but chuckle. She had a great sense of humor, he admitted to himself, and he appreciated it even though he was the butt of most of her jokes.

Following Elise back to the clinic offices, he watched her ponytail bounce against her shoulders and admired the feminine sway of her hips. She'd shoved her hands into her pockets, and the lab coat she wore was pulled tight across her curvacious derriere. But if she knew what he was looking at and thinking, she'd probably waste no time getting out her neutering instruments. He shook his head ruefully and forced himself to look away.

Being a practical man, Dylan decided to quit pouting and make the best of the situation, and even smiled at the three or four patients and their owners when he walked into the small waiting room. He was beginning to think he didn't absolutely hate his temporary job as veterinary assistant...but that was before the fat poodle and the dehydrated tarantula showed up.

"Mrs. Merryweather, I thought I told you that Precious was not to have between-meal snacks?" said Elise.

Mrs. Merryweather, an elderly woman in a pink suit, a matching hat decorated with silk roses, with pearls at her throat and a Liz Taylor–sized diamond on one arthritic finger, pursed her pink-painted lips till the delicate, papery skin around her mouth puckered into a hundred fine lines. She reached down and wrapped a protective arm around her pet's fat neck.

"How can you expect my poor Precious to live on

that dry, tasteless food you sent home with us last month? I was afraid she'd starve to death!"

Dylan gave Precious a judicious once-over and decided that it would take a month-long bread-and-water diet to starve all the fat off that pampered poodle. She was a round ball of kinky hair, with two tiny black eyes, a black nose and a diamond-crusted designer collar. She wasn't even sniffing around the room like most of the dogs did when they were brought in on their leashes, but was just sitting there in a seeming stupor, her substantial canine fanny spread out on the cold clinic floor.

"I've explained to you before, Mrs. Merryweather, that the extra weight Precious carries around puts a tremendous strain on her vital organs. And her bones, too. Precious isn't a very large dog under all that fat and fur. If she doesn't lose weight, she's going to get a crippling case of arthritis."

Mrs. Merryweather scowled. "Dogs live such a short time, Dr. Allen, I've always thought they should eat, drink and be merry while they can, you know." She cupped her dog's face and peered adoringly into the beady little eyes, speaking in the coochy-coo voice people sometimes used when talking to infants. "Isn't that right, Precious?"

Elise exchanged an amused glance with Dylan, then turned back to Mrs. Merryweather. "It's obvious you love her very much," she said tactfully, "and that's why you indulge her so much, but—"

"I don't indulge her," Mrs. Merryweather insisted.

Elise folded her arms across her chest and cocked her head to the side. "Tell me, Mrs. Weatherweather, what you fed Precious yesterday. And don't leave anything out."

Mrs. Merryweather's cheeks turned bright pink. "Why, I fed her that horrid food you gave me."

"What else did you feed her?"

Mrs. Merryweather lifted her pointed chin. "Well, I guess she had part of my breakfast croissant," she added reluctantly.

"Was it buttered?"

Mrs. Merryweather bit her lip and stared at the floor. "Er...yes. And there was just a dab of cream cheese on it, too."

"That's a lot of fat, Mrs. Merryweather. Is that all?"

"Well...no. My husband has half-and-half on his cereal in the morning, but he never eats it all. The flakes get soggy while he's reading our horoscopes out loud, so I just put the bowl on the floor and Precious laps up what's left."

Elise sighed. "How about lunch?"

Mrs. Merryweather sighed, too, obviously resigned to a full confession. "Leftover pot pie, TV dinners, pasta or whatever. And sometimes Floyd feeds her part of his Mr. Goodbar." She lifted her faded blue eyes and looked at Elise imploringly. "He always has a Mr. Goodbar after lunch...he has for twenty-five years. Floyd and I have always been thin as rails and can eat whatever we want."

"But Precious can't," Elise countered. "And, if you don't mind my plain speaking, you're going to seriously shorten her life if you don't limit her treats, Mrs. Merryweather. She's only five years old. If you start controlling her diet now, Precious can still live to a ripe old age."

Dylan could tell the message was finally getting through to Mrs. Merryweather. She was looking soberly and tenderly at her pet and probably making New Year's resolutions. Elise had a nice, firm way of speaking without offending…that is, when she didn't *want* to offend.

"Let's get Precious up on the table now," Elise said briskly, pulling on a fresh pair of gloves.

Mrs. Merryweather stood up, but made no effort to lift Precious onto the high table. It took a minute for Dylan to realize that, although all other pet owners had hefted their pets onto the table themselves, for Mrs. Merryweather to lift Precious was out of the question. Actually, for *most* people, lifting Precious would be a bad idea…if not an impossible feat. He, however, worked out with weights at the gym and was perfectly able-bodied. He bent over at the waist and propped his hands on his knees.

"Precious?" he said. "Are you going to let me lift you?"

All the response Dylan got was a glazed stare.

"I'll take that as a yes," he said, anticipating no trouble. He opened his arms wide and scooped up the beach-ball-shaped dog like a load of dirty laundry headed for the washer. But she was heavier than he expected, and he immediately realized he should have bent his knees before lifting the dog when a sharp pain knifed into his lower back.

"Yeow!" he exclaimed, scaring the dog out of her apathy and into a barking frenzy. Precious had a high-pitched, earsplitting yip, and once she was motivated to move, she could really move. She squirmed and struggled and barked, throwing Dylan off balance. He swayed and circled and tottered around the small room, trying not to drop the dog and trying to somehow get her on the table, right side up, where she was supposed to be.

Faintly, beyond the barking, Dylan could hear Mrs. Merryweather saying, "Oh, dear me," over and over again, and could see her standing frozen with her palms pressed flat against her withered cheeks.

"Settle down, Precious," came Elise's no-nonsense voice into the din, and she reached out, plucked Precious from Dylan's arms without further ado and set her on the table. As soon as her flailing paws hit the stainless-steel surface, the dog sat still and shut up.

Rubbing his aching back, Dylan looked sheepishly at Mrs. Merryweather. "Geez, I'm sorry about that, Mrs. Merryweather. I guess I startled her."

Mrs. Merryweather was patting her bosom as if to slow the beat of her heart. She glanced up at Dylan and gave him a nervous little smile. "Never mind, young man. No harm done."

Except to my back, thought Dylan.

"There's probably an astrological explanation," she went on.

"Pardon me?"

"What's your sign, young man?"

"I'm a Gemini, but what's that got to do with—"

"There, you see?"

Dylan didn't see.

Mrs. Merryweather raised her thin, penciled eyebrows and said slowly and emphatically, as if tutoring a child, "Precious is a *Leo!*"

To avoid further explanation, Dylan simply smiled and said, "Ah, *now* I understand."

Sure you do, thought Elise, holding back a chuckle. In fact, Elise barely managed to get through Precious's exam without breaking into gales of laughter.

Having Dylan McAllister in the examining room was proving to be quite a hoot. She didn't think Precious had ever been in any danger while Dylan danced her about the room, or she would have stepped in sooner. She just hoped he would see it as additional proof that she needed help and that it was a darn shame she couldn't afford any.

"You should have bent your knees, McAllister," said Elise as they both watched Precious waddle out of the room behind her doting owner.

"Tell me about it," grumbled Dylan, stretching backward at the waist with his hands pressed into his lower back. "She's even heavier than she looks. I think I pulled something."

Elise subdued the surge of sympathy she felt for him—and the feminine stirring of awareness she felt as she watched him stretch like a sleek panther after a nap—and called in the next patient, who entered the room in a screened box that was carried by a gangly teenage boy.

"Is that a tarantula?" Dylan inquired with a grimace.

"Yeah, dude," said Rick, hooking his thumbs in his empty belt loops, dragging down his already saggy, oversize shorts. "His name is Spike, and he's sick, dude. I mean…like…*major* sick."

"You keep a tarantula as a pet?" Dylan drawled.

"Oh, he's not mine, dude," said the boy, tossing his chin-length sandy hair out of his eyes with a jerk of his head. "I've been taking care of him for a friend who's on vacation and…like…all of a sudden, dude, he started looking kind of shriveled up, ya know?" He turned one hand palm up and cramped his fingers into claws to demonstrate.

"Have you been feeding him, Rick?" asked Elise, studying the spider through the mesh lid.

"Sure, dude—I mean, Dr. Allen. I feed Spike bugs and lettuce and stuff every day."

Elise's brows furrowed as she opened the lid and reached inside. She lifted out a shallow plastic bowl. "Is this Spike's water dish?" Then she turned it upside down to show that it was bone-dry.

Rick's mouth fell open. "Wow, dude—Dr. Allen," he said at last, obviously dumbfounded. "You mean…like…spiders *drink?*"

An injection of water perked up the hairy arachnid nicely, and Rick took Spike home, relieved that his friend wouldn't have to come home from vacation to a dead pet.

"Geez, a spider for a pet! You can't throw it a Frisbee, and it can't fetch your slippers, so what's the point?" Dylan commented as they cleaned up after the last patient. "You get all kinds in here, don't you?"

"People or animals?" Elise asked.

"Both, I guess," Dylan replied. "I wish I had a dollar for every time that kid said 'dude.'"

Elise smiled. "I've known Rick since he was six. He's a good kid, and perfectly normal. As for dealing with the occasional eccentric that comes along, it's worth it because I love my work," she finished, using tongs to pull some sterilized instruments out of an ultrasound cleaner.

"You'd have to love it," Dylan muttered, scrubbing down the examining table one last time.

Elise turned and stared at Dylan's dark head bent over his task. He'd pushed his sweater sleeves above his elbows, and she could see the tight, corded mus-

cles in his arms flex as he worked. She felt a pang of
remorse that this man was so inaccessible to her. He
showed promise with the way he interacted with people and their pets, but she could never forget his ruthlessness in court. She reminded herself that he was
here so she could teach him a lesson, and not so she
could stare at him and wish he wasn't who and what
he was.

Suddenly he looked up, and their eyes locked. Was
there ever a bluer blue than those eyes of his? she
wondered as sexual awareness rippled through her.

"You like them that much, eh?" Dylan inquired,
and Elise was startled speechless. How could he know
she was admiring his eyes, and what kind of conceited
guy asked that kind of question?

"They're…they're *okay,*" Elise admitted, too flustered to evade the question.

Dylan's dark brows furrowed. His expression was
half amused, half puzzled. "If that's all the praise you
can dredge up for your patients and their owners, I
don't know why you put up with the long hours."

"My p-patients?" Elise stuttered.

"That *was* what we were talking about, wasn't it?"
Dylan prompted with a perplexed look.

Elise quickly gathered her scattered wits and turned
back to her instruments. What an idiot she was! Of
course he was talking about her patients and not his
bluer-than-the-summer-sky eyes! She could kick herself for misunderstanding him, and she only hoped
she hadn't revealed her unwilling attraction.

"I love my patients, and it gives me a great deal
of satisfaction knowing that I'm contributing to the
happiness of people and their pets," she answered
stiffly. "Which is more than I can say for *your* job.

You have to rake the party of the first part over the coals to make the party of the second part happy, don't you? There's always a loser."

She could hear his huff of exasperation. "I don't purposely hurt people, if that's what you're implying, Elise. I just do what I can for my clients within the limits of the law."

Elise didn't want to hear about the law. She was convinced that the law didn't serve everyone fairly. It was up to the lawyers to see that people got a fair shake, but Dylan was only out for himself and his male clients. She wasn't in the proper frame of mind to discuss that volatile subject at the moment, however, so instead she said, "Why don't you go over to the store now and get the things you need for the night? I'll finish up here and start dinner."

Without replying, Dylan left the room. When Elise turned around, she felt curiously lonely in a place where she'd never felt lonely before. "Damn the man," she muttered to herself.

DYLAN WALKED QUICKLY through the dark house as a clock somewhere chimed the half hour. It was six-thirty and well past sundown. As he passed through the kitchen, lit only by a night-light near the sink, Geraldo screeched his name and hissed. Dylan ignored the insult. It was difficult enough shouldering the guilt Elise piled on his shoulders; he wasn't about to let a bird get him down, too.

He strode to the main hall, snatched his coat from the coat tree, shrugged into it and buttoned up. He went outside and stood on the sheltered porch, morosely watching the snow fall. By the glow of the porch and streetlights, he estimated that it was a good eighteen inches deep in some places, with drifts up to two feet and higher against the buildings and fences.

He glanced down at his loafers and knew they'd be full of snow before he got back to the house after his jaunt to the store. His socks would be soaked, and he hoped Elise didn't hate him so much she wouldn't loan him a spare pair her ex-husband might have left behind. But then, Ted Muldare was a "taker," wasn't he? His type would pack everything he could and even take things that didn't belong to him. *Like half the equity in her business?* his conscience railed.

Dylan shook his head. He considered himself an ethical person. True, he was a champion of divorcing men, but he'd never considered his legal tactics irresponsible or ruthless. But then, he'd never had to spend the night with anyone he'd beaten in the courtroom, either.

There had been whole minutes in the past few hours when he'd completely forgotten he was spending time with Elise because she'd bought him at an auction for revenge…times when he found himself really enjoying her company. And if he wasn't being too conceited to think so, he felt a grudging attraction on her side, too. No, she didn't hate him. But she probably wanted to. And maybe she had plenty of reason to.

Tired of brooding, Dylan pulled his collar up and made a sprint across the lawn to the edge of Alpine's main street, spraying snow in his wake. A snowplow had come through minutes before, so the road was slushy and spotted with puddles of icy water that splashed up and stung Dylan's ankles as he hurriedly crossed to the small grocery store named Pop's.

Already wet from the knees down, he slogged and

squished around the store and quickly found a tooth-brush, toothpaste, shaving items and some analgesic tablets made especially for back pain. What he prob-ably needed was a muscle relaxant, but he'd have to have a prescription for that, unless… No. Scratch that idea. The type of muscle relaxants Elise kept around probably had to be administered with a dart gun, and there was no way he was going to provide her with a target.

At the checkout stand, he was greeted by a bub-bling blonde in jeans and a Levi's jacket. "Hi!" she chirped, much too cheerful for a man with Popsicles for feet and a wrenched back.

"Hi," he responded, squeezing out a weak smile. "Great weather for penguins and polar bears, eh?"

"It's too much like the Arctic for me," the thirtyish woman admitted as she quickly rang up his goods on an old-fashioned cash register. "Luckily I live next door and I don't have to drive back and forth to Salt Lake for work."

"Yeah, you're lucky, all right," Dylan agreed, pull-ing a twenty-dollar bill out of his wallet. "Seems like a nice little town," he added conversationally.

"The best!" the perky checker replied enthusiasti-cally as she handed him his change. "But I guess you'll have plenty of time in the next week to make up your own mind about Alpine and its peo-ple…right, Mr. McAllister?"

Dylan's head jerked up. He felt as if his face had just been recognized from a mug shot in the post of-fice. "How did you know who I was?"

"It was easy," she replied, her blue eyes dancing. "Elise and I are buds. I've heard about you ever since Elise kicked out Ted and he countersued for divorce.

Besides, I saw you crossing the street from her house. This is a small town, Mr. McAllister."

Dylan was uncomfortable. He even glanced into the sack of toiletries, half-expecting Elise's "bud" to have slipped in something repulsive, like a loose night crawler, as a gesture of support for Elise. He didn't like being thought of as a villain. It was making him paranoid.

He decided to act nonchalant. He grinned. "I'm surprised you didn't bolt the door when you saw me coming."

She shrugged. "You may not get a visit from the local welcome committee while you're here, but you won't get tarred and feathered, either. Besides, it's a free country and I'm running a business here."

"I admire your attitude, Ms...?"

"Call me Jan."

"Some people can't separate what a person does and who a person is."

Jan held up her hands. "Whoa! Don't expect me to comment on that loaded statement. Like I said, Elise is my friend. Besides, she won't kill you, dissect you and put you in a specimen jar full of formaldehyde and set you on a shelf alongside some dog's appendix...if that's what you're worried about!"

Dylan shuddered. "Actually such a horrible idea hadn't crossed my mind...till just now."

Jan waved a hand breezily. "She'll work you hard for a week, then forget she ever knew you."

Dylan smiled grimly. "Well, hard work never killed anyone, I guess," he conceded. "But this storm's no picnic. I have to spend the night in Elise's attic and share a bathroom with that cheeky ape, George. At least things can't get any worse."

Dylan's words still hung on the air to taunt him when the lights went out.

"What the hell...?"

"Oops! There goes the power again!" exclaimed Jan, cheerful as ever.

"Again?"

"It goes out every time we have a bad storm and stays out for hours. Alpine has its own power plant, y'know. Electricity's cheap here, but unreliable. You wanna buy a flashlight, Mr. McAllister?"

DYLAN BOUGHT a flashlight and, training it on the slick ground beneath his feet and clutching his bag of toiletries to his chest, he returned to Elise's house in a grimmer mood than when he left. He had been looking forward to a hot shower to help ease the knot in his back, but now it looked as if that tiny indulgence was going to be denied him, too.

Rowena greeted him at the door with an earnest look of welcome, and if her curled tail could wag, he was sure it would be going ninety miles per hour. He stooped to scratch her between the ears, grousing to himself, "At least someone in this house likes me."

"What was that, McAllister?"

Dylan started to straighten up, then winced and groaned when his back went into a painful spasm. "I shouldn't have stooped down just now."

"You should have bent your knees when you—"

"Yeah, yeah," Dylan replied, his eyes squeezed shut. "I know. I should have bent my knees when I picked up Precious. You're beginning to sound like my mother, Doc."

"Sorry, McAllister," she replied ruefully. "Do you have something for the pain?"

Dylan opened his eyes. Elise was holding a brace of three tapered candles. In the soft glow of candlelight, with her dark hair loose and haloing her face, Elise didn't look anything remotely like his mother. She'd changed into an off-white oversize sweater and a pair of matching leggings. Her only accessory was George, who was hanging on to her free hand and lifting his upper lip in a belligerent sneer. Elise looked comfortable, casual and damn alluring. George looked peeved.

"What's this? Pity for the prosecutor?" he inquired with one raised brow. "Shouldn't you be glad I'm hurting?"

She lifted her chin and stared down her lovely nose at him, her green eyes gleaming. "I'm not a sadist. I bought you to make a point, McAllister, not to incapacitate you. Really, what good would you be to me with a bad back?"

As soon as she'd said them, it was obvious Elise wished back the unintentionally suggestive words. Her eyes grew wide, and her cheeks took on a rosy hue that was plain to see even in candlelight.

"Don't worry, Doc," Dylan assured her with a grin. "I know why I'm here and I know it's not for stud purposes."

She gasped and laughed. "McAllister, you really are—"

"What?" he taunted her in a teasing whisper. "What *am* I, Doc?"

Her smile fell away, and she stared at him. He'd asked the sixty-four-thousand-dollar question. The tension between them crackled. *What was he?* Was he, as Geraldo liked to reiterate, a snake? Or just some poor schnook trying to make a living? If she decided he was just a schnook, did that mean it was okay for them to be attracted to each other? And to act on that attraction?

George started to hoot and pound the top of his head with his hand. The jealous ape apparently didn't like the way he and Elise were staring at each other, which only served to prove to Dylan that there was definitely something basically male-female going on here if George was picking up vibes.

George's tantrum jolted Elise out of her reverie. "What you are, McAllister," she informed him briskly, "is all wet. If you don't get out of those soaked shoes and pants, you're going to catch your death."

"Worried about me?"

"Worried you'll sue me if you catch the sniffles."

"Hmph. I assume you have other clothes I can put on?" he inquired.

"Of course," she snapped efficiently. "Follow me."

Dylan followed Elise though the living room—which was softly lit with candles placed here and there—to a staircase. They climbed to the next floor, traversed a dark hall to another narrower, much steeper staircase, then climbed those squeaky steps, too. At the top was a small, slope-roofed bedroom and a miniscule bathroom.

Elise hurriedly lit a hurricane lamp in the bedroom and another one in the bathroom. Dylan decided that Jan hadn't been exaggerating when she said the electricity went out frequently in Alpine, because Elise seemed to have backup sources for light stashed and ready all over the house.

"Hopefully you weren't planning to shave tonight," she said, turning to face Dylan as he stood in the tiny, low-ceilinged hall. "It might be dangerous with so little light to see by."

"I only shave at night when I've got a good reason to," he informed her with a wink.

"Then I guess you won't be shaving," she replied tartly, then gestured toward a chest of drawers in the bedroom. "There's some socks, shirts and even a couple pairs of jeans in the bottom two drawers. You can be thankful they were in the wash when Ted left, or you'd be up a creek about now." She flicked a glance over him that left goose bumps in its wake and said, "He was shorter than you, so the jeans might not be a perfect fit, but it's better than running around the house in your boxers."

He raised his brows as if to say *How do you know I wear boxers?*

She caught the suggestive look and pointedly ignored it. "If the power's off long enough, the temperature in the house can drop to below freezing."

"You're kidding, right? It's not going to get that cold, is it?"

"Without electricity to run the central heating, this drafty old house gets chilly fast. It could be hours before the utility crew gets the generator cranked up again. But we can stay close to the fire in the living room till bedtime, then bundle under lots of blankets when we…er…go to bed." She blushed again. "I'll have dinner ready in half an hour."

"You can fix dinner without power?"

"I'm a resourceful woman, McAllister," she tossed over her shoulder as she headed for the stairs. "You'd be surprised what I can do." She gave the tuft of hair on the top of George's head an affectionate tousle, then turned away.

Dylan watched her go, her slim back straight as a board as she descended the stairs with George in tow, the ape's face wreathed in a smug smile.

Dylan sighed. "Nothing you could do would surprise me, Doc," he whispered to himself. "You've already made me wish I were one lucky ape."

Chapter Four

When Dylan came down twenty minutes later, Elise was dishing the vegetarian chili into bowls. She hadn't heard him coming, but she knew he was in the room when Rowena scampered off in his direction. The pig was obviously smitten.

Elise turned to find Dylan standing just inside the kitchen door, looking like an awkward teenager with his fingers stuffed into the front pockets of Ted's jeans...which were about three inches too short.

"You're showing a lot of ankle, McAllister," she couldn't resist saying. She also couldn't resist noting that, despite the wrong inseam length, Ted's jeans looked a lot better on Dylan than they'd ever looked on Ted. Encased in the soft, tight denim, every lean muscle in his long legs was plain to see.

He raised a brow. "At least I'm ready if the next disaster happens to be a flood," he grumbled.

She wrenched her appreciative gaze away from his legs and laughed nervously. "You're not being very optimistic."

"I don't need a psychic to tell me that if things keep going for the next week like they've been going today, I should be prepared for the worst."

"You're just hungry. Grab that basket of corn bread and follow me. I've got the coffee table set near the fireplace in the living room. It's already getting cold in here." George was sitting on a chair eating a banana and glaring at Dylan, so Elise called over her shoulder, "You come, too, George, but make yourself useful and bring napkins."

"How did you cook chili without power?" Dylan wanted to know as he dutifully picked up the basket of corn bread and followed Elise into the living room.

"Even though I've got an electric range, I kept the old wood-burning stove that was installed when the house was built a hundred years ago. It's come in handy on more than one occasion. The chili was already made—I just warmed it up. I cooked the corn bread in a cast-iron skillet."

"Well, you said you were resourceful." He set the basket on the coffee table and winced as he straightened up.

She felt that unwilling surge of sympathy again. "Oh, I forgot about your back. Can you sit on the floor?"

"I can probably get down, but I might not be able to get up again."

"We could go into the kitchen or the dining room—"

"No, this is fine," he insisted with a polite smile, then dryly added, "I like a little challenge now and then."

Elise frowned. He was being much too cooperative. "Well, okay, as long as you promise not to show up in a body cast in a few days and blame the whole thing on Mrs. Merryweather's Precious and an aggravated injury from sitting on my floor."

"Geez, Doc! You must really think I'm a sleaze-bag if you're afraid I'll sue you on top of everything else I've—"

Elise was momentarily speechless. She stared at Dylan, and he stared at the floor...obviously wishing he could rephrase that last sentence. "Excuse me?" Elise said at last. "Am I imagining things, or were you just about to implicate yourself?"

"I plead the Fifth," he groused.

"You started to say just now that you regretted your part in helping Ted ruin my life."

"Now you're being overdramatic, Doc," Dylan objected. "You have a perfectly good life."

"Which could have been even better if you and Ted hadn't—" Her frown deepened. "You're trying to change the direction of this argument."

He grinned. "It's a good defense tactic."

"We're not in a courtroom now, McAllister, so why don't you just be honest with me?"

He shrugged. "You'll only consider it honesty if I say exactly what you want to hear."

She heaved a beleaguered sigh. "You've been a lawyer too long. You probably couldn't be straight with me if your life depended on it."

"I make it a point not to be 'straight' with a woman holding two full bowls of piping-hot chili," he responded with another wry grin.

Elise shook her head. "Why can't you just admit you were wrong?"

Dylan's smile fell away. "Because I didn't do anything wrong," he insisted stubbornly, carefully levering himself onto the pillow at his end of the low rectangular table.

"Maybe not in the eyes of the law," Elise muttered as she set the bowls down, "but *morally* speaking—"

"Indigestion is not something I'm keen on getting on top of this sore back, Doc," Dylan said with an edge of irritation in his voice. "Could we save the recriminations for after dinner?"

Elise decided to drop the subject. She wasn't getting anywhere, anyway. He'd probably never admit he'd done anything to hurt her. But she wasn't giving up yet. She had several more days to work on getting him to admit he'd used the law to get an unfair settlement for Ted, and to get him to apologize to her.

She knew then that that's what she wanted…*an apology*. She needed closure. She needed to get over the bitterness that Ted's greed had created, and an apology from Ted's lawyer might just do the trick.

She sat down, and that's when the awkwardness between them really set in. The whole scene was just too cozy. Except for Rowena, who had settled down next to Dylan on the floor, and George, who was perched on the sofa arm keeping close watch on the two of them, they were entirely alone. The snow fell quietly outside, and the fire crackled cheerfully within. Beyond the golden glow of firelight that bathed their small grouping, soft shadows enclosed them in an intimate circle apart from the world. It was the perfect setting to inspire confidences between friends…or lovers.

But they weren't friends, much less lovers, Elise reminded herself. She didn't know anything about Dylan McAllister beyond the fact that he was highly intelligent, drop-dead gorgeous and a good dresser. He avoided any serious talk about the divorce case by evading or making jokes, so it seemed ridiculous to think he'd be interested in personal chitchat that might actually give her an inkling of what kind of man he really was behind the high-powered image. They'd be lucky to choke down a little chili, then trudge off to their separate beds like the two strangers they were and would always remain....

"So, are you originally from Alpine?"

Elise was so surprised by the friendly question, she dropped her spoon into her bowl of chili, sending a splatter of spicy sauce flying through the air and into Dylan's left eye. He groped for a napkin, and Elise quickly handed him hers, since George had only brought one for her and none for his archrival. As Dylan pressed the napkin to his eye and cursed under his breath, the ape bounced his bottom on the sofa cushions and hooted gleefully.

"I'm so sorry," Elise said sincerely, anxiously watching Dylan blink and blot his eye with the napkin. "I hope you believe it was an accident."

"I'm not that paranoid, Doc," he informed her ruefully. "I know you didn't plan to blind me. You were just lucky. But at this rate—hunched over with a bad back and with one eye out of commission—the townspeople will start mistaking me for the Hunchback of Notre Dame and come after me in the dead of night with torches. Do they need someone at the town hall to pull ropes in the bell tower?"

Elise chuckled. "You're being a good sport. But how does your eye feel? Maybe you should flush it with water."

"I'm fine," he insisted, opening his eyes wide to prove his point. "Do I look fine, Doc?"

Elise stared into Dylan's eyes and noted—as a shiver ran down her spine—that they were bluer than ever in the firelight. Her gaze wandered. And his brows were more wickedly intriguing, his cheekbones more chiseled, his jaw more firm and masculine, and his lips more sensuous. She dare not go below his neck to note that his shoulders were broader, his chest—

"Doc?" Dylan's voice broke into her trancelike inventory of body parts. Obviously God had been in a good mood when He'd shaped a hunk of clay into Dylan McAllister.

Flustered, Elise stammered, "Your eyes…your *eye*…looks fine. Just fine."

"Can I depend on you not to flip chili in my other eye if I repeat my question?"

Elise picked up her spoon and absently stirred her cooling chili. "I remember the question, though I must say I'm surprised you want to know anything about me."

He raised one of those wicked brows again. "We can be civilized, can't we? Let's small-talk."

"All right. Yes, I am originally from Alpine. My father was a G.P. and practiced just down the street in a small office that has since been torn down. My mother was a stay-at-home mom who canned fruit and made all my clothes. She even made my prom dress."

"Was it pink and demure?"

She wrinkled her nose at him. "Yes, but it was still quite lovely."

"Bet your mom would never have made a dress for you like that little black number you wore New Year's Eve."

"No, but she's a little more open-minded about my wardrobe now that I'm a divorced woman approaching the big three-oh. Besides, she and dad live in Florida now. He retired right after Ted and I got married in that big white church down the block."

"Siblings?"

"One brother...a dentist in Idaho. He's married and has three kids."

"Sounds like you had a great childhood. Rural and stable, and all that. Kind of like the Waltons."

"With considerably fewer kids to call good-night to each other by the end of the day. But it really was great. I was lucky. I only wish I'd had as much luck in picking a husband as my mother did. What about you? What was your childhood like?"

"Well, my home wasn't like the Waltons'," Dylan admitted ruefully. "We were more like the Bundys."

Elise's eyes widened. "Not Al and Peg?"

"The same. My folks stayed together for twenty-five years, but they should never have married in the first place. They weren't happy. They stayed together for 'the kids' sake.' We'd have all been better off if our parents had been a little more selfish and tried to make themselves happy by splitting up. They fought constantly."

"How many kids were there in your family?"

"Five."

"You're kidding! I'd have never guessed you came from a large family."

"Well, I do. I've got three brothers and one sister." He broke eye contact and buttered a piece of corn bread. "She—my sister, Beth—died, though."

Elise could tell he was trying hard not to show any emotion. She wasn't sure if he'd appreciate an expression of sympathy or not, but she felt compelled to say, "I'm sorry."

He shrugged, unconvincingly nonchalant. "It was a long time ago. She was just a kid."

Elise's heart ached for him. She resisted a strong urge to reach out and stroke his hair consolingly. "Was it an accident?"

"It was leukemia," he said grimly.

Suddenly Elise understood why Dylan was willing to give up a week of work for the Make a Wish Foundation. His fight against cancer was personal. She bit her lip, not knowing what else to say, and wishing he didn't suddenly seem so touchingly vulnerable.

He smiled as if he understood her dilemma and went on, "My brothers and I are really close. With our parents squabbling all the time, and Beth's death, we learned to depend on each other for stability and support."

Elise nodded and was about to ask another question, when Dylan abruptly changed the subject. "Know any good jokes, Doc?"

Startled, Elise said, "What?"

"I asked if you knew any good jokes. The conversation was getting a little too heavy for me."

Elise took that to mean he didn't want to talk about himself anymore. Maybe he didn't want to show his vulnerability, his humanity, because it wouldn't go along with his cold, corporate image. But if he wouldn't talk about himself, Elise could never understand why he did what he did in the courtroom. Maybe he didn't want to be understood.

Well, if he refused to talk about the big issue between them, she decided fatalistically, maybe she'd have to torture him a little more....

"I don't know any good jokes," she said finally, "but Geraldo does."

"Geraldo?"

"Yes, and he loves to tell them. Shall I bring him in and let him put on his little comedy routine for us? He's a big hit at parties!"

"Do you think he can refrain from calling me names?"

"I can't promise anything," she admitted.

"Oh, well," Dylan said, resigned. "I'll put up with a little abuse for a few good laughs."

"Okay. I'll be right back."

I certainly hope you can put up with a little abuse for a few good laughs, thought Elise, *because you're going to get a lot of abuse.* But she also rationalized that he might actually laugh, and he could probably use a good laugh about now.

Elise went into the dark kitchen and roused Geraldo from a nap by taking down his cage from the hook by the window and carrying it into the living room. By the time she'd placed the cage on an end table nearby and sat down again on the pillow opposite Dylan, Geraldo was already pacing up and down his bar and chirping nonsensically.

"Are you ready, McAllister?"

Dylan popped the last bite of corn bread into his mouth and nodded, then turned around on his pillow to face the entertainment. Elise felt a little guilty about springing Geraldo's stand-up-comedy routine on Dylan when it was obvious he had no idea what he was in for. She chewed on her lip for a minute, considered warning him, then decided she was getting way too soft.

"Okay, Geraldo, let 'er rip, boy. Let's hear about those *lawyers!*"

Out of her peripheral vision, Elise could see Dylan's head swivel her way, but she kept her eyes trained on Geraldo. Then, as soon as Geraldo started his barrage of lawyer jokes, the bird was the center of everyone's attention.

"What looks good on a lawyer? *Squawk!*"

"I don't know, pretty bird," answered Elise. "What looks good on a lawyer?"

"A doberman, that's what! *Squawk!*"

George hooted and clapped vigorously, but Dylan didn't make a sound. He sat with his arms folded, watching Geraldo with a steely gleam in his eye and a firm set to his jaw.

"What's the difference between a carp and a lawyer? *Squawk!*"

"What, pretty bird?" said Elise on cue.

"One's a scum-sucking bottom dweller, and the other's a fish!" he screamed. *"Squawk!"*

George liked that one even better. Making primal sounds, he circled the sofa with his arms raised above his head, shaking his hands like pom-poms.

"What do you call a bunch of lawyers on the bottom of the sea? *Squawk!*" Pacing ever faster, egged on by George's enthusiastic approval of his performance, Geraldo didn't wait for prompting. "A good start!" he screeched.

After a couple more jokes, Elise finally had to calm down George by taking him into her lap and giving him his Cookie Monster doll to cuddle. It was impossible to silence Geraldo until he'd gone through his repertoire of lawyer jokes. By the time he was through and dipping his beak in the water holder, Elise was afraid she'd pushed Dylan McAllister a tad too far.

He sat still as a stone with a disgruntled look on

his face, his legs crossed Indian style and his arms folded over his broad chest. Elise was afraid they'd have to finish out the rest of the week in stony silence, when George squirmed out of her lap and stood up, crossed his long, hairy arms and mugged Dylan's grim expression to perfection.

Elise couldn't help it; she laughed. And Dylan laughed, too. His arms and legs unfolded like a spring-release card table, and he rolled onto his back, held his stomach and roared.

She'd heard him chuckle before, had been unwillingly charmed by his rueful half smiles and wicked grins, but Dylan's all-out laughter was something else. The sound of it warmed her to her toes. It was so damn attractive, it was scary. It definitely wasn't what she expected from a courtroom cad like him. He sounded absolutely...human.

Eventually they settled down and wiped their watery eyes. Elise hadn't laughed as hard as Dylan had, and her laughter was more of a release of tension than anything else. After all, she'd heard the lawyer jokes a hundred times; in fact, she'd taught them to Geraldo. But Dylan's reaction was a pleasant surprise.

"You really are a good sport," she told him.

"Well, I tried to be stiff about it, but George's mimic kind of broke the ice. I figured I had a choice to either laugh or cry," he joked. He studied her in the firelight, making her blush. "I can't believe you were so ticked off at me you went to all that trouble to teach that bird all those jokes!"

"It was right after the last hearing," she replied with an embarrassed shrug. "I'm sure it seems juvenile to you, but it helped me cope back then. Like you, I felt I could either laugh or cry." She smiled sheepishly. "I chose to laugh."

"I'm glad you did," he said softly. "Laughter's good. But, you know, I haven't laughed so hard since the last get-together with my brothers."

Elise was flattered to be compared with the siblings he seemed to care so much about. She felt her cheeks flush with gratification.

The table wasn't between them anymore. In fact, they were sitting quite close together. With only an arm's length separating them, Elise found herself spellbound by Dylan's eyes. She could almost forget he was the reason she was up to her ears in debt. She could almost forget he wasn't sorry he'd pulverized her in court. She could almost forget that he refused to represent women in divorce hearings. She could almost forget he was a sssssnake....

Suddenly Elise felt something gooey in her lap, glanced down and found her chili bowl resting upside down on her off-white sweater. She was at a loss to understand how the bowl had leapt off the table and into her lap, but then she looked up and saw George standing next to her, his bottom lip thrust out and his arms tucked behind his back.

"Oh, George," she groaned, "why did you do this?"

But she knew why, and so did Dylan. George was jealous, and he'd had reason to be. The air had been sizzling with sexual tension between Elise and her ex-husband's divorce lawyer...the one she'd bought to wreak revenge upon. My, wasn't she doing a famous job.

Apparently made unhappy by Elise's disapproving

scowl, George stalked out of the room with a sulky look on his face, leaving Elise and Dylan…alone.

"Hey, you know what, I know it's early, but—" Dylan performed a gigantic yawn "—I'm really exhausted. I think I'll go on up to bed now. Maybe read a little by gaslight, or…something."

"Sure," Elise readily agreed, as anxious for him to go as he was to get away. It was insane to be attracted to your ex-husband's divorce lawyer! She stood up carefully and scraped the chili off her sweater, just as carefully avoiding Dylan's eyes. "You should have everything you need…just bundle up under the extra blankets I laid out on the bed, and you'll keep warm even if the electricity doesn't come on all night."

Dylan stood up, too, but with difficulty. His back appeared to be worse, but he said he'd bought some pills to take for the pain and there really wasn't anything she could do to help him…short of a massage. And that was out of the question!

"Well, good night then," he mumbled, and limped off toward the stairs.

Elise lifted her embarrassed gaze just as he turned the corner to the hall. Man, what a tush he had, even in Ted's jeans. She shook her head, amazed and appalled by her runaway libido. She sighed, almost wishing Dana hadn't goaded her into buying the guy for a week. She smiled. Almost…but not quite.

DYLAN FELT A PAIN in his back for each step he climbed. His back muscles were as tight as a miser's fist. He'd kill for a good spa massage about now. The pills he'd bought just weren't doing the trick.

He finally made it to the attic bedroom, where the hurricane lamp was still burning. He pulled off his sweater and Ted's jeans, gathered his toiletries, then headed for the bathroom. It gave him a bit of a start when he saw George inside, lifting the toilet seat. When George saw Dylan in the hall, the ape lifted his upper lip in a disdainful sneer and closed the door in Dylan's face. He even heard the lock click.

"I hope you didn't take a newspaper in there, George, 'cause you're not the only one who needs to get ready for bed," Dylan snarled. He heard a muted "eee, eee," on the other side of the door, but it was a full ten minutes before Dylan heard the toilet flush and the door finally opened.

"Did you wash your hands, you little bozo?" Dylan inquired, trying to slip past the ape and into the room so he could close and lock the door, too.

Dylan had meant the question rhetorically, but George pulled a little stool up next to the sink, squirted a great deal of liquid soap onto his pink palms and thoroughly washed his hands. Dylan waited with as much patience as he could muster, but he was getting cold standing in the unheated hallway in his boxers.

When George was finally through, he just stood on his stool and stared at Dylan.

"Are you going to get out, George? Or am I gonna have to throw your hairy little rear down the stairs?"

George didn't like such aggressive talk, and he made that clear by pounding the top of his head and squealing.

"Oh, all right. I was only kidding. Settle down, George," said Dylan, resigned to sharing the bathroom with an ape while he brushed his teeth. He scooted next to George at the sink, carefully laid out his toiletries where he hoped George couldn't reach them, then squeezed toothpaste onto his brush.

George immediately reached for his own toothbrush, which was propped up in a plastic Cookie Monster toothbrush holder, and shoved it next to the tube of toothpaste Dylan was still holding.

"Where's your tube of toothpaste?" Dylan demanded. "Already sucked it dry?"

George bounced on the stool and waggled his brush impatiently. "Oh, all right," Dylan relented, squeezing some toothpaste onto George's brush, too. "But that's all you're getting, so don't eat it."

George immediately went about the business of brushing his teeth while Dylan watched in the mirror, mesmerized. Just as the dentist recommended, the chimp brushed vertically and even made a couple of swipes at his back teeth, too. When he was through, he pushed his hairy mug close to the mirror and bared his teeth, admiring his shiny-clean set of ivories.

For a minute Dylan couldn't get over the fact that he was standing in his boxers, in a bathroom, next to an ape with a hygiene obsession. "What's wrong with this picture?" he grumbled, staring at himself in the mirror. Then he shrugged his shoulders, bent over and brushed his teeth.

Trouble was, once he'd rinsed, he couldn't straighten up. He tried, but even a little movement made his lower back knot up like a charley horse. The muscles had tightened up down there, and there was no way they were going to loosen up without taking some kind of drastic measure. He needed a muscle relaxant, a hot-water bottle or a massage. Actually he needed all three, but how was he going to get any help when the only one who knew he was in trouble was a chimp who hated his guts?

"George. George? Are you up there? Come on down, hon, it's time for bed."

"Elise?" called Dylan, relieved to hear her voice. "Hey, I need some help. Can you—?"

But Elise didn't wait to hear more. He heard her footsteps quickly ascending the stairs, then her sharp gasp when she saw him bent over the sink dressed in nothing but his boxers. He turned his head and favored her with a chagrined smile.

"What's going on?" she asked faintly. "I thought maybe George had got into mischief."

"No, George is fine, although he's annoyingly persistent in guarding his territory. It's my back. I can't straighten up."

"Oh, dear," she said, taking another couple steps closer but still hovering near the stairs as if she were about to bolt any second. "You can't straighten up at all?"

"Not without a foist," he said dryly. "Maybe I could do it," he amended, "but I think I'd pass out and then George would steal my toothpaste. Can't let that happen, can I?"

"What do you want me to do? The muscle relaxants I have are for animals, and it would be unprofessional to give them to you...not to mention illegal. I wouldn't want to do anything *illegal,* you know."

"Of course not," Dylan drawled. "All I want you to do is massage my back for a few minutes. It's gotten like this before, and a good massage—"

He stopped talking when he saw the color drain out of her face. "Don't look so petrified. Surely you don't think I'm doing this to seduce you, Doc? Because if

I were trying to seduce you, I'd think of something a lot smoother than this back routine!" Then, remembering her comment earlier that day, he grinned roguishly and added, "Besides, what good would I be to you with a sore back?"

Elise was at her wit's end. This man might not be trying to seduce her, but he was succeeding quite nicely anyway. Even bent over the sink with an ape peering over his shoulder, he was a charmer. And it really wasn't fair that she had to see him in his boxers.... *Legal briefs* took on a whole new, and very disturbing, meaning.

His legs had looked wonderful encased in tight denim, but they looked even better au naturelle. They were lean and muscular and lightly furred with dark hair, and she could almost imagine how sensual they'd feel intertwined with her own legs. And his chest and shoulders... *Wow* said it all and said it best. *Wow.*

"Honest, Doc, I won't bite," Dylan assured her with another appealing smile. "Just rub a little of that tension out of my back, and maybe we won't have to call 911."

"Well, I'll massage your back," Elise capitulated reluctantly, "but I think you're expecting results you're not going to get. If your back's this bad, McAllister, maybe we *should* call 911."

"No, a massage is just what I need. A muscle relaxant would definitely help, but I won't be able to call my doctor and get a prescription till tomorrow. You're my best and last hope, Doc, so don't fail me."

As Elise walked into the bathroom and stood behind Dylan, she suddenly realized that for this moment, in connection with this particular situation, she had complete power over her ex-husband's divorce lawyer. This pathetic guy, bent helplessly over her sink, had no other means of help but from her. And she had the power to refuse to give help.

A wise man once said that power corrupts and that absolute power corrupts absolutely. Well, that wise man knew what he was talking about, because Elise was ashamed to admit that for a split second she was tempted to let Dylan McAllister suffer. But only for a moment, because she didn't even like to squash spiders with her shoe, much less allow another human being to suffer.

"Well?" he prompted. "Are you going to do it or aren't you? Or have you finally found the best revenge, Elise?"

He was staring at her in the mirror. Those blue eyes challenged her...implored her...seduced her.

"Of course I'm going to do it," she replied a little testily. "But you've got to show me where it hurts."

He seemed to heave a relieved sigh, then he reached back and rubbed a section of his back right above the elastic band of his boxer shorts. "The knot's here, but the pain radiates clear up to my shoulder blades. It might help if you rubbed a little baby oil or something like that on your hands first," he tentatively suggested.

Elise found baby oil in the medicine chest, rubbed her palms and set to work. George sat on the tank of the toilet and watched, growing more and more agitated. He obviously didn't like Elise "grooming" another primate, but she tried to ignore him.

Actually it wasn't that hard ignoring George. Elise became immediately absorbed in what she was doing. As her hands slid over Dylan's smooth back and her fingers kneaded the tight muscles, she generated heat. And not just the warmth that comes naturally from the friction of skin rubbing against skin. She was feeling warm all over.

And it didn't help that Dylan wasn't at all shy about telling her what felt good.

"Um…yeah, that's just the right spot," he'd say in a throaty, pleasure-filled voice.

"Yeah, great…but just a little lower," he'd croon.

"Wow, you've got the greatest fingers in the world, Doc," he'd sigh. "Your strokes are so firm and strong."

He closed his eyes and arched his neck. She stared at his sensual expression in the mirror. "Mmmmm…" he moaned. "That feels soooo good."

Elise closed her eyes and focused on the feel of his skin under her sensitive fingers. Her breathing had quickened, and her heart was beating as if she'd just run a sprint. And her breasts were even feeling tender and aching and—

Elise abruptly straightened up and stepped back, removing her hands from his back. Her palms pulsed and her throat was as dry as tinder. She'd become practically orgasmic just rubbing Dylan McAllister's back! And such a lack of scruples and control scared her spitless!

Dylan opened his eyes and looked dazedly at her in the mirror. "Are you through?" he asked.

"I…I thought you ought to try to straighten up. No point in…in rubbing your back raw if the knot's gone. Can…can you straighten up?"

Dylan looked disappointed but resigned. He had apparently enjoyed the massage as much as she had. He straightened up slowly and gradually, one inch at a time. Finally he stood straight and tall, beaming with satisfaction.

"Hey, it worked great, Doc. You've really got the magic touch." Then he turned around and faced her, the two of them standing chest to chest in the tiny bathroom.

Elise couldn't help it; she stared. From this vantage point his chest was almost too tempting to resist. She wanted to ask him if he needed a massage there, too, but recovered her wits just in time. Scooting out of the bathroom as if she'd just heard a fire alarm, she turned in the hall and called to George. He immediately joined her and grabbed hold of her hand possessively.

"I'll...I'll find you a hot-water bottle," she stammered, embarrassed to look Dylan in the eye. "George will bring it up. Good night."

Yes, George would bring it up, she said to herself as she hurried down the stairs, because she couldn't trust herself to be around that man another minute. Her hormones were already doing cartwheels. Dylan McAllister might be a snake, she decided, but he was the sexiest, most tempting snake in the world.

So now maybe she understood Eve's downfall in the Garden of Eden just a little better....

Chapter Five

Dylan was stretched out on the bed when George showed up about ten minutes later with the hot-water bottle, which, by the bulging looks of it, was already filled. Elise must have heated the water on the wood-burning stove, because the tap water was already tepid. Dylan knew. Instead of a shower, he'd endured a cool sponge bath.

"Hey, buddy, thanks for bringing that all the way up here for me," he said with a smile, rolling onto one shoulder and extending his hand over the side of the bed. He'd hoped he could make points with the chimp by showing his gratitude, but he'd apparently been much too optimistic. Instead of walking five feet into the room and handing the hot-water bottle to Dylan, George bared his squeaky-clean teeth, dropped the bottle on the floor by the door and stalked away.

"I wouldn't advise you to open a bed and breakfast, George," Dylan called after him. "Your attitude needs a little work."

Then he rolled onto his back on the soft feather mattress, which lay on top of a much firmer mattress, and stared at the ceiling. He'd turned out both hurricane lamps and had lit a thick candle by the bed, hoping not to have to get up again before morning. But if he wanted the hot-water bottle, he had no choice but to get up.

Elise's massage had been very effective, and along with the hot-water bottle and a second dose of pain pills, he just might get his sore back under control without having to call his doctor for a prescription.

But Elise's massage had been effective in another way, too. Her warm, skillful hands on his back, the nearness of her in the tiny bathroom and the womanly scent of her had been damn arousing. But it wasn't just her obvious physical charms that Dylan found so attractive.

She was fiesty.

She was principled.

She was intelligent and witty.

She was up-front and honest.

And despite plenty of reason to hate him, she still had enough compassion to put aside her feelings and actually give her ex-husband's divorce lawyer—the guy who had taken her to the cleaners—a back massage.

Dylan sighed and eased out of bed, standing up carefully. He walked to the door and bent slowly down, then picked up the hot-water bottle…all without excruciating pain in his back.

Encouraged, he climbed into bed and lay down on his side with the hot-water bottle tucked against his lower back, blew out the candle on the bedside table, then pulled the blankets over his shoulders.

He yawned and snuggled into the sweet-smelling linen. Nothing felt better than getting into a warm bed on a cold night after a hard day's work. The only improvement he'd make would be to exchange the hot-water bottle for Elise.

He grinned before falling into an exhausted sleep, muttering to himself, "And I sure as hell wouldn't let a bad back stop me from taking advantage of the situation. Any setback in my recovery would be well worth it."

DOWNSTAIRS, Elise put out the fire in the living room and snuffed all the candles. Finding her way with a high-powered flashlight, she put George to bed in his pen, locked it, took Geraldo's cage into her bedroom where it was warmer than the drafty kitchen and dragged Rowena's piggy bed in there, as well. Having tucked all the pets in, so to speak, she got ready for bed herself, thanking her lucky stars that she didn't have any overnight patients to take care of in the clinic.

Once she was snuggled under several blankets, she expected to go right to sleep. She'd had a hectic, taxing day, but she was used to having hectic, taxing days. And even though—or maybe *because*—Dylan McAllister had been around to add to the stress, her mind simply would not quit racing. And neither would her pulse when she thought about that legal eagle in his briefs....

It seemed as if she'd just dozed off when a loud ringing roused her from a disturbing dream. She sat up abruptly and fumbled for the alarm, then remembered her digital clock wasn't working and it was the phone making all that racket. She grabbed the receiver and mumbled, "Hello?"

"Dr. Allen?"

"Yes, this is Dr. Allen." Elise blinked, trying to

clear her vision and her groggy brain at the same time. It appeared that the snow had stopped falling, and moonlight was filtering in through the sheer drapes and bathing the room in a soft radiance.

"This is Pete Thompson...up at the Circle J?"

"Yes, Pete. What's wrong?"

"Got a horse with colic. She's hurtin' pretty bad, and Doc Spencer's stuck in Salt Lake overnight 'cause of the storm. This mare has had bowel obstructions before and nearly went into shock once. Don't want to lose her. Think you can help?"

Elise specialized in small and domestic animals, generally leaving the larger farm and ranch animals to Dr. Spencer's expertise. But Elise had frequently pinch-hit for Dr. Spencer, and he for her, when one or the other was out of town.

"I haven't treated a horse with colic in years, Pete, but I think I could get her through the night with some emergency measures, then tomorrow Dr. Spencer could take over, or you might even want to call in an equine surgeon if this mare is prone to obstructions."

"That's all I'm asking, Doc Allen. If you could just help out tonight, keep her from gettin' sicker and help ease her pain, I'd be mighty grateful."

"Have you got power up there, Pete?"

"Came on about midnight. How about you?"

"No, it's still cold and dark down here. I don't even know what time it is."

"It's three in the morning," he told her with a tired chuckle. "Isn't that when all the emergencies happen?"

"Yep. Par for the course," said Elise, throwing off her blankets and swinging her legs off the bed. "I'll get there as soon as I can, but if the roads haven't been plowed recently, I'll probably have to snowshoe in."

"You're not coming alone, are you?"

"Who would I bring, Pete?" she inquired dryly.

"I don't like the idea of a woman walkin' alone two miles through the snow in the dead of night."

"You'd have to be crazy—or a vet—to be out on a night like this. Don't worry, I won't run into a soul. And even if I had an assistant, I wouldn't call them up and drag them out of bed just to keep me—"

Hey, wait a minute, thought Elise. *What am I talking about? I do have an assistant, and he's right here under my roof!*

"Come to think of it, Pete, I *will* be bringing someone along."

"A man?" he inquired hopefully.

"I'll pretend not to notice the suggestion of sexism in your tone," Elise retorted with wry humor. "I'll just be touched that you're concerned about me. See you soon."

After Elise hung up the phone, she sat for half a minute and contemplated what she was about to do. She was going to drag an exhausted, frustrated lawyer with a sore back out of bed at three o'clock in the morning. On the one hand, it seemed the height of cruelty. On the other hand, she'd bought him at the auction so he'd get a taste of how hard she worked and to make him see what a shame it was she had to give half of what she earned to her deadbeat ex-husband. What better way to make her point?

She touched her feet to the floor, and when the icy impact sent a chill up her spine, steely resolve pumped into her bloodstream. Hey, if she had to get up in this refrigerator of a house, throw on some clothes and snowshoe two miles over a frozen land-scape to treat a horse with colic, Dylan McAllister was going to share the experience!

As Elise took off her flannel pajamas and dressed, shivering like crazy, remnants of the disturbing dream she'd been having when the phone rang came back to her.

The dream had been about McAllister, of course. They were in court, and she was on the witness stand. He was cross-examining her...in his boxer shorts. He wore a tie, which hung tantalizingly over his bare chest, navy blue socks and a pair of Gucci loafers. But even sans clothes, his courtroom demeanor hadn't changed one iota. He was as ruthless as ever and try-ing to get her convicted of some ridiculous crime she was somewhat fuzzy about—cruelty to animals, maybe?

She was being judged by a jury of her "peers," made up of pets of every variety—furred, feathered and scaled. And the judge, decked out in a black robe and wielding a monstrous gavel...was George.

"Maybe it was the chili," Elise muttered, but re-membering the dream only made her all the more determined to drag McAllister out of bed by the seat of his boxer shorts.

Dressed and on the march to the stairwell, Elise gathered a few things Dylan would be needing for the trek. Then, training the flashlight on each step, Elise climbed the flight of stairs with her load of gear.

Rowena stood at the bottom, curious but not curi-ous enough to attempt following. Rowena never climbed the stairs, which was probably the only rea-son the little snout-nosed devotee hadn't spent the night in Dylan's room lying loyally by his bed.

Elise made enough noise on her way up that she was surprised to find Dylan still asleep. Total exhaustion must account for it, she decided, unable to squelch a smug smile. But it felt good to feel a little vindictive again; she'd been *way* too nice last night, massaging his back and all. For all she knew, he could even be faking his injury.

Having psyched herself into a nasty mood, Elise positioned herself at the foot of the bed, pointed the flashlight square at Dylan's face and yelled, "McAllister! Get up!"

Probably unused to being woken up in such a manner, Dylan jerked to a sitting position, struggled in a tangle of blankets, then fell off the bed.

"What the hell?" he muttered hoarsely, obviously stunned to wake up and find himself seated on a cold floor.

"It's just me, McAllister," Elise briskly informed him, holding the flashlight under her chin with the beam shining up so he could see her.

"Elise? My God, don't do that. It makes you look like a ghoul."

"Well, you're going to wish I were a ghoul instead of a veterinarian when I tell you why I'm here. There's an emergency."

"An emergency?" He stood up, rubbing his eyes with the heels of his hands. His hair was tousled and he looked sexier than ever. He was still wearing only boxer shorts. "What kind of emergency?"

Elise tore her gaze away from his gorgeous chest and swallowed hard. "A horse with colic."

Dylan groaned and climbed back in bed, throwing the blankets over his head. "A horse with a bellyache is not an emergency," he announced, his voice muffled. "Have his owner feed him a bran muffin every morning, for crying out loud."

"So suddenly you're an expert in veterinary science?" Elise taunted. "I'll have you know, colic can be very serious for a horse, and very painful. If you have any decency in you at all, Dylan McAllister, you'll haul your carcass out of bed and help me out here."

Elise didn't really think she needed Dylan's help, but guilt was a good motivator. But maybe lawyers didn't allow themselves to feel guilty....

Suddenly Dylan threw off the blankets and stood up. "All right. Go warm up the car, Doc, and I'll be down in a sec."

When she didn't budge, he asked, "What's the matter? Don't you trust me?" He grinned. "Or do you just want to watch me dress?"

How about watching you undress? her traitorous libido suggested. Desperate for him to cover that hunky chest of his, she plucked his sweater off a nearby chair and threw it at him. "I'm surprised you can get your swelled head through this neck hole, McAllister. No, I couldn't care less about watching you dress," she lied. "I've pretty much seen it all, anyway, and I'm not the least impressed."

"Is that right?" he teased her, tugging the sweater over his head. "Then George is jealous for nothing. But then, you really haven't seen it *all*, have you?"

"You—!"

"If you don't want to watch me dress, why are you still here? Why aren't you warming up the car?"

He was much too frisky for 3:00 a.m., so Elise took a great deal of pleasure in telling him, "Because we can't take the car."

With one leg in Ted's jeans, he paused and scowled. "Why the hell not?"

"There's too much snow on the roads. We wouldn't get far without getting stuck or sliding into a ravine somewhere."

"Your snowplow drivers belong to a union or something?"

"Our snowplow drivers are volunteers who use their own vehicles. On nights like this, they generally get a few hours of sleep, then get up early and clear the roads for school buses, etcetera. This is a small town, McAllister."

"So how are we going to get there? Don't tell me we're walking?"

"I won't."

"Thank God!"

"We're snowshoeing."

"Swell," he grumbled. "So how far away is this place?"

"Only two miles."

"*Only* two miles, she says," he griped as he buttoned the front placket of the jeans. Elise tried to look away, but she couldn't. It was all she could do to keep the flashlight beam from spotlighting every movement of his long, dexterous fingers. It had been quite titillating watching him dress; she could only imagine how arousing it would be to watch him *un*dress…and all for her.

When he sat down on the bed to pull on his loafers, she made an effort to shake free of her lustful thoughts and handed him a pair of boots. "You'd better wear these. Loafers just won't cut it, I'm afraid."

Dylan took the boots. "Are they Ted's?"

"No, they're my dad's, but he doesn't need them in Florida."

"Lucky man." Bending over to put on the boots, Dylan winced.

"How's your back?" she couldn't help asking, although she was afraid his answer would make her feel guilty about dragging him out of bed at 0-dark-thirty in the morning.

"Actually it's a lot better than it was...thanks to your wonderful way with baby oil," he said, turning his head and grinning up at her.

"Good," she said briskly, her conscience appeased. "Put on an extra pair of socks, too, and I'll meet you downstairs by the back door."

USING THE FLASHLIGHT he'd purchased at Pop's, Dylan hurried down the stairs in his borrowed boots and met Elise at the back door. She was wearing a blue ski jacket and had a white muffler wrapped snugly around her neck. She was also wearing a knit ski hat she'd pulled low on her forehead with her hair tucked up inside.

Despite all the extra padding and no makeup, she still looked darn cute. That was a bad sign. He had either turned self-destructive and was getting a serious infatuation for a woman who detested him, or lack of sleep was distorting his judgment.

"Here's a muffler for you, a knit hat and a pair of gloves. Not as snazzy-looking as your wool coat, but you aren't going to care about style when that icy mountain wind hits you in the face. We'll put our snowshoes on outside on the porch. Hurry, McAllister," she urged. "This is taking too long."

For once, Dylan didn't mind Elise ordering him

around. He could tell by her anxious tone that she was worried about the horse. He hurriedly wrapped the muffler around his neck, tugged on the knit hat and pulled on the gloves. The hat and gloves were both too small and pinched, but he wasn't about to complain.

Elise had to shoo Rowena away from the door so she could shut and lock it behind them, then they sat down on a bench on the porch and strapped on snowshoes. Elise picked up a large black bag and stepped off the porch.

"That looks heavy, Doc," Dylan observed.

"Horse pills are big," Elise explained dryly.

"Let me carry it for you."

"No, that's—"

"I insist." He snatched the bag and started walking. She didn't put up an argument, and soon they were crossing the yard and headed for Main Street.

Once he'd gotten the hang of moving briskly along in snowshoes, Dylan finally had a moment to notice that he was walking in a Currier and Ives winter wonderland.

The low gray clouds full of snow that had obscured the sky all day and all evening were gone. A few feathery wisps still skimmed across the moon, but they were fleeting.

And what a moon. It was full and white and stood out as crisply against the black sky as an opal against velvet. And the stars... There must have been a zillion.

Things on earth were pretty appealing to the eye, too. The little town of Alpine was covered in snow...sparkling white snow that was unblemished by human footsteps and tire tracks, and not yet polluted by the exhaust of passing cars.

Snow. It laced the fences, made crescents in the windowpanes, perched precariously on the branches of trees in delicate piles and formed deep drifts against the outside walls of every building.

Here and there the golden glow of a lantern or candlelight warmed a window.

Dylan had never seen such a perfect depiction of winter Americana except in those miniature towns and old-fashioned villages people displayed on fireplace mantels and under Christmas trees. He couldn't help but say out loud, "Is this real, or am I dreaming?"

Elise turned and stared, but kept up her brisk pace as she led the way. Both of them carried flashlights, but they were unnecessary. With the full moon and the reflection off the snow, Dylan could see Elise's look of surprise quite clearly.

"That sounded dangerously sentimental, McAllister," Elise warned him. "Watch out or someone might think you're human."

"But not you, eh, Doc?" he shot back.

"I just never took you for the type that would appreciate a night like this—" she raised her arms as if to encompass everything around them "—a scene like this."

"Even a snake will crawl up on a rock to watch a sunset."

When she didn't immediately respond, he added, "But you're right. I don't appreciate scenes like this very often because I'm just too busy making a living to pay much attention to anything but the files on my next case."

"Scraping and bowing to the almighty buck, eh, McAllister?"

"You sure as hell think you've got me pigeonholed, don't you, Doc?" huffed Dylan, tired of the way Elise constantly jumped to conclusions about him…conclusions that always painted him in the very worst light. "I'll bet I'm paying a hell of a lot more alimony to my ex-wife than you're paying the bank to cover your ex-husband's settlement. I work just as hard as you do. It's less physically challenging than your job, I'll grant you that, but there's a ton more paperwork." He paused, then added, "In fact, our situations are very similar. We're a lot more alike than you think."

"In a pig's eye," Elise muttered, trudging on.

"I don't think Rowena would appreciate that comment," Dylan remarked, quickening his pace to catch up with her. Side by side now as they continued up Main Street, he peered into her face. "How are our situations different, Elise?" he demanded to know. "We're both paying a lot of money to our ex-spouses."

"I put myself through vet school, then I worked hard to get my clinic going."

"I put myself through law school and I worked hard to build a clientele for my law practice," he countered.

"Ted did nothing but sit around and watch sports on TV and drink beer."

"Brenda did nothing but shop and get manicures."

"Yeah, but you're a man and—"

Abruptly she stopped speaking.

"What was that, Doc?" Dylan prompted her. "Were you going to say that because I'm a *man* I'm supposed to support my ex-wife, and because you're a *woman*, you have no responsibility for your ex-husband? That's just the attitude men have been up against for decades. It's not fair. Look at it this way, Elise—I have to pay Brenda alimony till she remarries. You only have to pay the bank till the loan's paid off. Would you like to trade places?"

"If you're trying to convince me that the settlement you got for Ted was fair, you're wasting your time."

"The only point I'm trying to make is that *my* settlement wasn't fair, either. For crying out loud, why can't Brenda get a job and support herself?"

Elise stopped in her tracks and turned to face Dylan. "You said 'either,' McAllister. You said your settlement wasn't fair *either*. Are you admitting something? Are you *apologizing?*"

Dylan clenched his jaw stubbornly. She wasn't going to force an apology out of him. He slipped into his Sargeant Friday voice. "I'm just stating the facts, ma'am."

Elise shook her head and starting walking again. "And you think you and I are two divorced peas in a pod. What a laugh."

"The only difference between my divorce and yours, Doc, is that I don't blame Brenda's attorney for what happened. I've gotten on with my life. Can you say the same?"

She turned on him, her eyes gleaming. "I *have* gotten on with my life."

"Then why do you take such glee in torturing me? Why did you buy me at the auction, Elise, if not to get revenge?"

She turned off the main road and started across an open field. Dylan followed. With the east view no longer blocked by buildings, Mount Timpanogos loomed up before them in all its magnificence, its craggy, snow-covered angles sharp and white against the deep purple of the sky.

"I bought you because I wanted to prove a point," she finally answered. "Revenge was only a *minor* factor in my decision."

"Doc, you have a problem."

"You mean besides you?"

"You're bitter."

She laughed harshly. "And you're not?"

He sighed. "Yeah, I guess I am, too," he admitted.

They walked in silence for a while, both deep in their own thoughts.

Elise eventually spoke, saying wistfully, "I just wish—"

Dylan had to lean close to catch what she said. "What do you wish?"

"I just wish things were simpler...that two people could meet, fall in love and get married, have a couple of kids and grow old together...happily."

"Sounds like you bought the fairy tale," he observed, not without compassion.

"Hook, line and sinker."

"Do you still believe it could happen?"

She laughed self-consciously. "I do. Despite my disastrous marriage to Ted, I still believe in the fairy tale. Isn't that pathetic?"

Not pathetic, he thought to himself. Just naive. And awfully sweet. Maybe he'd believe it could happen, too, if he didn't have to face divorce day after day.

"I should have been a minister," he said.

"You?" She turned to gape at him, amused and faintly appalled.

"Yeah. I'd see people beginning their marriages instead of ending them. And then maybe I wouldn't be so cynical."

Again they walked in silence, but now it was a companionable silence. Despite the mandatory exchange of insults, they'd been honest with each other. And despite Elise's poor opinion of him, Dylan had a high regard for honesty. It was especially important in relationships.

Mind you, not that he wanted a relationship with Elise. But it would be nice to be…friends.

Dylan nearly laughed out loud. Elise would never accept him as a friend. She barely considered him as part of the human race. Besides, friendship required respect and trust, neither of which she felt where he was concerned.

"There it is…the Circle J. I expect Pete's in the barn."

Dylan had been so absorbed in his thoughts, he hadn't realized how close they were to the ranch. They'd covered two miles very quickly, but then the company had been stimulating, and sparring with Elise had kept his thoughts off the cold and the difficulty of hiking in snowshoes. His back seemed no worse for the wear, either, but maybe it was just numb.

The lights of the ranch house and the nearby barn looked warm and welcoming. Hopefully this Pete fellow would have a thermos of coffee ready to help them defrost from the inside out. Just a few steps more, and they'd be home free….

Suddenly Elise let up a whoop of surprise, slipped on a patch of ice under the barn's rain gutters, teetered as she tried to balance, then fell backward into Dylan's arms. He dropped the flashlight and Elise's black bag, clasped her around the waist, then plopped onto his rear in the soft snow.

Once he was over the jarring impact of falling, Dylan found himself in a very interesting position. Elise's knit hat was askew, and Dylan's nose was buried in her hair. It was as soft as silk and smelled great.

His legs straddled her hips, the womanly curves seeming to fit perfectly against him.

He embraced her around her midriff just under her breasts, their firm shapes resting lightly against his arms.

He had to admit, she was one nice bundle of woman. Did she like where she was as much as *he* liked where she was?

"Oh, great," she said, her voice dripping with frustration and disgust. "What next? I think I've sprained my wrist."

Chapter Six

All romantic ideas fled from Dylan's mind. "You hurt your wrist?"

"Yes, I tried to break my fall by putting out my hand, but I guess I came down on it too hard."

"I was right behind you. I caught you and cushioned your fall, Elise," Dylan said, exasperated. "You didn't need to put out your hand."

"It was a knee-jerk reaction, McAllister," Elise grumbled, sitting up and trying to scoot away. "Besides, I wasn't sure you'd catch me."

In other words, *I don't trust you, McAllister.*

She had scooted away far enough to have cleared Dylan's legs, and now she was trying to stand up. He scrambled to his feet, ignoring his own aching back, and exclaimed, "Don't be stubborn, Doc. Let me help you get up and save some wear and tear on your injured wrist." He took her arm and gave it a firm but gentle tug.

"I don't need any help," she was saying, still resisting assistance as he pulled her to her feet, when suddenly they both slipped on the ice. They each lurched toward the other and instinctively grabbed on. She ended up with her arms wrapped around his waist, her face flattened against his abdomen, and with one leg stretched between his two. His hands clenched her shoulders, and he stood, stiff-legged, trying to maintain his balance.

"Great, just great," she muttered, her voice muffled as she spoke against his coat. "Now what?"

Dylan tried not to laugh. "We're in a ticklish situation here, Doc." And he meant that two ways. One false move, and they'd both be spread out flat on the ice…and her mouth so close to his abdomen was giving him butterflies. "Maybe I should just ease you to the ground and we can…er…start over again."

"I told you I didn't need help," she reminded him testily.

Dylan couldn't help it. This time he laughed. "Don't talk. It tickles."

Her head jerked up, and she scowled at him. "*Where* does it tickle, McAllister? No, don't tell me! Just let go of me!"

"Hey, who's got hold of who here?" he countered.

"Fine," she groused. "*I'll* let go of *you*, then."

"Not so fast," he cautioned, but he was too late. She let go, slipping to the ground and landing on her fanny with a thud. In the meantime Dylan was thrown off balance, his knees buckled, his feet flew out from under him and he toppled over…right on top of Elise.

Pushed up on his elbows, with his forearms flattened on the ice, Dylan stared down into Elise's dazed expression. They were face-to-face, hip to hip. Her lips were inches away from his. He decided he liked this position…a lot. Even through all the padding of sweaters and coats, he was very aware of her warm, womanly body beneath him.

Through the fog of arousal, it occurred to him that

he probably ought to ask her if she was hurt, or if she could breathe with him virtually pinning her to the ground. But he could see she was breathing. Each breath was a plume of white in the icy air. She was breathing fast…just like him.

And if she was hurt, she'd say so, wouldn't she?

It would be so easy, so natural, just to lower his head a notch and kiss her. He wanted to. And if she didn't like the position they were in and the ever-diminishing, scant distance between their lips, she'd waste no time telling him to get up or else.

Her eyelids lowered slightly, and her lips parted. Dylan interpreted such telling body language as a silent invitation. He closed his eyes, bent his head and—

"Doc Allen? That you?"

Wincing from the strain on her injured wrist, Elise shoved Dylan off of her with the strength of an Amazon and was on her feet in seconds. "Pete," she said with a nervous laugh, furtively straightening her clothes. "My…er…assistant and I fell on the ice."

From Dylan's position—flat on his back on the driveway—he could see the doubtful and slightly aghast look on the lanky, middle-aged man's sun-leathered face. "I threw some salt on the concrete after I shoveled, but I guess I missed a spot. Sorry about that," he apologized. Then, when Dylan continued to lie there, he stepped forward and asked, "Do you need some help getting up, mister? You're not hurt, are you?"

"No more than usual," Dylan replied dryly. "But I could use a hand up. I wrenched my back yesterday, and it's a little stiff."

Pete helped Dylan up without any further catastrophe, and the two men exchanged short introductions, then followed Elise into the barn. She'd retrieved her black bag and was now all business. She avoided Dylan's eyes, removed her snowshoes and briskly went to work. He noted that though she didn't complain or comment about it, she favored her injured right hand. Again he admired her professionalism and determination.

The horse was a beauty. Penny was a sleek, copper-colored mare with a glossy mane. But even to someone like Dylan, who was uneducated in vet medicine, it was extremely apparent that Penny was in pain. Her big eyes rolled, she tossed her head and she gave an occasional plaintive whinny. Pete held her by the bridle he'd obviously put on her for the purpose of control, crooned in her ear and stroked her neck.

Dylan watched as Elise examined the horse, running her hands along the mare's bloated middle and taking her pulse and respiration with a stethoscope pressed against her neck.

"Her pulse is fast but strong. So's her breathing, so I don't think she's in any danger from shock at this point, but it's obvious she's in a lot of pain. We'll bypass IVs for now, but is it all right if I give her an analgesic, Pete? It won't fix the problem, but she'll be much more comfortable and manageable while we work on her."

"Go ahead, Doc," Pete replied. "I hate to see her in pain."

Elise nodded and reached inside the black bag for a large hypodermic needle. She filled it with liquid from a small bottle and held it up to the light to check the measuring lines on the syringe. Unlike Elise's house, the barn was lit up brightly with electricity. It must have been heated, too, because Dylan felt quite warm suddenly. He pulled off his knit cap and gloves and unwrapped the muffler from around his neck. Was the barn that warm, or was he just overheated from his recent close encounter with one sexy vet?

"How much does she weigh, Pete? About a thousand pounds?"

"Only nine hundred last weigh-in. She's still growing."

Elise squirted out a tiny bit of the liquid, then approached the horse. As if she suddenly remembered something, she turned and gave Dylan a quick, impersonal glance and said, "McAllister, there's alcohol and cotton balls in the bag. I want you to wipe the area before I give her the shot."

Actually quite glad to be able to help in some way, Dylan hurriedly did what he was asked to do. When he got near the horse, she turned her head away and whinnied. "I won't hurt you, girl," Dylan said softly as Pete held Penny's massive head. She must have believed him, because she held still while he swabbed the area that Elise indicated over the mare's jugular vein.

Minutes later Penny was acting less agitated. Dylan was sitting on a bale of hay a few feet away while Elise stood next to the horse, stroking its flank.

"So, what next, Doc?" Dylan asked her.

"I think we'll give her some precautionary antibiotics, Pete," said Elise, ignoring Dylan but answering his question anyway. "The fluxinin meglumine I gave her for the pain will prevent laminitis, so—"

"What's laminitis?" Dylan persisted, growing irritated with Elise's cold-shoulder treatment and genuinely interested in Penny's condition.

Elise gave him an annoyed look and said, "Laminitis is a foot problem that sometimes occurs after a bout with colic. The painkiller I gave her will help that."

"That shot you gave her?"

"Bingo," she replied sarcastically.

"I thought you said he was your assistant, Doc?" Pete said under his breath, but loud enough for Dylan to hear him...while he scraped snow off his boots and pretended not to be listening.

"He is, but he's still as green as grass, Pete," Elise explained in the same low voice, focusing her attention on the horse.

Pete bent his head near hers. "Well, the only way he's going to learn, Doc, is by asking questions. Don't you think you're being a mite hard on 'im?"

Dylan watched Elise shake her head ruefully. "I'm not being nearly hard enough, Pete," she answered, then leaned close and whispered something in his ear so quietly Dylan couldn't make out a word of it. He watched, frowning.

When Elise was done whispering, Pete turned and glowered at Dylan, nodding knowingly. "Ah, now I understand," he said.

Just what do you understand, Pete? Dylan wondered, getting that post-office mug-shot feeling again. Was the whole town familiar with Elise's hard-luck divorce story featuring Dastardly Dylan as the black-caped, mustache-twirling villain?

Then, as Elise whispered something else into Pete's ready ear, a wide grin formed on his weathered face. "Yeah, Doc, I think that's a great idea. Go for it."

Dylan had a terrible feeling of foreboding. Any minute now, he'd probably be tied to a railroad track somewhere while Pete and Elise watched and waited gleefully for the next train.

"Pete's right, McAllister," Elise said, walking toward him with a sweet smile that reeked of duplicity.

"About what?" Dylan asked suspiciously.

"You should be more involved in helping with Penny's treatment. How else will you learn?"

He stood up, nervously pulling at his clothes. "Yeah, so what do I do?" he asked hesitantly.

"Since we don't have the right-size nasogastric tube needed to start Penny on a mineral oil or a psyllium regimen—"

"What?"

"We don't have the right-size tube to put down her nose to administer lubricants or fiber into her stomach, which would then work its way into her intestines, so we're going to have to go with another procedure."

"What kind of procedure?"

"One that will give Penny much more immediate relief, although it's a little…messier."

Dylan was no dunce. He smelled a rat, or something worse. "Are you saying you want me to give this horse…an *enema?*"

Elise smiled. "You guessed it! You're absolutely right, McAllister. Penny needs an enema."

He felt his jaw clench and his neck muscles tighten clear down to his toes. "And you want *me* to administer this…*procedure?*"

"Yes, I do. I think it will be a good learning experience for you."

"No, you don't," he snarled. "You want me to do the dirty work because you're determined to mete out as much punishment as possible over the next few days."

"I can understand how you would think I was just being mean spirited, McAllister," Elise replied in an infuriatingly soothing tone. "But there's a perfectly logical reason why you should do the deed and not me or Pete."

Dylan raised a haughty brow. "And that is?"

"Pete's needed to keep Penny calm. And—as you must have forgotten—I fell and hurt my wrist. I don't think it's sprained, but it really is weakened. I don't know if I would have the strength to do what's… er…necessary to conduct the procedure."

"How convenient," Dylan muttered, but there was a ring of truth somewhere in that condescending explanation. Elise's wrist *was* sore…probably more sore than she'd like anyone to know. Dylan had noticed her surreptitiously favoring it ever since the fall.

He unbuttoned his coat and threw it on the hay behind him, then rolled up his sweater sleeves. Elise watched with a look of amused surprise. *I'll show her,* Dylan thought with determination. Besides, what were a few more spots on his expensive hand-knitted sweater?

"So, tell me exactly what to do," he demanded, standing with his hands on his hips and his feet spread. "I don't want this to be any more traumatic for me or the horse than necessary."

"It won't be," Elise assured him. "You'll do a good job. You're a smart man, McAllister. After all, you graduated law school, didn't you?"

"Yes, I did, Doc," he replied grimly. "I finished first in my class. And all to prepare me for this shining moment in my career."

"All professions have their messy cases, McAllister," Elise informed him with another of her sweet, lethal smiles. "I'm so glad that I can share one of mine with you."

Two HOURS LATER Dylan and Elise returned to the house and both were relieved to find the electricity back on.

"I hope it's been on long enough for the water to be hot," Dylan hinted as they stepped into the warm kitchen.

Elise pulled off her gloves and stared with reluctant admiration at her obviously exhausted houseguest. He'd been through a lot in the past twenty hours. He'd worked hard at an unfamiliar job, wrenched his back, endured the scorn of a jealous chimp and the indignity of being the butt of a mouthy parrot's jokes, gone on a four-mile hike on snowshoes in teen-degree weather in the dead of night and had even given a horse an enema...successfully. And all this with no more than four hours sleep and no recent shower.

Elise had to admit to herself that Dylan McAllister was made of tougher stuff than she'd originally given him credit for. And except for some very understandable grousing now and then, he'd been a better sport about the whole thing than most men would be under similar circumstances. He was certainly better natured, more flexible and more useful in emergencies than Ted had ever been.

Elise shook her head. She didn't like the direction her thoughts were leading her. She didn't want to like Dylan McAllister. She didn't want to recognize his good qualities. After all, she'd spent the past few months resenting him. It was bad enough that she was so physically attracted to him. That near-kiss as they lay on the icy concrete at the Circle J was a clear indication that she definitely had to watch her p's and q's around her ex-husband's divorce lawyer...or they'd end up in the sack. Just the thought of her and Dylan cavorting on her feather mattress gave her shivers all over.

"Well, Doc, can I take a shower or not?" Dylan prompted her, sitting slumped in a kitchen chair. "I could sure use one. Or aren't you talking yet? You didn't say two words to me on the way back from the Circle J."

Elise shrugged. "I was thinking."

"About the horse?"

"Yes," she lied. Actually she'd been thinking about *him* the whole time, giving herself stern lectures on not getting in another situation where his lips were quite so close to hers, trying to rationalize away all the good points she seemed to be constantly discovering about him.

"Do you think she'll be okay?"

Elise looked at Dylan. There was a furrow of worry between his brows. Compassion for animals was a very appealing personality trait in a man. In Elise's opinion, when a man kicked a dog, that said something very negative about him. So why, if he could have compassion for a horse, was he seemingly so indifferent about pulverizing her and other women in the courtroom?

"You're an enigma, McAllister," she said, her own frown matching his.

He quirked his mouth into that ready grin of his. "What's that got to do with the horse?"

She sighed. "Never mind... I think Penny will be

fine. We got her through the night. She's feeling better, and maybe Dr. Spencer will be able to keep something like this from happening again."

He slapped his hands on his knees and stood up. "I'm glad for Penny, but I still need a shower, Doc. Can I go first?"

"Go right ahead," she answered, beginning to bustle about the kitchen. "But save some hot water for me."

"You know what they say, don't you? Save water, shower together," he suggested with a teasing leer.

She stooped for a pan to hide her blush. "Thanks, but no thanks."

"Suit yourself," he answered, heading for the door.

"Oh, just a minute," she called before he could leave. She turned and faced him across the room.

"Yes?" He flicked a searing glance over her, making her blood pump like crazy. "Changed your mind about the shower?"

"When pigs fly," she retorted.

Dylan looked dubiously at Rowena, who stood at his feet, staring up at him. "Not any time soon, then, I gather." His amused gaze shifted back to her. "So what do you want, Doc?"

I want you.

"I...I wanted to make sure you understand, McAllister, that there's no way you can go back to bed after your shower, no matter how much you may want to."

He frowned and darted a quick look at the teakettle-shaped clock over the sink. "It's only six o'clock. Surely I've got time for a nap. Your first appointment yesterday was at nine."

"Yes, but today's my surgery day. I start at seven-thirty."

He heaved a resigned sigh. "Great."

"Be glad all you've got to do is shower," she said tartly. "I still have to bathe myself, get George out of his pen, dress him and feed him, and fix breakfast for us, too."

"I get the picture," he murmured ruefully. "So, who or what's our first patient, Doc?"

"A Great Dane, named Bruno."

Dylan nodded appreciatively. "I like Great Danes. Good-looking breed. Big. A real man's dog. So what's Bruno going under the knife for?"

Elise bit her lip to keep from smiling. "Well, Bruno's coming in to be neutered."

She watched the color drain out of Dylan's face. "And I have to help?"

She shrugged and nodded. "'Fraid so."

Dylan grimaced and shook his head, muttering as he left the room, "The poor bastard."

DYLAN'S HOT SHOWER had felt wonderful. He'd put on a fresh pair of jeans and a clean denim shirt purloined from the drawer that contained a few clothes Ted had left behind. His eyes were a little gritty from lack of sleep, but he was used to occasional all-nighters as he pored over case files. All he needed to perk him up were a couple cups of strong coffee.

By the time Dylan returned to the kitchen, George was in his high chair eating cheerios and a banana, Rowena had her snout in her food dish, Geraldo was perched on his swing in his cage near the window and was peering curiously outside and Elise was standing over a steaming pot at the stove.

Dylan lingered at the door of the kitchen for a moment and surveyed the strange but oddly appealing domestic scene before him. Bright morning light spilled into the kitchen through the window, and a glimpse through the curtains revealed glistening white snow and a crystal blue sky.

The kitchen was warm and cozy and smelled of breakfast. He took a deep breath. Coffee, oatmeal, soft-boiled eggs, o.j. and toast. No bacon, of course. That would be a sacrilege in this particular kitchen.

And then there was Elise....

So far, no one had noticed he was there, least of all the cook. From the back she looked mighty appealing. She'd obviously made time to shower. Her hair was loose and curly and still slightly damp. She was wearing a crisp white blouse tucked into jeans.

If they were more familiar, if his overnight stay had been for the usual reason he stayed overnight at a woman's house, he'd creep up behind her, slip his arms around her slim waist and surprise her with a kiss on the neck and a friendly pat on the bottom.

His eyelids drooped as he imagined the scene with scintillating detail....

She'd laugh softly and melt against him, then turn and offer her lips for a good-morning kiss. They'd kiss...lingeringly. He'd ask her how much time they had before the first patient, and she'd say, *Enough time to repeat a little of that wonderful lovemaking we did last night. Oh, Dylan, you were so—*

"McAllister? What's the matter?" she asked him in a sharp tone, shattering his fantasy. "You in a stupor or something? Snap out of it! We've got a busy day ahead of us."

Reality bites, Dylan decided, moving to the table

and sitting down. Alerted to his presence, Geraldo hissed, Rowena came running and nuzzled his leg with her snout and George put his thumbs in his ears, waggled his fingers and gave Dylan a "raspberry salute," managing to spray his clean shirt with milk.

Elise observed the greeting George gave him, but made no comment about it. Instead, she plopped a bowl of oatmeal in front of him and inquired sweetly, "Cream or sugar?"

Grimly Dylan replied, "How about a little arsenic?" By the way the day had started out, he was sure a quick and painful death would be much more fun than the next few hours at the Allen Asylum.

By seven-fifteen, breakfast was over and Dylan was on his third cup of coffee. Elise was being thornier than ever. At the moment she had her nose buried in the *Salt Lake Tribune,* which had somehow gotten delivered despite the two feet of snow outside.

Now what had he done? he wondered. He thought he'd been a pretty good sport about everything so far. Why couldn't she cut him a little slack? One minute she was acting halfway pleasant and reasonable, and the next minute she was Mr. Hyde.

He was puzzling over her Jekyll-and-Hyde behavior when the front doorbell rang.

"Who could that be?" she wondered aloud, peering over the newspaper in the direction of the living room.

"The poor bas— Uh...the Great Dane?"

"No. It's too early, and they'd bring Bruno to the clinic door." She glanced at her watch, frowned, stood up and stalked out of the room. Dylan hoped whoever was at the door had a good reason to be calling so early in the morning, because it looked as if Elise's irritation with him might spill over on some unsuspecting brush salesman.

But if Mr. Hyde left the kitchen, Dr. Jekyll returned with a tall, broad-shouldered, Nordic-looking fellow in tow. Elise was all smiles, as bright and cheerful as sunshine.

So who the hell was this guy? Dylan wondered, taking an immediate and unreasonable dislike to the stranger. Big, blond, as wholesome looking as Mom's apple pie and dressed in a red parka and tall black boots, he reminded Dylan of Dudley Dooright of the mounted police. Even his teeth glinted.

"Thank you for shoveling the sidewalks for me, Lars," Elise was saying as they entered the room.

Lars?

"I was pressed for time this morning, and there was an awful lot of snow out there."

Dylan could have kicked himself. He'd been so intent on getting his hot shower and getting comfortable and warm again, he'd completely forgotten about the shoveling that obviously needed to be done after a gargantuan snowstorm. So she'd hired this overgrown Boy Scout to do it?

"It was no trouble at all, Elise," Lars replied, grinning as if he were in a toothpaste commercial. "You're just a hop, skip and a jump from my place and when I open my office across the street, you'll be even closer."

His office? What kind of office? Something with dumbbells and tanning machines?

"Well, you deserve a cup of coffee and a Danish for all your hard work," she informed him. "Please sit down at the table." She turned, still smiling, and inclined her head toward Dylan. "That is, if you don't mind sharing a meal with a chimp and a lawyer."

Dylan threw her a give-me-a-break look and stood up, extending his hand toward the studly fellow. "In case there's any doubt in your mind, *I'm* the lawyer," Dylan drawled. "Dylan McAllister."

Lars looked at Dylan as if he'd just noticed him. And the obvious question that was undoubtedly bombarding his brain was...what was this lawyer doing in Elise's kitchen having breakfast at seven-fifteen unless he'd spent the night with her?

Dylan's extended hand hovered in the air while Lars was probably deciding on the fastest and most efficient way to break his neck. Twisting it like a screw-off lid, maybe, or just a quick, clean snap?

"McAllister got stranded here last night, Lars," Elise explained hastily, seeming to have finally noticed the thick-as-fog tension in the room. "That was quite a snowstorm last night, wasn't it?"

Lars' chiseled features relaxed. "Oh, yeah. The snowstorm." He took Dylan's hand and squeezed...hard. "I'm Lars Peterson. I was surprised to see you here at first, but now I remember Elise saying something about having some help in the clinic this week. But why a lawyer?"

"I'm surprised you don't know the whole story," Dylan replied, surreptitiously shaking some blood back into his hand after Lars released it from his death grip. He glanced at Elise and smiled crookedly. "I thought the whole town knew."

Elise was returning to the table with a flaky, yummy looking Danish on a plate. She gave Dylan a repressive glare. "I won McAllister in a bachelor's auction, Lars. He's agreed to be at my beck and call for a week. I couldn't think of a single better way to put him to use than in my clinic."

Dylan wrinkled his nose at her. *Not a single better way?* he telegraphed suggestively. She sniffed and looked away.

Lars sat down and picked up his fork, immediately digging in to the Danish. Dylan wondered why he got lumpy oatmeal and the boy-toy got a tasty sweet-roll.

"I wish I'd known about the auction, Elise," Lars told her between bites of Danish and gulps of strong coffee. "I'd certainly enjoy being at your beck and call for a week. I'd make myself very useful."

"I'm sure someone would have outbid me, Lars," Elise said with a teasing smile. "You'd go for big bucks."

Yeah, thought Dylan, *slabs of beef cost a pretty penny these days.*

Dylan hated jealousy more than any other emotion. It made him feel out of control. But he wasn't the only one having difficulty tolerating the presence of someone so clearly anxious and ready to bonk Elise on the head with a club and drag her to his love cave. George was beside himself. He was glaring at the most recent threat to his corner of the jungle with obvious animosity. His teeth were bared, his chest was puffed up to the max and he was banging his spoon against the metal tray of the high chair.

"Settle down, George," Elise scolded him, taking away the spoon. "Be good or I'll put you in your pen."

George sulked and folded his arms across his chest.

For once, Dylan was on the ape's side. He didn't like Lars, either. There was a certain self-importance under that Dudley Dooright image. And he was looking at Elise as if she were ripe fruit and he hadn't eaten in a week.

"You say you're opening an office nearby?" Dylan prompted, forcing Lars to pull his hungry gaze away from Elise and look at him instead.

Lars turned reluctantly. "That's right. I'm the new dentist in Alpine."

Dylan's jaw nearly dropped. This guy had calendar-boy good looks *and* a brain? He could flaunt his physique in a Speedo and still do a root canal? Where was the justice? But he should have known Lars was a dentist. How else could he afford a full set of capped teeth unless he'd done them himself?

Now Dylan felt really threatened. Elise wasn't his girlfriend, but he was feeling damn proprietary about her. He crossed his arms—this time unconsciously mimicking George instead of the other way around—and seethed.

Then things got even worse.

Lars turned back to Elise. "Are we still on for tonight? I thought we'd go to Nino's after the ballet."

They had a date? He was *cultured?* And Nino's was Dylan's favorite night spot to take dates, so it proved again that the big lug had good taste. But the fact that he liked Elise was proof enough of Lars's intelligence and good taste.

"Sure, we're still on," said Elise. "My day ends early today, thank goodness."

"Good. Then we can go to dinner first, too?"

Elise shrugged and smiled. "Sure. Why not?"

Lars grinned from ear to ear. "Great. Pick you up at five?"

"My last patient should be out of recovery and ready to go home by four, so that's perfect."

All the particulars settled between them, Elise went to the stove for the coffeepot to refill Lars's cup. Hadn't she noticed that *his* cup was empty, too? Dylan groused to himself. He was no chauvinist who needed to be waited on hand and foot, but if Elise was being hospitable, why couldn't *he* be included in that hospitality?

Elise took George out of his high chair and set him down on a chair next to Dylan while she dampened a paper towel to wipe the milk off his hairy upper lip. Side by side, Dylan and George gritted their teeth and bored holes in Lars's broad back as he sipped his coffee and watched every move Elise made. His attitude was wolfish and predatory. Dylan was imagining his hands around Lars's thick neck when the doorbell rang again.

"Maybe they brought Bruno to the front door instead of the back," Elise commented, hurrying out of the room.

In the brief time Elise was gone, Dylan and Lars and George sat in stony silence. There was enough testosterone in the air to start a war.

Then Elise returned with the Great Dane on a leash, the big dog prancing along as if he hadn't a care in the world. He sat down in the middle of the room, his tongue lolling, his ears perked up and a friendly dog smile wreathing his face. He didn't have a clue what he was in store for.

"Poor bastard," breathed Dylan, crossing his legs.

Chapter Seven

"Bruno's here to be neutered," Elise cheerfully informed everyone. "Ready to go to work, McAllister?"

Elise's announcement had the desired effect. Evidently feeling a cringing empathy for the dog, Dylan had already crossed his legs. She could hardly refrain from bursting into a hearty belly laugh when Lars and George crossed their legs, too!

"I'd better get going," Lars said a minute later, standing up hurriedly. "They're laying carpet today in my new office, and I'd better make sure they get the right color down."

"That's probably a good idea," Elise agreed, smiling to herself. She knew Lars disliked the idea of the Great Dane being neutered. But since the dog was four years old and had already sired several offspring, she totally agreed with Bruno's owners that it was time to curtail his amorous activities. "See you at five, Lars."

"At five," Lars repeated, then he made a hasty exit.

Elise turned back to Dylan, who—along with George—was still sitting with his legs crossed. "You men act as though being neutered is the worst thing that could happen to Bruno."

"*I* can't think of anything more horrible," Dylan drawled.

"Well, it would be pretty awful if *you* were being neutered," Elise conceded, "but you're a human being."

"Ah, so you finally admit I'm human, do you?"

She ignored his interruption. "Bruno's a dog. Sex is different for animals. It's an urge, a basic drive to ensure proliferation of the species. With people it's more…"

"Sex is more…*what*, Elise?"

Elise couldn't believe she was discussing sex with Dylan McAllister. But she'd been the one to foolishly bring up the subject. How did she manage to get her foot in her mouth so frequently these days? She lifted her chin, determined not to show how flustered she felt as his teasing, sexy blue eyes challenged her.

"For human beings, sex is an emotional, as well as a physical, experience," she said in the instructive tones of a schoolteacher.

Dylan cocked his head to the side, considering. "Yes, I suppose it *is* an emotional experience when the two people involved are in love, or at least have some affection for each other. But sometimes sex is…well…just sex."

Elise stared at him, wondering if he'd ever been in love. Wondering if sex had always been "just sex" to him. Then her errant thoughts wandered. If she and McAllister made love, would she feel an emotional reaction or just a physical one? It was already achingly obvious to her that she was highly attracted to him, but could sex ever be "just sex" for her? Or would she always hold out for the emotional fulfillment that came with falling in love?

Impatient with the stupid romantic thoughts that filled her head these days—especially since they revolved around a cynical divorce lawyer—Elise snapped to attention and led Bruno down the hall toward the clinic.

"Come on, McAllister, we've got work to do," she called out as she marched along. "Bruno's only the first of three surgery patients this morning, and they've all got to be conscious and walking a straight line by four o'clock, when their owners come to pick them up."

"That's right. We'd better keep on schedule today because you've got a date," he said with mild sarcasm as he followed her.

She peered over her shoulder. "Anything wrong with that?" *She* could think of plenty of things wrong with having a date with Lars Peterson. She'd basically been pressured into it by Lars, and talked into it by her well-meaning friend Jan, but she really didn't want to go out with him. There was no chemistry, no—

"There's nothing wrong with you going out tonight. Nothing at all, Doc. But Lars Peterson, D.D.S., just doesn't seem your type."

She swiveled around, and Dylan had to put on the brakes quickly to keep from running into her. "How could you possibly know *my* type, McAllister?" she snapped, disconcerted by his ability to come to the crux of the matter so quickly. "You barely know me."

Dylan put his hands on his hips. "Have you ever been out with this guy before?"

She bristled. "That's none of your business."

"So this is your first date, I gather," he concluded with irritating accuracy.

"What if it is?"

"Just watch out, Doc. You may know your domestic animals, but you clearly don't recognize a wolf when you see one."

"Ha! Takes one to know one," she shot back childishly, not knowing what else to say. "But in this case, you're dead wrong, McAllister. Lars has always been a perfect gentleman. Now, if you don't mind, can we get down to business?"

Dylan's gaze dropped to Bruno, who was patiently waiting for the humans to quit arguing and get on with things. He was so clueless, even Elise felt a little sorry for him.

"If I had a choice, I think I'd rather give another enema to a horse than help you 'fix' poor old Bruno here."

Elise raised a brow. "Well, you don't have a choice." She turned and headed toward the clinic, Bruno following trustingly behind. "Coming?" she called sweetly.

She heard Dylan heave a weary sigh. "Coming," he snarled back.

Elise smiled to herself, then quickly sobered. It was pretty scary to realize that she'd much rather stay home and exchange insults with Dylan McAllister than go out with a hunky dentist. But it just made her more determined than ever to keep her date with Lars.

WHEN DYLAN RETURNED to his apartment late that afternoon, he was bone weary. He shrugged out of his coat, kicked off his loafers, turned up the thermostat and collapsed onto the black leather sofa.

"Home, sweet home," he murmured, relishing the silence of his high-rise apartment. No chattering chimp, no squawking parrot with a Don Rickles personality, no pig underfoot all the time and no Elise... The only sound was the quiet hum of the refrigerator and the muffled whoosh of the furnace as it poured warm air into the chilly room.

Dylan propped his head against the thick sofa arm and waited for much-needed sleep to steamroll him into blissful unconsciousness. And he waited, and he waited.

One eye flicked open. "Why can't I go to sleep?" he asked the empty room. Naturally there was no reply, so he stood up and paced the floor.

"It's *too* quiet," he finally admitted to himself, raking his fingers through his hair. He sat down, resting his elbows on his knees, and looked around.

His apartment suddenly seemed sterile to him. Except for his discarded coat and shoes, the spacious living room was immaculate. Every Friday a cleaning woman came in to dust the glass tables and chrome lamps, the sleek leather sofa and chairs and disinfect the stainless-steel-and-Formica bathroom and kitchen. She had a pretty cushy job, because his apartment never got really dirty. But how could it? He was the only one who lived there, and he was gone eighty percent of the time either working or socializing.

He wrinkled his nose. No wonder he was gone all the time. This place was about as cozy as a museum. Why would he want to spend time at home when it didn't really look or feel like a home?

Dylan paused to analyze that thought. So what should a home look like, feel like? he asked himself.

The answer was disconcerting. *A home is filled*

with comfortable clutter. A home has warm fires and smells of candle wax and corn bread. A home has overstuffed furniture with lots of pillows, antiques, feather beds, and books scattered and stacked in every corner...like Elise's house.

A home has someone in it besides yourself, someone to laugh with and quarrel with. Someone with a biting wit, soft green eyes and a cloud of dark, sweet-smelling hair...like Elise.

"Whoa," said Dylan, rising to his feet in a panic. "This isn't like you, McAllister. What you need is a hot shower, a cold drink and a cool blonde...not necessarily in that order."

First Dylan poured himself a Scotch on the rocks. Sipping the drink, he moved to the sofa table and pressed the Play button on his answering machine. Sure enough, among the several messages were three from Carol, whom he hadn't seen since New Year's Eve. He immediately got on the phone and made a date with her for that night.

"Can we go to Nino's?" Carol wanted to know.

Dylan tipped his glass and watched the ice swirl in his amber drink. Elise was going to Nino's with Lars, but that shouldn't keep him from patronizing his favorite night spot, should it?

"Sure, we can go to Nino's...if that's what *you* want." He'd just niftily shifted the responsibility for the decision to Carol.

"I love Nino's," she crooned across the wires. "That's the first place you kissed me...remember?"

He grinned. "I thought the first place I kissed you was behind the ear."

She giggled. "Oh, Dylan, you're so funny."

Dylan's grin fell away. There would be no snappy

comebacks from Carol, no humorous barbs delivered with a sweet, devious smile. His gaze wandered to the large picture window and the panoramic view of the Salt Lake Valley and the majestic Wasatch Mountains looming on the east. In the distance he could see the point of the mountain where the freeway curved and dropped down and around to the tiny rural towns of Lehi, Pleasant View, Springville and Alpine....

"Dylan, you still there?"

"Sure." He swallowed the rest of his drink. "Pick you up at eight, okay?"

"I'll be ready."

"Hey, and would you do me a favor and wear that sexy little black dress you wore New Year's Eve?"

There was silence, then, "My dress was red, Dylan."

"Right." He forced a chuckle. "I knew that. Wear the *red* dress, okay?"

"Sure, if you liked it that much."

"Yeah. It was sexy...and so were you."

"Can't wait to see you, Dylan," she purred. "Bye."

"Goodbye, Carol."

Dylan stood for a moment with the receiver in his hand, his gaze wandering back to the view from his window. Dusk was bathing the city in a soft orange glow, and lights were coming on, one by one, up and down State Street.

"I don't like this," he mumbled to himself, replacing the receiver and moving to the kitchen to set his glass in the sink. "I don't want to like that woman!"

Then he stalked off to his bathroom—which he didn't have to share with anyone, least of all a chimp—and turned the hot water in the shower on full bore.

AT TEN O'CLOCK Dylan sat with Carol at an intimate little table in a dark corner of Nino's. He had maneuvered things so that he was facing the door and could see everyone coming in. Not that it was all that important, but if Elise did show up with Lars, he wanted to see how the big ape looked in a coat and tie. And not that it mattered one whit, but he was curious to see how Elise looked and acted when she was on a date.

Carol was going on about some office politics at the travel agency where she worked, and Dylan was inserting the "hmm's" and "oh, really's" in what he hoped were all the right spots. So far, she hadn't complained. Once or twice he'd tried to really listen, but for some reason tonight her conversation seemed banal.

Then Elise appeared at the door, and Dylan wasn't hearing anything but the hammering of his heart. Had it only been five hours ago when he'd last seen her? It seemed like a month. She was wearing the same black dress she'd worn New Year's Eve. She looked drop-dead gorgeous. Carol's red dress was flashier, but no bright packaging was necessary to draw attention to Elise's classy beauty.

Lars came in behind her, took her arm with a proprietary air and guided her along behind the maître d' to a table in the opposite corner of the room. The lighting was dim, but Elise's corner was a little brighter than Dylan's, and he took great satisfaction in knowing that he could see her, but she probably would have to stare rudely and use a flashlight to see him.

"Don't you think so, Dylan?"

Carol was asking for an opinion about something, and Dylan didn't have a clue what she was talking about.

"I totally agree with you, Carol," he improvised.

She propped her elbows on the table, cupped her face in her hands and smiled dreamily. "I like talking to you, Dylan. You always see things so clearly."

He grinned and tapped her lightly on the nose. "Especially when I agree with you, right?"

She reached out and caressed his shoulder. "Want to go back to my apartment?"

He laughed uneasily. Strangely enough, that was the last thing he wanted to do. "We just got here, Carol."

"I've really missed you, Dylan. Why did it take you so long to return my phone messages?"

"Remember the bachelor auction? I was bought by a vet that lives in Alpine. I was stranded down there overnight during the snowstorm."

Carol frowned and straightened up. "Is this vet pretty?"

Dylan took a deep breath and lied. "No, not at all." *She's not pretty—she's beautiful,* he amended to himself.

"Good," Carol said, dismissing her competition easily. She usually had nothing to worry about when it came to competition, at least not in the looks department.

Suddenly Carol stood up and smoothed her hands down her short, tight skirt. He didn't like that, because it drew attention to their corner of the room. "I have to go to the ladies' room," she announced, then she bent down and gave Dylan a peck on the check. "Don't go away!"

He smiled and nodded at Carol till she quit looking back at him, then quickly glanced over at Elise. Carol didn't need to worry. He wasn't going anywhere. He just hoped Carol's sexy promenade across the floor to the ladies' room, which had caught every man's eye in the place, hadn't drawn Elise's attention, too.

But Elise's attention was being monopolized by Lars Peterson. While Elise sat stiffly in her chair, her fingers tightly curled around a full glass of some kind of drink, Lars was leaning very close. In fact, his Dudley Dooright mug was pushed up so close to hers, he was literally breathing down her neck! Then his muscular arm snaked around the back of the chair, and a big hand clamped over Elise's bare shoulder. Dylan could have sworn he saw her flinch. Or was that just *his* reaction?

In this case Dylan got no satisfaction from being right about Lars's wolfish personality. Dylan had a feeling that morning, given the way Lars had practically drooled while watching Elise move around the kitchen, that he would be hard to control on a date. But what he couldn't tell so far was whether or not Elise minded the way Lars was coming on to her. If she liked it, then it was a whole different ball game.

Dylan watched and brooded and sipped his drink and finally decided that Elise was definitely uncomfortable. Lars was drinking a lot. He was on his third drink in just fifteen minutes, and Dylan was still nursing his first in half an hour.

Dylan frowned and clutched his drink till his knuckles hurt. He couldn't fault Lars for finding Elise

attractive, nor, he supposed, could he blame the guy
for trying to seduce her while he had the chance. But
when a woman isn't interested, the signs are all there.
And when a woman says no, whether by word or
gesture or attitude, a decent man backs off. Lars
wasn't backing off.

"I'm back," Carol said as she slid into her seat.
"Sorry I was gone so long, but I broke a nail."

Dylan had forgotten all about Carol. "Oh, were you
gone long?"

Carol raised a brow. "You didn't miss me? Now,
that's flattering."

Dylan smiled weakly. "Do you want another
drink?"

"In a minute. Talk to me, Dylan. I've been yakking
all night. Now it's your turn."

Dylan didn't want to talk. He wanted to choke Lars
Peterson. Despite Elise scooting her chair and apparently making excuses to turn away and rummage
through her purse, Lars still persisted in malling her.
Finally she stood up…off to the ladies' room as a last
resort, he supposed. At least Lars couldn't follow her
in there.

"She's attractive, isn't she?" Carol commented
dryly as Dylan slavishly watched Elise cross the
room. "But she's not your type, hon. You like
blondes, remember?"

Dylan jerked his gaze back to Carol, quickly
drained his drink and croaked automatically, "Right.
I like blondes."

While he tried to figure out how to rescue Elise
without making her angry, since she was very independent and might resent his interference, thinking
she could take care of herself; without making Lars

angry, as Dylan remembered the handshake that morning and knew Lars had the strength of three mules; and without making Carol angry—she could pout with the best of them—Dylan managed to carry on a light conversation and still surreptitiously observe Lars.

Lars ordered another drink in Elise's absence and drained it immediately. If nothing else, Dylan had to make sure Elise was driving the car when she and her date left for Alpine that night. But how was he going to do that?

Dylan watched as a waiter brought a plate of appetizers—it looked like skewered, grilled shrimp—and set them down in front of Lars. His appetite for food seemed as voracious as his appetite for alcoholic beverages, because he dug right in, not even waiting for Elise to return. And this guy took her to the ballet? Dylan thought incredulously. It had to have been Elise's idea.

Dylan was still fuming, still agonizing over what to do, when Lars settled the matter. Suddenly he stopped stuffing shrimp into his mouth and grabbed his throat. His eyes got big, his mouth got slack and his face turned curry red. He was choking. It was the silent kind of choke that indicated his whole windpipe was blocked by food. He couldn't cough, he couldn't throw up and he couldn't call for help. But instead of grabbing a nearby diner and indicating his difficulty, he just sat there, too embarrassed or too panicked to move.

"For crying out loud," Dylan grumbled, leaping to his feet. "First I have to give an enema to a horse...now *this!*"

Like a runningback weaving his way through the

defensive line, he pushed his way past a waiter—
making the guy stumble and drop a plate of Buffalo
wings on some woman's lap—knocked down three
unoccupied chairs and nearly tackled a dessert cart,
but he made it to Lars's table in record time.

Strengthened by a rush of adrenaline, Dylan
grabbed Lars's forty-plus chest from behind and
heaved him to his feet. While the woman with the
chicken wings in her lap squealed with dismay and
excited murmurs rumbled through the room, Dylan
made a two-handed fist and placed it under Lars's
sternum.

He pressed hard, lifting Lars off his feet, once,
twice, three times, then…*whoosh*…the unlodged
shrimp popped out of his mouth and flew across the
room like a spitwad. Unfortunately it landed in some
guy's daiquiri.

People gathered around as Lars slumped to his seat
and breathed with a heavy rasp.

"You saved his life!" a woman gushed.

"You're a hero!" another one breathed reverently.

"I did the Heimlich maneuver, just like anyone else
would have done had they noticed him choking," Dylan replied modestly. He just wished they'd all sit
down again.

"You noticed him choking from clear across the
room?" Carol inquired, stepping out of the crowd and
standing next to Dylan. "Wow, you're observant."

"What's going on here?"

Suddenly Elise appeared. Her gaze darted from Dylan to Lars, and back to Dylan. Her eyes narrowed.
"What did you do to Lars, McAllister?"

Carol's mouth fell open. "Dylan, you *know* her?"

"I just saved his life, Doc," he informed Elise testily. "Got a problem with that? By the looks of things before you left for the ladies' room a while ago, you might wish I hadn't rushed to the rescue so fast."

Dylan watched Elise's cheeks blush bright pink. "What are you doing here, McAllister? Did you follow me? Are you *spying* on me?"

Carol tugged on Dylan's sleeve. "Who *is* this woman, Dylan?"

"Why would I follow you, Doc? Why would I spy on you? Believe me, I've spent more than enough time with you at the Allen Asylum for the past two days. You and your chimp and your parrot and your pig have nearly ruined my life...not to mention my wardrobe."

"I thought you liked Rowena," Elise protested.

"Who's Rowena?" Carol wailed.

Dylan continued to ignore Carol and address Elise. "I do like her. She's the only one that treats me with respect in that crazy place you call home."

"You're still mad about the enema, aren't you?" Elise accused, crossing her arms.

"The *enema?*" the crowd echoed.

"I want to go home!" insisted Carol, stamping her foot.

"Not till I make sure Lars is okay," said Dylan, suddenly solicitous of the man he'd wanted to choke himself a few minutes ago.

"Should I call 911?" a waiter inquired.

"No," croaked Lars, wiping his face with a napkin dipped in ice water. "I'm fine."

"You see, the man is fine," hissed Carol into Dylan's ear. "And we're making a scene!"

"I can take care of him, McAllister," Elise informed him, pushing past him to hover over her date. "Why don't you just take care of your date?"

"You're not a medical doctor, you're just a vet, Elise," Dylan snidely reminded her.

"She's the *vet?*" shrieked Carol. "I thought you said she was *ugly?*"

Elise raised a brow and glared at Dylan. "So, now I'm ugly, eh? I'd say this whole situation is getting pretty ugly."

The manager apparently agreed. Nino himself appeared and quieted down the crowd, urging them all to return to their seats and enjoy a round of drinks and a plate of appetizers on the house. He laughingly suggested that no one wanted shrimp…right?

Dylan dredged up all the charm he could and apologized to the woman with Buffalo-wing sauce on her skirt. Then he gave her his business card, asking her to send him the cleaning bill or, if necessary, the cost of replacement. To Dylan's surprise, the woman quickly got over her irritation and was soon flirting with him. Dylan saw Elise roll her eyes. He smiled weakly and shrugged, seeming to say, *Can I help it?* Soon things had returned to relative normalcy, so Dylan paid his tab and, urging a stony-faced Carol beside him, walked quickly to the door.

Outside in the foyer, Dylan breathed a sigh of relief, but discovered his ordeal far from over. Elise was helping Lars on with his coat…or trying to. One arm was in a sleeve, but she was following him around in a circle, holding the coat up while he tried unsuccessfully to slip his arm in the other sleeve.

"You're drunk, Lars," Elise said in a testy voice, obviously at the end of her rope.

"You're right. I saw him down several strong drinks in there," Dylan corroborated.

Elise's head jerked up, and she was about to say something, when Carol shouted, "You were watching their table all night, weren't you, Dylan? If you wanted to go out with *her*, why didn't you call *her* instead of me? Good night, Dylan! And don't call me again!"

Carol stomped away toward the stairs, too angry to wait for the elevator.

"Are you going to let her walk home?" Elise inquired, struggling to keep Lars steady as he swayed and fumbled with his coat.

"Carol doesn't walk anywhere. The doorman will get her a cab. She'll be fine," he said, adding curtly, "but I'm not so sure about you. I didn't think he was *that* drunk."

"He had two more drinks after he choked," Elise explained with an exasperated edge to her voice. "The manager was only too eager to keep him pacified. People sue for spilled coffee these days, so maybe they were worried Lars would file suit, too."

"Hey, buddy," Lars said, suddenly focusing on Dylan. "Aren't you the guy that saved my life?" His words were slurred, and he kept blinking.

"I plead guilty," Dylan admitted dryly.

"Name's McDonald, right?"

"No, it's McAllister, but it really doesn't matter."

"Sure, it does," Lars insisted, staggering forward to slap Dylan on the back. "If it weren't for you, I'd be dead."

"Well, no one's perfect," Dylan murmured, supporting the hulking dentist as he stumbled against him. "And it appears I'm going to have to save your life a second time tonight." He turned to Elise. "I'm driving you home."

"That won't be necessary. *I* can drive us home, McAllister," Elise quickly insisted.

"What if you can't handle this guy?" Dylan hissed over Lars's shoulder. "What if you get halfway home and he insists on taking the wheel? And what if—?" He raised his brows, leaving the rest to Elise's imagination.

Elise's shoulders slumped, and she nodded. Obviously she got Dylan's meaning and she was no more eager to fight off Lars's amorous attentions than she was to drive home on slick roads with a possibly unruly drunk.

"Hopefully he'll sleep the whole way," Elise commented as she tiredly poked the elevator button.

"He's already half-asleep," Dylan replied, his arm thrown around Lars's wide shoulders. "I just hope we can get him to the car before he collapses."

They stepped into the elevator, and Lars leaned heavily against the back wall. Then, as he blearily watched the doors close, he announced, "I think I'm gonna be sick."

Chapter Eight

Thank goodness, Lars didn't get sick in the elevator. He held on till they were outside, then he was refreshed somewhat by the cold, crisp air. With Elise and Dylan walking on each side of him and holding on to his arms, they made it to the parking lot half a block away without too much difficulty.

"There's his truck," said Elise.

"His...*truck?*"

Elise knew Dylan would be surprised to find out that Lars drove a truck and that they'd have to drive all the way home squeezed together in a small cab.

"It's a late model, but it's still going to be crowded," Elise warned him. "Lars will probably go right to sleep and sprawl as much as he pleases."

"In that case, I hope you'll put aside your aversion to me for a half hour, Doc, and sit in the middle. If Lars gets restless in his sleep, he'll be a definite hazard at such close proximity to the steering wheel and gas pedal."

"I think I can tolerate sitting next to you for a while if it means the possible difference between life and death," she informed him frostily.

Trouble was, sitting that close to Dylan McAllister

presented a different kind of hazard to her own peace of mind. She wished she did feel an aversion to him— she *should* feel an aversion to him, but as each hour passed in his company, she was more and more attracted to him.

Elise made Dylan search Lars's pockets for his keys, which he did most reluctantly. The keys located, they got Lars inside the truck, locked and closed his door, then Elise and Dylan both climbed in on the driver's side.

Sandwiched between Lars's massive thigh on the right and Dylan's muscular but much leaner thigh on the left, Elise realized all her aversion was directed toward the right. She instinctively leaned toward Dylan, her cheek pressed against his shoulder.

"Comfy, Doc?" Dylan inquired, grinning down at her. With his face mere inches away, his boyish dimples showing, his blue eyes twinkling wickedly in the glow of the parking-lot lights, his breath smelling pleasantly of brandy and breath mints and his tangy after-shave teasing her senses, how could she possibly be...*comfy?*

"I feel like a thin wafer of Swiss cheese between two thick hunks of pumpernickel, but other than that, I'm just fine," she assured him with dry sarcasm. "At least I won't get cold."

"Neither will I," Dylan murmured, leaving Elise to wonder again if he felt the same unwilling attraction to her.

"That was a nice thing you did in there," Elise finally said as they turned onto the freeway and headed south.

"You mean saving Lars's life?" Dylan inquired.

"Of course that's what I mean."

"I had no choice. I certainly couldn't sit there and watch him choke...although I was tempted."

Staring straight ahead, Elise timidly inquired, "Had you been watching us?"

Dylan sighed. "Yes."

"Why?"

"Because I was worried about you," he confessed in a grudging tone.

Elise couldn't help it; Dylan's concern gave her a warm glow. "You were right about Lars," she admitted, giving the devil his due. "He was much too friendly for a first date—and with no encouragement on my part, mind you—even before we got to Nino's. I was waiting till ten, then I was going to inform him that I had a headache and wanted to go home. I didn't want to make an enemy out of him, because he's going to be working right across the street from me and Alpine is a small town." Elise grimaced. "But then he started drinking."

"I noticed."

"Which proves you sometimes think you know a person, but maybe you don't."

The possible double meaning hung tantalizingly in the air as the conversation trailed off, but Dylan didn't pick up on the invitation to bare his soul.

Elise had already discovered that Dylan was much more than the one-dimensional villain she'd made him out to be for the past few months, and she was stoking up her courage to lead the conversation into more-dangerous territory. She truly wanted to understand why he was so prejudiced against women in divorce court.

Obviously he'd had a bad marriage and a nasty divorce. Her marriage had been no picnic, either, but it hadn't turned her against all divorcing men. She wondered if Dylan could possibly have been married more than once and been shafted badly by both ex-wives. Hmm...now, there was a theory worth pursuing.

As they went over the point of the mountain and began to descend into Utah Valley, they could feel the stiff winds buffet the west side of the truck, but inside the cab was toasty warm. Lars was sleeping like a rock and snoring like a buzz saw. Elise and Dylan might as well have been entirely alone. It was the perfect time to ask him what she was suddenly dying to know.

"McAllister, were you...er...married more than once?"

He stared straight ahead, but she could see his lips curve into a rueful smile. "What brought that on?"

"Curiosity."

"I make it a point of honor not to discuss my ex-wives."

"*Wives?* As in the plural?"

He chuckled grimly. "No, there was only one. It just felt like there were two of her."

Well, there went another theory down the tubes. But since he seemed not to be averse to the subject, Elise decided that this would be a good time to try to find out how bad his single, disastrous foray into matrimony really had been.

"Your marriage was not a pleasant experience, I gather."

"Sonny and Cher got along better than Brenda and I did."

"Then why—?"

"Why did we get married in the first place? I could ask you the same question about you and Ted."

"Touché," she conceded quietly.

"I'm sorry," he said, reaching down and giving Elise's hand a brief squeeze, which left her breathless. "That was uncalled-for. Everyone makes a bad call now and then. I don't know anything about you and Ted. In my case, I should never have married Brenda in the first place, but she dazzled me from the minute I met her. Trouble was I was so dazzled, I couldn't see clearly. About six months of marriage improved my vision tremendously, and I've been paying through the nose for my short-sightedness ever since."

Elise nodded understandingly, then began her own confession. "Ted didn't dazzle me. I've known him since we were kids. There were never fireworks between us, but he was a real nice guy. He changed after we married, though. He had no direction, no motivation. Basically he wanted me to support him."

And now she *was* supporting him, thanks to Dylan. But for some reason, the thought didn't rankle her as much as it normally did.

"So now you're off marriage for good, eh?" Dylan prompted her when she fell silent.

"Not necessarily," she replied thoughtfully. "But I'm definitely off divorce!"

He chuckled. "That's a good way to look at it. But as for me, I've concluded that the best way to avoid divorce is to avoid marriage."

Elise supposed that Dylan's bitterness was understandable, but it was affecting more than himself. He was taking his disillusionment out on all divorcing women. Suddenly her determination to convince Dylan to change his cutthroat courtroom capers took on the noble dimensions of a campaign. For divorcing women everywhere, she had to make him see the error of his ways. For herself, all she wanted was an apology....

They had left the freeway and were traveling down the highway between Highland and Alpine, and were just about to turn onto Alpine's quiet Main Street when it suddenly occurred to Elise that Dylan had no transportation home.

"McAllister! You don't have a car!"

"I know. I've been imagining the effect of sleeping on Lars's cold floor on my sore back ever since we left Salt Lake."

"You don't have to sleep on Lars's floor," she told him.

He turned and gave her a quizzical look. "I don't?"

She was glad it was dark and he couldn't see her blush. "I'll drive you home."

He returned his gaze to the dark stretch of road, still banked on the sides by a good two feet of snow. The temperatures had stayed quite cold after the storm, and nothing was thawing.

"I can't let you drive me home."

"The roads are fine."

"They might not be in another hour. With the wind blowing as hard as it is at the point of the mountain, there'll be patches of black ice to contend with. The whole idea was to get you home safely, Doc. If I let you drive me home, then you drive back alone, I'd undo the whole purpose for driving you down here in the first place."

"You have a point." She bit her lip, pondering the wisdom of what she was about to say, and in the end throwing caution to the wind. "You'd better stay at my place again."

He turned and searched her face in the brief snatches of light that brightened the truck cab. "You think so?"

"Sure," she answered. "In the attic, of course."

He chuckled. "Of course. And why not?" he asked some higher, wiser source, peering up into the starry sky through the windshield. "I'm going to be down here slaving away again tomorrow anyway. What's another night in the Allen Asylum?"

Elise grinned. "I'm glad you're being so sensible, McAllister."

DYLAN WASN'T BEING sensible. If he were being sensible, he'd have hired any kind of transportation available back to Salt Lake and the solitary safety of his empty apartment. A Gypsy caravan, a circus train, a pack of mules or even a cranky camel would do, because the bottom line was that he was going crazy trying to keep his mitts off Elise. But maybe George would help keep him in his place.

Unfortunately, when they finally got Lars tucked into his bed at a small basement apartment two blocks down, then walked back to Elise's house, George was already locked in his pen for the night and was sound asleep. Jan, the long-suffering baby-sitter for the evening, met them at the door.

"What's this?" she whispered, staring at Dylan. "You leave with one man and come back with another?"

"It's a long story," Elise whispered back.

"I want to hear all about it over tea tomorrow. Deal?" Jan said as she slipped into her Levi's jacket.

"Deal. So, George is sleeping?"

"Like a baby chimp."

"Did he give you any trouble?"

"He was a bit peeved when I restricted him to only one Dr Pepper, but after he clapped along with Vanna while we watched 'Wheel of Fortune' and ogled the beach-bunnies on 'Baywatch,' he was in a much more cheerful state of mind."

"Who wouldn't be?" Dylan added with a grin.

"You're cute," Jan informed him, poking his chest on her way out and whispering to Elise, "You must have turned Lars in for a better model."

"I thought you *liked* Lars," Elise called after her, obviously frustrated. "That's the only reason I went out with the guy!"

But by now Jan had hopped off the porch and was crossing the lawn, headed for her apartment over the store.

Dylan stooped to pet Rowena, who had greeted him at the door with ecstatic grunts. "Hi, girl. Miss me?"

"Keep your voice down, McAllister," Elise advised him, stepping around him and the pig. "The last thing I want right now is for George to wake up and start dragging his tin cup across the bars of his pen."

Dylan rose, and they stood face-to-face in the foyer. "You and me both, Doc."

Standing so close, knowing they were alone—relatively speaking—in the warm, dark, quiet house, was very hard on Dylan's self-control. Elise had expressed disapproval of Lars's forward behavior on a first date, so what made him think she wouldn't slug *him* if he kissed her? But he was so tempted to take his chances....

"Would you like some hot chocolate, McAllister?"

Elise suddenly asked him, her voice suspiciously—
and attractively— husky.

Drinking hot chocolate was an innocent enough
pastime, and it was hardly the beverage of choice for
seduction. But somehow Dylan felt the invitation
hinted at possibilities.

"You...you must be cold after that long drive," she
stuttered. "It's got to be ten degrees or less out there."

It might be cold outside, but it had never been cold
in the cab. Even the walk home from Lars's apartment
hadn't lowered Dylan's temperature below the point
of percolation. Having Elise's thigh pressed against
his during the entire trip down from Salt Lake, his
nostrils filled with the scent of Shalimar—which he
had come to connect only with her—and her soft
breast brushing against his arm whenever she tried to
scoot farther away from Lars had been exquisite
torture.

And now all he could think about was dragging her
into his arms. He would be smart to go straight to
bed, because what right did he have to kiss a woman
he'd crushed in divorce court?

"Sure, I'd love some hot chocolate," he heard himself saying, apparently not capable of being smart at
the moment. As she nervously smiled her approval,
he shrugged out of his coat, already feeling enough
at home at Elise's to know exactly where to hang it
up. She took her coat off, too, and he enjoyed the
view from the back as he followed her into the
kitchen.

That black dress was a killer. Her shoulders were
bare, and her loose mahogany hair brushed against
the pale skin like bent willow branches brushing the

soft grass in a warm breeze. It was too sensuous for words.

And the way her waist dipped in and her slim hips flared out, and the sexy way she walked without being obvious about it—the way Carol was obvious about it with her hips zigzagging like a loose trailer across three lanes of traffic—really did things to his hormones. And those legs. They were as long as a summer afternoon, as curvy as a mountain road.

He could go on and on, but he was running out of metaphors. In short, she was one classy, sexy lady.

He sat down at the table and watched her fill a teakettle with tap water, mesmerized by her every move. As if she sensed his keen watchfulness and repressed desire, she was disarmingly shy, hiding her face behind a cloud of dark hair as she bent over the sink. A self-conscious, highly charged silence filled the room. Dylan waited and watched....

But when she turned off the tap and lifted the kettle, she let out a small cry of distress.

Dylan quickly stood up and moved to hover over her at the sink. He lightly touched her shoulder, and she turned, staring up at him uncertainly.

"What did you do, Doc?" he asked her. "Did you burn yourself?"

"No," she said, ducking her head. "It's this darn wrist. It's still weak. If I try to lift something just a little bit heavy, I get this shooting pain.... But it's nothing."

He reached down and took her hand. "It's this one, right?"

"Y-yes. Why?"

"Why aren't you wearing an Ace bandage?"

"It…it gets in my way when I work. It restricts my movement."

"You take good care of your furry and feathered little patients, but you don't take care of yourself very well, do you?"

She rolled her eyes, clearly flustered by his concern. "It's really nothing. I'm just fine. But maybe you should lift the kettle and put it on the stove."

"I will. But first I think you need a little T.L.C."

Elise's eyes got as wide as saucers, but she didn't say a word or make a move. She seemed frozen with expectation.

Dylan dragged his gaze away from her flushed skin, her luminous green eyes and slightly parted, dewy-looking lips, and looked down at her wrist.

She had beautiful hands. The fingers were long and slim, the skin smooth. Her nails were clipped short and were immaculate and shiny. Her wrist was delicate and narrow.

He turned her hand over, then lifted it to his mouth and pressed his lips against the warm, scented pulse point at the base of her wrist. His eyes drifted shut as he savored the contact.

Elise thought she'd melt. Just like the Wicked Witch in *The Wizard of Oz,* any minute she was going to dissolve into a puddle of ooze on the kitchen floor. All that would be left were her black dress and an expensive pair of high-heeled satin pumps. Oh, but she didn't want him to stop.…

A thrill as electrifying as sticking a knife in a toaster coursed up Elise's arm. She gasped and stared raptly at his bent head, his long lashes black and stunning against his chiseled cheeks. Then her own eyes drifted shut, and she concentrated on the warm, intoxicating feel of his lips on her skin. She could hardly fathom the idea that such a simple, chaste kiss could send her senses reeling like a runaway roller-coaster.

He lifted his head and cupped her chin in his hand. When Elise opened her eyes, his face was mere inches away.

Then they kissed.

Oblivious to everything but Dylan and the need to get as close to him as possible, Elise slid her hands up his chest, around his broad shoulders and behind his neck. She loved the feel of his long, lean body against hers. His hands roamed her back and caught in her hair, and he kissed her deep and long and hard.

Somewhere in the recesses of her brain, Elise knew she shouldn't be kissing Dylan McAllister. He was a bitter divorced man and a hotshot lawyer with a penchant for winning unfair divorce settlements for his male clients. It was his fault she was a "valued customer" at the local savings and loan. So far, he'd refused to admit any fault in the matter or indicated any intention of behaving differently in the future. And where was her apology?

On the other hand, she thought dazedly as he trailed kisses along her jaw and nibbled her ear, he was kind to animals, was a good sport, had a keen sense of humor, saved obnoxious drunks from choking and had alienated his blond-bombshell date that night to assist Elise in getting safely home. These were not the usual activities of a sleaze-bag...although his date might disagree. But Rowena liked him, and the discerning little pig had always been a good judge of character.

Dylan just didn't make sense. He seemed to have a split personality. The only thing Elise was sure about, was that both personalities were very, very sexy. Too sexy. In fact...

Elise pulled away, wedging her hands between her chest and Dylan's. His heart was hammering like crazy, and so was hers. He was breathing fast, and so was she. But she was still surprised to find herself against the silverware drawer with Dylan's hands on her waist, as if he were about to lift her onto the counter.

"I get the feeling that you and I were about to make love somewhere between the toaster and the pasta maker," she whispered breathlessly.

He looked behind her, then down at his hands on her waist. Dazed, he said, "I think you're right." He swallowed hard and stepped back, raking a hand through his hair. He glanced down at Rowena and added, "And with a pig for an audience, no less."

"At least Geraldo's cage is covered, or we'd never hear the end of this," Elise joked, and they both laughed nervously.

Sobering, Elise concluded, "I think we're moving a little too fast here, McAllister."

Dylan took a deep breath and smiled crookedly. "Does this mean you don't hate me anymore?"

She licked her lips and racked her brain for an answer. She wasn't sure how she felt about him, and she wasn't about to give him the satisfaction of admitting she was confused, so she said, "I don't think what happened here has anything to do with feelings."

Was she imagining things, or did she see a flash of hurt in his eyes?

"I see," he said dully. "In other words, this little interlude of passion falls under the category of 'just sex'?"

That sounded good to Elise. At least it gave her an out for her out-of-control behavior. And to think it had all started with a little kiss on the wrist! But even the memory of that kiss gave her goose bumps.

"What else could it be?" Elise replied, turning away. "I don't know how you could expect me to feel any affection or have any sort of positive feelings for you." She could see his reflection in the window above the sink. His head was bent, and he was rubbing his jaw.

"You still hate me."

"I never said I hated you," Elise corrected.

Dylan gave a grim laugh. "You've sure nurtured a close facsimile of that particular emotion since the divorce hearing."

"I had good reason to—"

"I was within the limits of the law—"

She turned on him. "But does that make it right?"

He grabbed her arms. "You've been itching for me to cry uncle ever since I got here." His blue eyes blazed. "I don't like being pinned down, Elise."

"You don't like admitting you're wrong," she shot back.

"Neither do you," he accused. "And for all the spouting off you do about fair play, how fair is it to use sex to get me on your side?"

Elise bristled. "How dare you? I never *use* sex! I kiss someone when I feel like it. I sleep with someone when I have strong feelings for that person—"

Elise stopped when she realized she'd been trapped. Dylan released her and stepped back, folding his arms across his chest and smiling smugly. "So you do like me a little, eh, Doc?" he concluded. "In fact, even if I were the best-looking, sexiest guy in the world, you wouldn't let me anywhere near you—you wouldn't let me kiss you like I just did—unless you genuinely liked me as a person."

Elise glared at him, speechless. He was right, damn him.

"What's the matter, Doc? Is the truth hard to swallow? Are *you* ready to cry uncle?"

"Just because you have a few good qualities doesn't make up for everything you've done to hurt me and lots of other women, McAllister," Elise finally had the presence of mind to offer in defense. "You're the one that'll be crying uncle before this week's up." Then she turned on her high heels and stomped toward the door.

"So what are you going to do tomorrow, Doc, to try to make me miserable enough to confess and forsake my evil-lawyer ways?" he called after her. "I've already given an enema to a horse, nearly broken my back lifting a fat poodle and stood helplessly by while you emasculated a great male specimen of a dog. What else could you do to me?"

Elise stopped and turned to face him, one hand propped on the door frame. She threw him a sly smile that alarmed and charmed him at the same time. "I've got just the job for you, McAllister," she said with sweet malice. "The Circle J has a herd of breeding cows that need to be impregnated and only one bull. I'll send you out into the field with nasty old Ferdinand—"

Dylan laughed and held up his hands. "Whoa! Where's this leading, Doc?"

"—and you can collect sperm to use for artificial insemination!" Then she touched her tongue to her top lip, raised her brows and said, "Think you'll be able to handle that assignment all right?"

Dylan was still chuckling to himself long after Elise had left. He was sure he'd never be expected to take part in such a distasteful procedure. And he was sure that if such procedures were done routinely, Dr. Spencer, the "big animal" vet, was the unlucky schmuck that had to do them...not Elise.

Dylan looked down at Rowena, who still stood nearby, waiting for him to notice her. He stooped down and scratched the pig behind her little pink ears.

"She was joking, Rowena," he whispered. Then suddenly his smile fell away. "Wasn't she?"

BY THE FOLLOWING afternoon, Dylan was sure he'd rather be taking sperm samples from a raging bull than doing the project Elise had actually saddled him with.

He was balancing her budget.

That morning over breakfast, she'd announced that today was her day off and she would be spending it doing chores around the house. And while she scrubbed floors and chopped wood, he'd be trying to find a few extra dollars in her budget to put aside for the burglar alarm she desperately needed. Now, as Dylan had once suggested, if she wasn't "that strapped by her divorce settlement," it shouldn't be too hard to find those needed extra bucks.

By 2:00 p.m., Dylan was ready to admit defeat. Elise had been right about her finances. She wouldn't have a single spare dime till that loan was paid off. And it was a doozy of a loan, too, much bigger than he'd thought.

Dylan rested his chin in his hands and stared at the

wall. How many other women had he left in similar purse-pinched situations? How many kids had lost their dads *and* their allowances because he'd been overzealous in making sure the men in the divorce didn't get the shaft?

In his efforts to make things equal, had he really considered everything and looked at both sides? Or was he the biggest jackass and the most prejudiced divorce lawyer in recent history?

Dylan stood up and paced the floor. He couldn't think clearly. Lying awake half the night and reliving those all-too-brief minutes holding Elise in his arms didn't help to promote a clear head, either. Maybe he needed some more black tea. In a surprising show of thoughtfulness, Elise had brought him a cup a few minutes ago, generously laced with honey, and told him to mosey out to the kitchen for more when he was ready for a refill.

He was ready.

But just as he stepped onto the hardwood floor in the foyer and was about to pass through the dining room and into the kitchen, he thought he heard soft, muffled crying.

Elise?

Chapter Nine

Dylan stopped in his tracks and listened. His immediate reaction to the idea of Elise crying was one of disbelief. She seemed so strong, so unlikely to give in to a show of weakness.

Then he realized he wasn't being realistic. Everyone cried now and then. Sometimes it was good for you. But what was making Elise unhappy in the middle of the afternoon as she shared a neighborly cup of tea with Jan?

"I feel so stupid," he heard Jan say in a watery voice, and relief flooded through him. Elise wasn't crying; Jan was. He now realized he'd been horrified to think he might be the reason Elise was crying. He didn't want to hurt her. And if he had hurt her in the past, he'd never meant to.

Dylan stood there for a minute, unsure of what to do. The considerate thing to do, of course, would be to turn around and return to the living room, leaving the girls to work out Jan's problem in peace. But he could barely stand the thought of facing the condemnatory numbers on Elise's budget sheet, and he was admittedly curious about why Jan was crying.

"Don't feel stupid," Elise said soothingly. "If I

were in your situation, I'd be shedding a few tears, too."

"But you *were* in my situation," Jan protested.

"Yes," Elise said, sighing loudly enough for Dylan to hear her quite clearly in the foyer. "Jan, all the advice I can give you is to get a good lawyer."

Now Dylan was hooked. There was no way he was going to walk away from this conversation. He leaned against the wall and blatantly eavesdropped.

"Do you know a good lawyer?" Jan inquired, sniffling.

"Well, I definitely won't give you the name and number of the guy that represented me in *my* divorce. He was no match for McAllister."

Set off by the sound of Dylan's last name, Geraldo squawked, "Aawwk! McAllister! McAllister! McAllister's a *ssssssnake!*"

"Dumb bird," Dylan mumbled.

"Mike doesn't have a lawyer yet." Dylan could hear the panic in Jan's voice. "What if he does hire McAllister?"

"Then you might as well kiss the store goodbye. McAllister won't care that you inherited the store from your father. He'll figure half of it ought to go to Mike, no matter how little help he's been in running it. And isn't it interesting to note that Mike didn't sue you for divorce till after your father died?"

"If Mike gets half equity in the store, I won't be able to buy him out, Elise. I can't get a loan like you did. I'm barely making ends meet now. I'll have to close down."

"Then hold your breath till Mike hires a lawyer, and hope that lawyer isn't McAllister or some other hotshot who's got it in for women and knows how to stick it to them."

"I just wish Mike and I could settle this fairly and amicably."

"There's a chance you can. Just hope that Mike doesn't get too greedy."

"All I want is what's fair."

"That's all I wanted, too," Elise replied wistfully.

"Men," said Jan.

"Yeah, *men,"* Elise echoed on a dismal note.

Silence followed this final pronouncement of all that was generally wrong with the world—*men.* And Dylan was feeling just low enough at the moment to agree with them. Before meeting Jan, if her soon-to-be ex-husband had come to his office and wanted representation, Dylan would have taken the case unhesitatingly. And he'd have won it, too, thereby closing down Pop's.

But now his victim had a face, a cute personality and a sob story that made the last woman-in-jeopardy movie of the week look like a fairy tale.

He could almost believe he'd been set up, that Jan was only pretending to be on the brink of a divorce and in danger of losing her beloved family grocery store. But she sounded so genuine.

And Elise would never be that dishonest. If there was one thing he particularly admired about her, it was her sense of fair play. She'd never ask her friend to put on a phony show just to make him feel guilty.

Having settled it in his mind that Jan was on the level, he skulked back to the living room and sat down at the desk again. As he gazed down at Elise's budget sheet, he forced himself to face the fact that maybe she was right after all.

Such a humbling conclusion had been coming on all week, but now he was facing it head-on. Though it had never struck him as the case before meeting Elise, perhaps he *was* a tad prejudiced in divorce court. Perhaps he *had* overcompensated for what he'd always perceived as men's disadvantages in divorce settlements and had swung the pendulum too far the other way.

Now he was making sure women got a raw deal every chance he got...just like the raw deal his brother Craig had gotten when he divorced five years ago. And Elise was just one example of his expertise in delivering raw deals. Was Elise an innocent victim in an unconscious quest to revenge himself and Craig?

Resting his chin on his fists, Dylan gave himself up to deep, troubled thoughts.

"IS HE GONE?"

Elise craned her neck and peered into the dining room. "I don't know," she whispered. "I don't see him. I heard his footsteps on the wood floor when he walked into the foyer, but I can't tell whether or not he's gone back to the living room. I'll send George in to investigate."

Elise took George out of his high chair and whispered in his ear. "George, go into the dining room and look by the front door. If you see McAllister, make a big noise, okay? Do you understand?"

George hooted and nodded his head vigorously, then ambled off into the dining room. Seconds later he returned.

"Did you see McAllister, George?"

George "hee-hee'd" and gave a negative shake of his head.

"How convenient to have your own spy," Jan drawled.

Elise closed the kitchen door, sat George in a chair, gave him a hug and handed him a bunch of grapes. "He's come in quite handy over the past couple of days. He sees Dylan as a rival."

"Is he?"

Elise scowled. "Don't be silly. You know what he did to me last spring."

"But what's he doing to you this winter?"

"Don't be a smart aleck, Jan," Elise advised her. "It's very unattractive."

"I see we're still in revenge mode," Jan observed dryly. "Only you seem even more determined today to help McAllister see the error of his ways. Did something happen last night that you haven't told me? Something besides the Lars fiasco and the teakettle tryst?"

Elise felt her jaw clench as she remembered Dylan's attitude last night after their kiss. "I just realized that McAllister is an incredibly stubborn man and I decided that he needed a little boost to help him see things my way."

"So you hit him with the budget and my sad story all at once. Very tricky, Elise! But did I do my part okay? Was I pathetic enough?"

Elise chuckled. "You're no Meryl Streep, but I think your high-school drama classes are finally paying off."

"Not to mention three years of community theater," Jan reminded her. She took a sip of tea, then frowned thoughtfully. "But you know, Elise, as much fun as all this is, I'm wondering if maybe you've gone a little too far this time."

Elise nibbled on a blueberry muffin. "What do you mean?"

"You pride yourself on being up-front with people. You hate dishonesty and you're always on the bandwagon about being fair and equal."

Elise's gaze shifted to her plate. She could feel her color rising. "And your point is?"

"You know what my point is. This whole routine is a hoax. I love Michael to death, and we're never going to divorce. My store is paid off, and there's no danger of ever closing the old mercantile down. None of this is true."

"But it could be true," Elise said stubbornly. "And that's really the point here. McAllister needs to see how unfair divorce settlements affect real people. If my situation alone can't prick his conscience, then he needs a little live soap opera to help things along."

"Yeah, but if he ever found out you threw out the bait and reeled him in, he'll never forgive you."

"Like that's a consideration? After this week is over, I'll probably never lay eyes on him again."

Jan shrugged and took another swallow of tea while Elise let the impact of what she'd just said sink in. *After this week is over, I'll probably never lay eyes on him again....*

Now, why did that idea depress her? After all, last night had been a mistake, a giving in to her baser urges. Despite what she'd admitted to the contrary last night, she didn't really *like* Dylan McAllister, she firmly told herself. She just enjoyed his kisses... right?

The phone rang, and Elise was grateful for an interruption of such confusing thoughts. She grabbed the receiver from the wall phone and said, "Hello?"

When it became obvious that Elise was talking to a pet owner with a problem, Jan pointed to the door to indicate she was leaving, waved a breezy goodbye and was gone.

Two minutes later Elise walked into the living room and found Dylan hunched over the desk, looking miserable. Her initial reaction was one of triumph. Her scheme had worked. Then she felt the inevitable guilty letdown. Her conscience told her she wasn't playing fair, that she should never have involved Jan in her battle with McAllister.

He turned and smiled wanly. "Hi. Jan gone?"

"Yeah, she had to get back to the store," Elise answered. Then, afraid he'd ask her something about Jan's fictitious divorce and be forced to lie again, she hurriedly added, "But I got an emergency call anyway, and I've got to make a house call. You want to come?"

Dylan raised his brows. "You're asking me and not telling me?"

"I thought I'd give you a choice between budgets and BBs."

"Another BB-gun accident?" Dylan stood up, pressing his hands briefly into the small of his back, which apparently still bothered him.

"The call was from Amber, the same little girl that was in here on Monday with Fluffy. She's home alone and she saw some neighbor boys shooting BBs near her yard again, then Fluffy came in the back door in a lather. She's afraid the cat might have been hit again, but Fluffy's too agitated to stay still long enough for Amber to get a good look. It could be nothing, but she's really attached to her cat and sounds pretty frantic."

"Then we'd better get going," Dylan prompted, headed for the foyer.

Elise followed, amused, impressed and, yes, touched by the way Dylan shook off his glum mood and sprang to action when he heard the emergency involved Amber and Fluffy. Just then, George came in from the kitchen, carrying a half-picked bunch of grapes.

Elise sighed. "I forgot about George. He'll have a fit if I put him in his pen so early in the day, so we'd better take him along."

"Whatever you say, Doc," Dylan replied in a resigned tone.

"Come here, George," said Elise, motioning to the chimp. "We need to put your coat on. We're going for a ride."

George responded with enthusiasm, pounding his head with the flat of his hand and bouncing from foot to foot.

"Doesn't get out much, I gather," Dylan observed, slipping on his own coat.

"Both he and Rowena like to go on rides," Elise answered, helping George into a blue parka with a Cookie Monster patch on the pocket.

"Then why don't we take Rowena, too?" Dylan suggested.

Elise peered up at him dubiously. "Are you sure? She likes to stick her snout out of the window on the passenger side and snort the fresh air while I drive."

Dylan shrugged. "Is that a problem?"

"Only if you don't like a pig sitting on your lap."

Dylan's brows furrowed. "You mean—"

"I mean I have a truck and we'll all be together in the cab. And since I'll be driving, you'll be the one with the pig in your lap."

Dylan shook his head, smiling wryly. "Does everyone in Alpine own a truck? Never mind. It doesn't matter. Besides," he added with a flirtatious gleam in his sky blue eyes, "cabs are cozy."

Elise's heart skipped a beat, but she gave him a quelling look and led the way through the kitchen, out the back door and into the garage. She glanced back and saw Dylan picking up Rowena when the pig seemed hesitant to cross the snow-covered lawn. Then he carried her into the garage, opened the door of the truck and gently set her down inside.

"You're going to spoil that pig," Elise warned.

"So sue me," Dylan retorted with his signature killer grin.

"I wouldn't dare," Elise shot back.

Once they got her older-model truck warmed up and were on the road headed south, with George strapped into a child's car seat between them, and with Rowena's front feet perched on Dylan's knee and her snout hanging out the window, Dylan remarked, "It's kind of like taking the kids for a Sunday drive, eh, Doc?"

"These 'kids' must look like your side of the family, 'cause they sure don't resemble anyone I know and love," Elise said, laughing.

"George reminds me a little of my uncle Ralph," Dylan said, glancing at the chimp as he yanked the toy steering wheel on his car seat back and forth and

Elise laughed again, feeling more relaxed than she had a right to. Dylan McAllister could be so much fun to be around with his wry sense of humor and his boyish grin. At the moment he was holding on to Rowena by her plump middle so she wouldn't fall forward if the truck came to a sudden stop. It struck her again what an enigma he was. He was ruthless in court, but he showed a disarming kindness and consideration for a potbellied pig!

The day was beautiful, and pint-size puffs of white clouds dotted the sky like Indian smoke signals above the granite peaks of Mount Timpanogos. The air hitting Dylan in the face from the open window was icy cold—Elise could feel it, too—but, though his complexion was turning a little ruddy, he didn't complain. If the drive to Amber's house hadn't been so short, Elise would have insisted he roll up the window for all their sakes.

Amber's family, the Tates, lived in a rambling, ranch-style home in the foothills of Mount Timpanogos. Frank Tate, Amber's father, worked in Salt Lake at an office job, but he'd moved the family out to Alpine five years ago so they could enjoy a more rural life-style.

Amber had told Elise over the phone that her mom had taken her brother down to nearby Provo for an appointment with the eye doctor, and left Amber alone for the hour she expected to be gone. But her mom was running late, and Amber had gotten so worried about Fluffy, she decided to call Elise on her own.

As they pulled into the driveway, Amber's white face appeared at the window, then disappeared, then showed up again at the open front door as Elise and her entourage walked up the driveway.

"Dr. Allen," said Amber, her blue eyes wide and worried, "I'm so glad you're here." She opened the door, and Elise hurried in with her black bag, Dylan following behind with George and Rowena.

"Oh, hi, Mr. McAllister," Amber said as Dylan passed her into the house. "You still workin' with Dr. Allen?"

"Day *and* night," he drawled, throwing Elise a long-suffering look. "I hope you don't mind that my assistants and I tagged along," he teased, making Amber giggle and helping to erase some of the tension from her face.

"Where's Fluffy, Amber?" Elise asked.

"She's in the laundry room, hiding under the table Mom folds the clean clothes on. I kept trying to catch her so I could see if she was hit again, but she finally just squeezed under the table and won't come out."

"Well, we'll coax her out somehow, and I'll check her over."

"I'm *so* glad you came," Amber repeated as they headed for the laundry room. But Elise noticed that Dylan wasn't following, and she peered over her shoulder to see what he was doing. He stood at the kitchen window with his hands on his hips, staring out across the yard.

"You can admire the view later, McAllister," Elise said. "I might need you in here."

Dylan turned toward her and raised a brow. "What did you ever do without me, Doc?"

"Are you coming or not?" she countered irritably.

"In a minute," he said, turning back to whatever

he was looking at through the window. "There's something I need to do first."

Elise frowned as she watched him leave through the back door. "Now what's he up to?" she wondered aloud.

It took about five minutes to get Fluffy out from under the laundry table, and still Dylan hadn't returned from wherever he'd disappeared to. It took another fifteen minutes to check the cat for new wounds and give a brief but thorough exam. Finally Elise concluded that Fluffy had not been shot again, but she'd been badly frightened. Boys aiming BB guns at her, even if they hadn't intended to actually shoot her again, was turning the poor cat into a basket case.

"Have your parents talked to the boys who are shooting BBs in the field behind your house, Amber?"

"Yes. My dad talked to 'em, but those boys know my dad's at work all day. And this afternoon, with both cars gone, they prob'ly thought no one was home to see 'em outside with their dumb guns again."

Elise frowned thoughtfully as she put away her instruments. To entertain George, she'd allowed him to listen to his own heart with the stethoscope, and he put up quite a squawk when she took it away. "Sounds like those boys are going to have to be talked to again or their parents notified."

"No need," came Dylan's voice from behind her. She turned to see Dylan standing at the door to the laundry room, looking pleased with himself.

"Why?" Elise asked, alarmed. "What did you do?"

"Hey, don't look so nervous," he admonished her, laughing. "I'm not an ogre. I didn't eat the little stinkers. I just explained a bit about the law to them concerning shooting your neighbor's cat, and I don't think they'll bother Fluffy again."

He turned to Amber. "If they do, you just give me a call, okay?" He reached inside his coat pocket and pulled out a business card and handed it to Amber. "Here's my number."

Amber took the card and blushed with pleasure. "You mean you'd really be my lawyer, Mr. McAllister?"

"In a New York minute."

"In a *what?*"

Dylan grinned and bent over so that his face was level with Amber's. "Any time you need a lawyer, kiddo, I'll make myself available. But I don't think you'll have any more trouble with the neighbor boys. I made it pretty clear to them that what they were doing was against the law."

"Do you think they'll be mad at me?" Amber asked him, a furrow of worry appearing between her brows.

"No. In fact, they didn't even see me come from your house." He looked to Elise to share his amusement. "Actually I think they just thought I was out 'patrolling' the area or something."

Elise shook her head ruefully. "You mean kind of like those lawyers who chase ambulances, only you chase boys with BB guns?"

"Yeah, kind of like that," he concurred, grinning.

Elise couldn't help but grin back. She could just imagine what a grim authority figure Dylan must have seemed to the misbehaving boys as he waded through the snowy field to confront them. In his tailored coat and with his stern, chiseled features, all he needed was a fedora to look like the media's image of the FBI's famous Eliot Ness.

"That was decent of you, McAllister," Elise said at last.

"I'm a decent guy," Dylan replied. "At least, most people think so."

When Elise didn't respond to the bait, Dylan added, "Anyway, I couldn't let those boys keep terrorizing Fluffy and Amber."

He reached down and stroked Amber's dark hair, her eyes beaming gratefully—and adoringly—up at him. Obviously Dylan had won the girl's affection and trust.

Just don't call him fifteen years from now and ask him to represent you in a divorce hearing, Elise thought to herself.

"When's your mom coming home, Amber?" Elise asked her.

"She's supposed to be home already, but maybe she got caught in traffic."

"I know you're old enough to stay alone—and you showed how smart and responsible you are when you called us about Fluffy—but do you want us to stay till your mom comes home?" Dylan asked.

Amber smiled. "I'd like that."

That issue settled, Amber took Dylan by the hand and led him into the kitchen for milk and cookies, Rowena scurrying along on her short legs behind them.

Elise finished packing her bag and ruefully acknowledged the power of Dylan's considerable charm. If she didn't know better, she'd swear that McAllister, attorney-at-law, and McAllister, vet assistant and charmer of pigs and little girls...well, *big* girls, too...were two different men.

Elise and George joined Amber and Dylan in the kitchen, and together they worked their way through a package of Oreos and a half gallon of milk. Fluffy finally got brave enough to creep into the kitchen, and Amber set down a small bowl of milk for the skittish cat. Even Rowena, whose figure Elise watched carefully by limiting the pig's sweet treats, enjoyed a few bites of cookie when Dylan slipped them to her under the table.

"No wonder she likes you," Elise murmured, wanting him to know she realized he was sneaking food to the pig. "You bribe her."

"What would I have to do to bribe *you* into liking me?" Dylan inquired with a wink.

It would take a heartfelt apology, she said to herself, but out loud she said, "It would take more than plying me with food and scratching me behind the ears."

Dylan's brows shot up. She could tell he was about to make a suggestive remark, when he seemed to suddenly remember that they were in the company of a child. He clamped his mouth shut and refrained with an effort, but his blue eyes danced with mischief.

"Don't you like Mr. McAllister, Dr. Allen?" Amber asked ingenuously.

Elise bit the inside of her lip and tried desperately to think of a way to sidestep the question.

"It's not that I don't like Mr. McAllister—" Elise began.

"Then you *do* like him?"

With his elbow on the table, Dylan rested his chin on his hand and watched Elise squirm.

"It's hard to explain my feelings for Mr. McAllister, Amber," Elise said, stalling. She scowled at Dylan's handsome face with its smug, amused smile. "He's definitely one of a kind."

Suddenly Amber brightened. "Oh! I think I understand now! You must *love* Mr. McAllister! And that means you're going to marry him...right?"

Elise was so stunned and embarrassed by Amber's naive assumption, she just sat there, speechless, while Dylan held back a laugh. The silence was just long enough to firmly plant the idea in the little girl's head.

"No, Amber," Elise finally began. "You don't under—"

Elise's explanation was abruptly interrupted when the front door opened and Amber's mother and little brother entered the house. Excited, Amber ran into the living room and exclaimed, "Mom! Mom! Guess what? Dr. Allen's getting *married!*"

Elise dropped her head to the table and groaned.

"Hey, you should be flattered, Doc."

Elise lifted her head and glared at Dylan. "Because that sweet, trusting little girl thinks I've nabbed a prize?"

He chuckled. "No. Because our engagement got top billing over Fluffy's narrow escape from a BB barrage. Don't worry. I'll tell them that you'll only marry me—" he reached down and gave Rowena a scratch behind the ear "—when pigs fly."

"You've got that right, McAllister," Elise agreed wholeheartedly.

AFTER AMBER EXPLAINED to her mother why Dr. Allen was there in the first place and Fluffy was displayed and declared to be in fine fettle, Mrs. Tate came into the kitchen and warmly congratulated Elise on her coming marriage.

Dylan was tempted to let Elise flounder through an explanation, but a gallant urge took over and he explained to Mrs. Tate how Amber had come to the wrong conclusion about his...er...relationship with the local lady vet. Enjoying Elise's look of surprise and relief, he even explained about the bachelor auction and how he'd ended up being Elise's assistant for the week. He did leave out the part about being her ex-husband's divorce lawyer, but he was frankly surprised that Mrs. Tate didn't know the whole story already.

Mrs. Tate, an attractive woman Dylan placed in her mid-thirties, found the incident amusing. She also expressed her gratitude to both him and Elise for coming to her little girl's rescue and easing Amber's mind about Fluffy. Then, when Amber explained how Dylan had taken care of the BB bullies, too, she insisted that he and Elise stay to dinner so the Tate family could show their collective appreciation.

Feeling a warm family spirit in the Tate home— the same sort of spirit that pervaded the house on those rare times when Dylan was able to get together with his brothers and their families—he impetuously agreed to the invitation without consulting Elise. When both he and Mrs. Tate turned to Elise, she simply stood there looking dazed.

"Is that all right with you, Dr. Allen?" Mrs. Tate inquired, looking so eager Dylan knew Elise wouldn't have the heart to disappoint her.

Elise smiled but avoided Dylan's eyes. "Sure, I'd love to stay to dinner. But only if you'll call me Elise. Remember, I went to school with your sister, Ann.

I'm just a hometown girl. You don't need to be formal with me."

"Then call me Vicky," Mrs. Tate insisted.

"And I'm Dylan, although some people call me by my last name," he added, sliding a glance toward Elise.

"Some of the guys, I'll bet," Vicky suggested. "I hope you two like fried chicken with all the trimmings."

When Frank Tate got home, Dylan found him to be outgoing and talkative. After hearing a brief but entertaining explanation of why they were there, he welcomed Dylan and Elise into his home and then immediately engaged them in friendly conversation.

Despite Elise's looks that hinted they should be going, Dylan couldn't resist an invitation to play Pictionary after dinner, and later he and Frank romped with the kids, the pig and the chimp on the family-room floor while Elise and Vicky cleaned off the table and filled the dishwasher.

Dylan enjoyed the relaxing evening immensely. In fact, it had been a long time since he'd had such fun, even though the food and the entertainment were simple and certainly not as sophisticated as he was used to.

Things had gotten a little crazy when, during the roughhousing on the floor, George climbed on Dylan's back and grabbed his hair, hopping up and down and hooting like an Indian on the war path. But Elise had promptly pulled the excited chimp off his back and settled him down. Dylan supposed that George couldn't resist the primal urge to turn a playful romp into a serious match between rivals.

"It's okay, Elise," Dylan assured her. "He just went bananas for a minute, that's all."

Apparently George didn't like Dylan's use of the term *went bananas,* and he stuck his thumbs in his ears and flapped his fingers at him. The kids thought that was hilarious and rolled on the floor, convulsed with laughter.

After chocolate cake for dessert, Dylan and Elise said a warm good-night and left. Elise gave George a piggy-back ride to the truck, and Dylan carried Rowena in his arms. Inside the cab, while the truck's sluggish engine warmed up, Dylan sighed and settled back in the seat...and now that they were alone, an awkwardness set in.

"I'll try to get her warmed up fast, McAllister," mumbled Elise. "Do you want to go back to my house first, or should I drive you to Salt Lake from here?"

"With these two driving you nuts all the way back to Alpine? It would be worse than having an amorous drunk in the car. By the way, have you heard from Lars since last night?"

"He called to apologize. But I don't want to talk about Lars, McAllister," she said, dropping the subject abruptly. "So, you think I should take the 'kids' home before I drive you to Salt Lake?"

"It's too late to drive me home, Elise."

She turned away and stared straight ahead, clenching the steering wheel with white knuckles. "If you keep spending the night at my house, pretty soon the town will think there's something going on between us."

He sighed, wishing there *were* something going on between them. "Okay, I won't stay the night. But I don't want you driving me home this late. I'll call a cab."

She drummed her fingers on the dashboard. "A cab to Salt Lake will cost you a fortune."

"I'll just add it to my list of charitable donations related to this bachelor-auction deal."

She gave a huff of exasperation. "No. Stay the night. I don't care what the neighbors say. Besides, I'm an adult. I can do what I want."

He turned to stare at her in the dark, craning his neck to peer around George and the toy steering wheel. "You don't care what the neighbors think?"

"No."

"Not even Lars?"

Elise clicked her tongue. "*Especially* Lars."

Dylan paused, then plunged ahead, saying, "I'm glad I can stay the night, Elise, because—"

"Because?"

"Because we need to talk."

"We do?"

"Yes. Big time."

"Well, okay," Elise agreed at last, sounding as enthused about the prospect as Dylan did. But the fact of the matter was, this little talk was way past due.

Chapter Ten

The fact that Elise wasn't eager for a heavy-duty talk with Dylan struck her as more than a little ironic. Wasn't that what she'd been hoping and waiting for? He was finally taking her seriously. Maybe she'd made her point after all, and he was going to apologize.

The problem was, the memory of her scheme involving Jan and that whopping lie about her marriage being on the skids was weighing heavily on her conscience. She knew now she shouldn't have resorted to tricks to teach a man to play fair. What if he brought up Jan's divorce? Would she keep on lying to protect her credibility?

It was too confusing. And besides that, Elise had had such a wonderful time at the Tates', she'd enjoyed Dylan's company so thoroughly, she didn't want to spoil the mood with a knock-down, drag-out debate on divorce settlements.

In short, if the world were a perfect place, instead of ending the day with a heated discussion laced with legal terms, she'd be headed home to a different kind of heated conversation in a feather bed with Dylan's strong arms around her....

Too soon they were parked in the garage and taking the pets inside. Worn-out from roughhousing with the Tate children, George gave his teeth a cursory brushing and went willingly to his pen in the spare bedroom, cuddled up to his Cookie Monster doll and fell immediately asleep. Even Rowena toddled off to bed, too tired to chase after her idol any more that day.

As agreed upon, fifteen minutes after getting home, Dylan and Elise met in the living room for the much-awaited confab. Elise had stoked up a small fire in the fireplace, changed into some demure flannel pajamas and wrapped herself in a huge, shapeless robe. She thought of the extra padding as armor…protection against her own desire to fling herself into Dylan's arms and shower him with kisses. That would be just a tad forward, not to mention disastrous. She was growing rather too attached to a man she was supposed to hate.

When Dylan came into the room, he looked surprised to see her in her pajamas. Elise shifted uncomfortably, even though she knew she was more covered up now than she'd been earlier in her jeans and sweater.

"Just thought I'd get comfortable," she mumbled.

"You should have told me we were having a pajama party, and I'd have dressed accordingly," Dylan commented teasingly as he eased down on the opposite end of the long sofa from her.

"You don't have any pajamas here," she said.

He grinned. "I know."

"I thought this was going to be a serious discussion," Elise reminded him, blushing. She could just imagine him coming downstairs in boxer shorts, bare chested and with his hair tousled by sleep. The tantalizing image gave her goose bumps.

"I'll be serious," he promised, schooling his face into a properly sober expression.

"What did you want to talk about?" Elise prompted him, eager to get the talk over with so she could escape to hose down her hormones with a cold shower and some stern mental lecturing.

Dylan turned and looked earnestly into her eyes. His own eyes shone brilliant blue in the soft glow of Elise's Victorian-style hurricane lamps. He took a deep breath, then said in a rush, "I wanted to tell you that I was wrong, Doc, that I made a mistake in finagling that settlement for Ted. He didn't deserve half equity in your business, and I'm sorry it's caused you so much hassle and grief."

Elise stared at him, dumbfounded, unable to grasp that he was actually admitting he was wrong, that she was actually getting the longed-for apology.

"McAllister, I don't understand—"

"What don't you understand? I just said I was sorry."

"But I didn't expect it. You certainly haven't led me to think you were relenting over the past few days. Just last night you seemed as convinced as ever that you had every right to help Ted win all he could get from me."

"Legally I did have every right. I'll never budge about that. But a lawyer can counsel his client in what's fair, and that's where I loused things up and hurt you...and probably lots of other women. I didn't take the time to consider everything involved. I plan to change that kind of one-sided thinking."

"You never gave me the slightest hint you were

starting to see things my way," she protested, still in shock. She wished he'd given her *some* indication of his change of heart, because then she wouldn't have felt so desperate and she wouldn't have asked Jan to help her with that afternoon's sudsy little skit. Darn it, she wouldn't have *lied!*

"I was having far too much fun crossing swords with you to admit too soon that you'd effectively made your point," he confessed, looking chagrined. "Besides, I don't think I realized how much sense you were making till today when I was faced with those irrefutable numbers on your budget sheet, and when—" He stopped suddenly.

He was probably going to mention Jan and her divorce, then thought better of it when he realized he'd have to admit he'd been eavesdropping. Elise was so relieved that she wouldn't have to either resort to more lying, or fess up and tell the whole truth, that she pretended to ignore his abrupt hesitation. She was afraid to tell the truth, because things were going far too well to throw a wrench in the machinery at this point.

He'd apologized. He'd really apologized. So did that mean...?

"McAllister, I want to thank you sincerely for your apology. It's exactly what I'd hoped would be the outcome of our week together. But I was wondering, does this mean you'll be taking on female clients in future divorce cases?"

Dylan chuckled. "Don't push it, Doc! I've done all the major policy changing I'm going to do for one day. You've got me thinking, and who knows where I'll go from here? But give me a little space, okay?"

"Okay," Elise agreed, smiling. "But can I ask just one more question?"

"Shoot."

"Why have you been so one-sided in these divorce cases? Was it primarily because of your own marriage?" In other words, she wanted to know just how bad his marriage to Brenda had been. At this point she was ready to believe the worst about his ex-wife. She wanted to understand and excuse Dylan for being so prejudiced. For some reason she wanted to exonerate him from all wrongdoing, if possible. Maybe then she wouldn't feel so guilty about liking him so darn much.

"My costly divorce from Brenda was just another straw on the camel's back. Before Brenda and I even knew we were headed for a split, my brother Craig went through the divorce from hell. Although he and Joyce were probably equally to blame for the breakup, he felt so guilty about what he perceived as a failure, he wouldn't contest anything Joyce wanted. They had three children together, and Craig wanted the best for the kids."

"That speaks well of him," Elise put in.

"Yes, but he went overboard. Joyce and the kids ended up with the best of everything, all right— bought and paid for by Craig's more-than-generous alimony and child-support checks—and Craig ended up with barely enough money to live in a crummy little apartment. All he did was work. He had no life. He was so depressed, it scared me.... Thankfully, as time passed and when Joyce finally remarried, things eased up a bit. Craig's experience, then mine, reinforced what I'd suspected all along— that divorced men in America were getting the shaft."

"And now you don't believe that anymore?"

"Now I've seen the other side up close and personal, and I realize that every divorce is different. You can't lump them together and deal with them all the same way."

"You're a smart man, McAllister," Elise remarked. "You should have known that all along."

"As you've probably learned in the past week, I'm a stubborn man, too, Doc. Sometimes, especially when people I care about are involved, I have a hard time forgiving. Then my emotions, instead of the brains God gave me, rule the day."

Elise knew all about emotions getting in the way of cool, clear thinking. For example, if she hadn't been so obsessed with teaching Dylan a lesson, she wouldn't have lowered her standards and concocted that scheme with Jan. It was putting a damper on everything. She couldn't feel completely happy about Dylan's apology with her own guilt hanging over her like a dark cloud.

She knew she ought to tell him the truth about Jan, but he'd just said he sometimes had a hard time forgiving. She couldn't bear the thought of Dylan looking at her accusingly, distrusting her, blaming her—

"There's something else you ought to know, Doc," Dylan said, interrupting her self-condemnatory thoughts.

"Yes?" Gosh, he looked especially attractive tonight, she thought, unconsciously pulling her robe more snugly together in the front. But when had he ever looked less than one hundred percent gorgeous?

He leaned on the sofa arm, resting his chin in his hand, and smiled at her. She could have sworn there was admiration in those sexy, cobalt blue eyes of his…admiration for her. She swallowed hard and waited for him to speak, as nervous as a teenager on her first date.

"I didn't apologize to you because I'm attracted to you—"

Elise's heart plummeted to her toes. *He wasn't attracted to her.*

"I did it because I meant it."

"I'm glad," she said dully, forcing a smile. "But you didn't need to explain. I never thought you were attracted to me anyway, so—"

Dylan sat up, a furrow appearing between his brows. "Hey, I think you misunderstood what I just said. I was trying to tell you that my attraction to you had nothing to do with the apology."

Elise's heart started racing again. "So you *are* attracted to me?"

Dylan slid closer to her on the couch, leaned forward and traced a line down her cheek with his finger. To Elise, his touch was electric. And his smile was teasing, tender and irresistible.

"I should have thought our kiss yesterday was proof enough of how crazy you make me," he said, "but if you need more proof…"

As he leaned closer still, with his finger tilting her chin just so, Dylan's mouth hovered near Elise's. There was a question in his eyes, but there was also a persuasive seductiveness. He was asking her, and urging her at the same time, to say yes.

Elise said yes with a soft, surrendering sigh and a small, rueful smile. Life was strange, she thought as her eyes drifted shut and her lips tingled with expectation. Who'd have ever thought she'd want to kiss

Dylan McAllister, divorce lawyer extraordinaire, more than she'd want her next breath?

When she felt Dylan's warm, firm lips make contact with hers, every nerve in Elise's body took notice. Just like the first time—only much, much worse—she was melting, melting....

No other part of their bodies was touching—just their lips. The kiss was warm, lingering and sensual. It was a prelude to what Elise knew could be pure bliss...if only she'd allow herself to let go.

Bliss with Dylan McAllister, the man whose courtroom ruthlessness had filled her with resentment for months, should have been as unlikely as snow in August. But now she understood him better. She knew him as a complex person with a past and a family, a great sense of humor, an appreciation for the ridiculous and a weakness for children and potbellied pigs. Amber liked him, Rowena liked him and she liked him...a lot. As each moment passed, bliss was sounding better and better.

"Elise," Dylan groaned against her cheek when their lips finally broke contact. Then his hands were on her shoulders, pulling her against his chest. "I've felt a chemistry between us from the moment our eyes connected at that silly auction."

"Funny how you didn't feel that chemistry at the divorce hearing," she couldn't help countering with a wry chuckle.

"I'm totally focused when I'm in court, Elise," he whispered in her ear, rubbing her back in all the right places. "I'm the kind of guy that puts his all into his work...while I'm working. And when I'm with a woman, I'm totally focused, too. Right now all I want to think about, to concentrate on, is you."

Elise wasn't about to argue with that kind of thinking. She slipped her hands around his broad shoulders and did a little concentrating of her own.

She loved the firm feel of him against her. She loved the sensation of his hard, muscled back beneath her sensitized fingertips, and the way his silky hair touched the top of his collar. She cupped the back of his head, splayed her fingers and sifted them through his hair with the reverence an old-time miner might feel as he sifted a hard-won handful of gold dust.

While Elise enjoyed the tactile paradise of Dylan's hair, he bent his head and trailed kisses and nibbles down her neck and into the sensitive hollow at the base of her throat. Her head fell back, and she moaned with the pure pleasure of it. Then, with his face buried in the V of her pajama top, he moved his hands slowly up her arms, grasped the lapel of her robe and pulled it off her shoulders.

"If you're going to stop me, now would be a good time," he warned her, cupping her face and forcing her to look him in the eye.

Elise opened her eyes and stared dazedly at him through a fog of arousal. "I don't want you to stop," she said with a betraying huskiness to her voice. "I want you to make love to me, Dylan."

He smiled. "That's the first time you've ever called me by my first name."

"'McAllister' seems a little formal under the circumstances, don't you think?" she whispered.

"You can call me whatever you like, Doc," Dylan assured her. "As long as you do it with that same look in your eyes."

"Do lawyers always talk too much?" she teased

him, breathless with desire and anxious to feel him kissing her again.

"I know when to shut up," he assured her, then bent his head and kissed her again, deeply and luxuriously.

Soon Elise felt Dylan gently pushing her back against the plump throw pillows and aligning his body with hers as they both stretched out full-length on the large sofa. She had never imagined it could feel so good, so right to be this intimately connected with Dylan. But the best was yet to come.

While keeping her senses reeling with kisses, he untied her robe at the waist and parted the heavy material to slip his hands inside. Seeking bare skin beneath the warm flannel, soon his hands were tracing the dip of her spine, the soft jut of her rib cage, then up to her tender breasts with their hardened nipples.

"You feel like heaven," he murmured. "So soft, so smooth."

"You feel like heaven, too," she countered, pulling his shirttail out of his jeans and easing her hands underneath. She pressed her palms against his hard chest with its light furring of hair and stroked his nipples.

Soon touching wasn't enough; they had to enjoy each other with their eyes, too. Dylan unbuttoned Elise's pajama top, while she unbuttoned his shirt. She shrugged out of her robe and pulled off her pajama bottoms while he stood up and took off his jeans. Completely naked now, she leaned back against the cushions and he stood in the glow of the fire, each looking at the other.

"Wow," he said.

"Yeah, wow," she agreed, repeating the word that

said it all and said it best. He was beautiful. Every lean, muscled inch of him was to die for.

"If George were awake, he'd probably kill me about now."

"If George were awake, we'd both have our clothes on," Elise corrected. "But please don't spoil the mood, McAllister, by mentioning an ape in the middle of lovemaking."

"Nothing could spoil the mood for me," he assured her, approaching.

She raised a brow, observing the obvious state of his arousal. "Apparently not."

He chuckled. "But like I said before, I know when to shut up."

And he was a man of his word. Except for the sometimes playful, oftentimes passionate, occasionally desperate words that well-matched, expressive lovers murmur to each other while making love, Dylan did indeed shut up.

The next hour was bliss.

But what surprised Elise the most was that there was nothing of "just sex" about this romantic tryst with Dylan. It was sex, and the sex was fabulous, but something else was going on inside her heart and mind.

While she trembled and ached and shivered with ecstasy in his arms, watching with awe and delight as his pleasure matched her own, she felt a connection on a deeper level, on a higher plane. Then, when their physical climaxes came, leaving them deliciously spent and blissfully sated, Elise felt something else, too.

For the first time she could ever remember, she felt complete, whole and utterly content. And she had this dreadful realization that she'd like nothing more than to feel this way for the rest of her life. And all this in the arms of a cynical man who was determined to avoid divorce by forsaking marriage.

With her cheek pressed against Dylan's chest, listening to his heart gradually slow to a less-frantic rhythm in the aftermath of lovemaking, she acknowledged again the strange twists and turns of life. Who'd have thought she'd fall in love with her ex-husband's divorce lawyer?

DYLAN WOKE UP to the smell of coffee brewing. He was wrapped in a quilt, still stretched out on the sofa. He rolled on his stomach, plumped the pillow under his cheek and, for a few precious moments, allowed himself the indulgence of remembering last night.

He and Elise had made love three times, each time better than the last, then they'd fallen asleep wrapped in each other's arms. It was everything he'd ever imagined it would be, only better. He smiled to himself, his eyes drifting shut as he conjured up an especially wonderful memory...when suddenly he felt something whack him right between the eyes!

Mumbling an expletive, he blinked his eyes open and found himself staring into the bared teeth and protruding upper lip of an irate ape!

George was no dope, and the fact that Dylan was lounging around in Elise's living room in the buff was a sure giveaway to the jealous chimp that someone had been monkeying around.

Dylan sat up, rubbing the bridge of his nose. George watched him like a hawk ready to swoop. A folded newspaper—no doubt the weapon he'd used to launch his assault on Dylan—was tightly clenched in one hand. George was pounding his hairy chest with his free hand and hopping from foot to foot in some sort of war dance. His high-pitched "hee-hee's" were loud enough and sharp enough to break an eardrum.

Just when Dylan was wondering if you could get rabies from a chimp bite, or how much time in prison he'd get for defending himself against a love-crazed ape, Elise rushed into the room. The sight of her was enough to make Dylan forget for a minute all about the possible danger he was in.

She had on his denim shirt from the night before, her long legs showing from mid-thigh all the way down to the fuzzy slippers on her feet. The shirt, the slippers and a pair of fish-shaped, gloved pot holders were all Elise was wearing. The overall effect was funky but still a definite turn-on. A rush of longing swept through him that was downright scary.

"George!" Elise exclaimed. "What are you doing? I told you to lay the paper down on the coffee table, not try to wake the dead by screeching at the top of your lungs!"

George toned down the screeching somewhat, but he wasn't ready to cease and desist with the war-dance portion of his performance. He bounced and gestured and continued to beat his chest with wild abandon.

"He's gone off the deep end this time, Doc," Dylan stated grimly. "He hit me with the newspaper, and I'm sure he was wishing he'd had a hammer handy." In a lower voice, he added, "He knows what we did last night."

"How could he possibly know that, McAllister?" Elise scoffed, but with an edge of uncertainty in her voice. Dylan noticed that Rowena was standing next to Elise, uncharacteristically keeping her distance. She must have been intimidated by George's behavior, too.

"I don't know how he knows, but he knows," Dylan insisted.

"When I got him out of his pen this morning and brought him through the living room, he saw you on the couch but he didn't act perturbed."

"Maybe there's some kind of rule of the jungle that you can't go bananas before breakfast," Dylan drawled, then laughed.

Not immune to the absurdity of it, Elise laughed, too. "I've never seen him so out of control. What should we do?"

"Got a tranquilizer gun?"

"That's a little drastic."

"Got a better idea?"

Elise was silent for a moment, then left the room and returned seconds later with a can of Dr Pepper in her hand.

"George," she called. "I've got a treat for you, but you've got to quit threatening McAllister if you want it. What's it going to be?"

George caught sight of the aluminum can of Dr Pepper, glinting provocatively in the morning light that peeked through the drapes, hesitated for only a second, then laid the paper down on the table as he was supposed to do in the first place and ambled over to Elise.

Elise held the can just out of his reach and bent down, waggling an admonitory finger in the chimp's face as she laid down the law.

"This is yours, but only if you promise to behave yourself. Do you understand, George?"

George seemed reluctant to promise good behavior in exchange for his precious soft drink, but finally gave in and nodded his head vigorously, then signed a word.

"Hey, that's the first time I've seen him do that. What did he say?" Dylan asked suspiciously.

"He just said 'please.'"

"How polite," Dylan remarked dryly. "Someone should tell him it's impolite to swat people with newspapers."

When Elise handed him the can, George signed something else. Elise duplicated the motions and said, "I love you, too, George."

"He must really like that stuff," Dylan said.

"Apparently even more than he likes me," Elise returned with a chuckle.

Sporting a cheesy grin, George popped open the tab, then took a long sip before sitting down in a chair opposite the couch. While guzzling his drink, he made sneering faces at Dylan.

"I suppose I can put up with the evil eye, as long as he doesn't attack again," Dylan remarked.

"Why don't you come into the kitchen and have some coffee before your shower?" Elise suggested. "I'm sure he'll follow you in, but at least you'll have Rowena and me to keep you company, and *we* like you." Elise bent down and addressed the pig. "Don't we, Rowena?"

Rowena seemed to take this as a sign that it was safe to enter the living room, though she eyed George warily as she crossed the floor, inched up to the sofa and presented her head to Dylan for petting.

After giving Rowena her morning scratch behind the ears, Dylan wrapped the quilt around his midsection and followed Elise into the kitchen. Sure enough, George followed and perched himself on a chair to keep an eye on his indecently clad rival.

As Elise set a cup and saucer on the table and poured Dylan some coffee, he couldn't help but skim his palm up the back of her leg, enjoying the cool smoothness of her skin. Then he pulled her by the waist onto his lap and nuzzled her neck.

"I've got a hot pot of coffee here and an ape who's quickly losing his cool despite the bribe," she cautioned.

"How much time before your first patient?" Dylan asked her, incredibly living the fantasy he'd dreamed up just the day before. "Can't we put the pot on the stove and the chimp in the pen?"

"We don't have time," she said, sounding truly sorry. She smiled flirtatiously. "But there's always lunch break."

"Yeah, who needs to eat?" Dylan agreed, letting go of her reluctantly. He watched her walk back to the stove and lifted his cup of coffee with a sigh. He couldn't remember ever being this beguiled. She was everything he admired in a woman. Beautiful, sexy, smart, funny and honest. Yet most of all, she was honest...sometimes brutally so. That was a rare trait in a person these days.

When the doorbell rang, Elise turned with a surprised, almost panicked look on her face. "Who could that be this early?"

Dylan smiled reassuringly and pulled the quilt more securely around him. "Don't worry. I'll stay hidden. Just don't let whoever it is into the kitchen."

"I'd better grab a robe," Elise said, sounding irritated by the interruption as she rushed out of the room.

Dylan sipped his coffee and listened to Elise's slippers scoot across the hardwood floor as she hurried to her bedroom, then into the front hall. There was a pause as she probably peeked through the narrow window next to the door to see who was outside.

He heard the door open and Elise say, somewhat nervously, "Hi, guys. What can I do for you?"

Dylan rested his chin in his hand and smiled. He could imagine Elise blushing just from the knowledge that she was harboring a naked man in her kitchen.

"Aren't you going to invite us in, Elise?" came a cheerful masculine voice that Dylan didn't recognize as belonging to Lars or Pete, the only two men he'd met in Alpine. He sat up straighter, paying attention.

"It's cold out here," a female voice added. "And we could sure use a nice hot cup of coffee before we open up the store." That voice Dylan recognized. It was Jan's. She and her husband—who else could it be if she was talking about the two of them opening up the store?—sounded quite chipper for two people on the brink of divorce.

"I'm in kind of a hurry this morning, Jan," Elise said, an edge of anxiety apparent in her tone. "Will you take a rain check? I need to get dressed, and I've got an early appointment and I—"

"We get the picture, Elise," Mike said, chuckling amiably. "It was Jan's idea. She woke up all perky this morning and she was sure you'd want company. I told her if you two wanted to talk, she'd be better off coming alone, but she insisted that I— "

"Come on, Mike," Jan's voice abruptly interrupted,

as if she'd suddenly realized that Elise might already have company. "We'll see you later, Elise."

There was another pause, then the sound of the door closing. Before Elise had time to return to the kitchen, Dylan hurried to the window, craned his neck and pressed his cheek against the glass to see Jan and a tall man walk across the street to the store...holding hands. Hmm.

When Elise returned to the kitchen, she walked straight to the stove. "You'd better get that shower, McAllister," she called briskly over her shoulder. "Breakfast will be ready in ten minutes."

Dylan didn't like the way events were shaping up. He'd be crazy not to suspect at this point that Elise and Jan had staged that conversation about her marital woes yesterday just to yank his chain. But if he came right out and asked Elise about it, he'd be admitting to eavesdropping. He wanted to clear things up right here, right now, because he didn't want to believe Elise—honest Elise—had pulled a scam. But how?

"Don't worry. I usually take quick showers," he said casually.

"Usually?" she repeated without turning around.

"When I shower alone," he explained teasingly.

When she didn't chuckle or blush or throw him a snappy comeback, he knew she was probably feeling too uncomfortable to respond easily to his teasing. And he knew it was most probably guilt that was making her feel so uncomfortable. He decided to give her a chance to explain. He desperately wanted to hear a reasonable explanation.

"Who was at the door?"

She darted him a quick, keen look before turning

back to her cooking. "Oh, didn't you hear? It...it was Jan."

"What did Jan want?"

"A cup of coffee."

"She doesn't strike me as the type of woman that easily takes no for an answer."

"I think she figured out that I already had company."

"I see." He took a sip of coffee. "I've never met her husband. Is he a nice guy?"

Elise turned, holding a spatula, her face flushed from the heat of the stove...or something else. If Jan were really getting a divorce, this would be the logical time for Elise to say so. It would also be the perfect time to make a confession if she'd misled him into believing that a rock-solid marriage was on the skids and some poor woman was being taken advantage of by her avaricious husband.

She stared at him, seeming to search his face for a clue about what he was thinking...what he knew. She took the safe route. She avoided the issue entirely. "I'm serious about the time, McAllister. You've got about five minutes to shower and dress. You'd better get a move on."

To say the least, Dylan was disappointed. But he wasn't ready to confront her with his suspicions just yet. He was going to give her a little time to think about it, and hopefully she'd decide to tell him the truth.

He rose with a sigh, clutching the quilt around his waist. He smiled roguishly. "I wish there was time for a long shower, Doc."

She wet her lips and turned slowly back to the stove. "So...so do I."

Elise could barely concentrate on the blueberry pancakes she was flipping on the grill. That last, suggestive comment Dylan had made before exiting the kitchen, wrapped up in nothing more than a quilt, had further rattled her already severely rattled nerves.

Was it really possible he hadn't heard her conversation with Jan and Mike at the door, or was he just playing dumb? She was beginning to suspect that the best thing she could do would be to confess her scheme with Jan and throw herself on Dylan's mercy.

Mercy from a bitter divorce lawyer with a ruthless reputation like Dylan's? she chided herself, shaking her head as she absently watched bubbles form on the pancake batter. Sure he'd said he was sorry about her own unfair settlement, but he'd admitted to being a stubborn man and not quick to forgive. By blabbing, she'd just be sealing her fate. If she kept mum, maybe there was a chance he'd never find out that she and Jan had conspired against him. And if, down the line, the state of her friend's marriage came up, Elise could always tell Dylan that Jan and Mike had reconciled.

Elise quickly finished cooking the pancakes and placed them in the oven to keep warm. She took George's hand and settled him in the living room in front of the television, turned on *Sesame Street,* then hurried to her bedroom to change into jeans and a sweatshirt. Despite the nearness of her first appointment, she actually found herself fussing with her hair as if she were going on a date instead of going to work in a vet clinic. Frustrated with her moonstruck behavior, she finally just pulled it into the usual ponytail.

When she returned to the kitchen not more than five minutes later, however, there was a note on the table from Dylan that read, "Gone to the store to buy more pills."

Elise crumpled the paper into a ball and bit her lip. Was the jig up? Or did she still have time to tell him the truth before he found out on his own?

She rushed into the hall, nearly tripping over Rowena in the process, grabbed her jacket and pulled it on, then picked up George and hurried out the door.

Chapter Eleven

As Dylan showered, he found himself getting angrier and angrier as he thought about Elise's collusion with Jan to portray a pitiful case of material inequity just to make him feel guilty. By the time he'd dried off and dressed, he'd decided that Elise had had her chance to tell him the truth and now he was going to find it out for himself. He was tired of waiting.

Dylan wasn't sure why he didn't just confront Elise with his suspicions instead of going the roundabout route through Jan. Maybe he was still resisting the idea that she'd tricked him. He wanted to be able to trust her, and if he couldn't trust her...what then?

The store had just opened up for business when he pushed through the door and the bell jingled overhead. Jan and the tall, blond man he assumed was Mike were standing behind the counter stocking a candy display. Jan turned at the sound of the bell to greet her first customer of the day, but when she saw Dylan, her smile froze. She quickly recovered, however, and called, "Morning, Mr. McAllister. You're up early."

"The early lawyer catches the worm," Dylan

quipped, and he enjoyed watching this particular worm squirm.

"Haven't got my stock of night crawlers yet," Jan gamely joked back. "Plan to do some ice fishing?"

He planned to do some fishing, all right, Dylan thought to himself. But not for trout…for the truth.

"Thought I'd buy some more of those back pills," he said, biding his time as he moseyed down the over-the-counter-medicine aisle. "They didn't help much, but some pain relief's better than nothing."

He picked up the pill bottle and headed for the counter. By now—just as Dylan expected—Mike was through with his candy display and looking curiously at the famous lawyer-turned-vet assistant. "So you're McAllister," he said.

"The very same," Dylan replied, smiling amiably. He pulled out his wallet while Jan quickly rang up the pills, no doubt extremely eager to get him out of there. "I'm sure you've heard a lot of bad things about me from Elise, but I want you to know I've changed my methods recently."

"Oh?" said Mike, his brows furrowing. "How's that?"

Along with the five-dollar bill to pay for the pain pills, Dylan pulled a business card out of his wallet and offered it to Jan. "I plan to represent women, as well as men, in divorce court from now on. Give me a call if you need a good divorce lawyer, Jan."

The alarmed look on Jan's face as she stared at the card was worth a thousand words, and the stunned look on Mike's face was worth a thousand more.

"What's the idea, McAllister?" Mike said gruffly. "My wife doesn't need a divorce lawyer."

"Oh?" said Dylan, raising a dubious brow. "That's not what I inadvertently heard yesterday."

Her cheeks suddenly drained of color, Jan turned and stared up at her grim-faced husband. He glared down at her. "What the hell's he talking about, Jan?"

"I...I can explain, Mike," Jan stuttered.

"Why don't you explain to me, too, Jan," Dylan suggested dryly. "No, don't bother. I think I already get the picture."

Leaving the pills, Dylan stuffed his wallet back into his pants pocket and headed toward the door. Just as he reached it, Elise pushed through and entered the store. She was carrying George on her hip, and for once it was easy for Dylan to ignore the ape's dirty looks.

Dylan could hear Jan's hushed and harried explanations in the background as Elise and Dylan faced off. She sighed. "You know, don't you?"

"I'm not a mathematician, but let's just say any idiot can put two and two together," Dylan said harshly.

"I was coming to—"

"To finally tell me the truth? Why? Because you knew I was about to find out the truth on my own? You had plenty of chances to tell me."

Elise flinched. "I was afraid to tell you. I knew you wouldn't understand why—"

"What's to understand, Doc?" Dylan shot back. "You set me up, it's that simple. You and your 'bud' made up that whole sad story about her divorce and her avaricious husband, didn't you? If nothing else, I should give you credit for being creative." He turned to Jan. "I'll bet your father didn't even start Pop's, did he?"

"Well, actually that part's true," Jan said meekly. "Only he's not dead. He's just retired."

"Ah, but his death was a nice touch," Dylan replied sarcastically, then turned back to Elise. "What else have you made up to bring this snake to justice, Doc? Was the budget sheet I sweated over filled with phony numbers? Do you really work such long hours and have so many patients, or did you just arrange with the friendly townsfolk of Alpine to inundate your office for dramatic effect? Was the *enema* really necessary?"

"I didn't lie about anything else, Dylan," Elise assured him, her eyes glistening with unshed tears. "Honest. You just seemed so stubborn about everything, I thought I needed something more immediate and close to home to make my point."

George was squirming in Elise's arms and hooting agitatedly. Dylan ignored him and said, "Your point was that I wasn't being fair, Elise, and you went about proving that point by cheating me with a lie," he stated coldly. "You see the problem, don't you? Now I don't know what to believe."

Elise did not reply. But what could she possibly say to him that Dylan could be absolutely sure wasn't just another lie?

Angry and sad and feeling like a first-class fool, Dylan walked out of the store to the pay phone and called a cab.

"So, HOW DID YOUR DAY go without your hunky urban assistant?"

Elise rested her chin in her hand, staring out the kitchen window as a glorious sunset gave the snow-covered landscape a mellow, golden glow. She sighed and reached down to scratch Rowena behind the ears as the unusually subdued pig lay on the floor at her feet. "How do you think my day went?"

Jan nodded understandingly. "Feeling pretty low about what happened this morning, aren't you? I wanted to talk to you sooner, but I had to calm Mike down. Then you were busy with patients all day."

"That's okay," Elise replied, lethargically stirring her tea. "There's nothing you could say that would make me feel better anyway."

She motioned to George, who was chowing down on a boiled egg and fruit salad. "At least the ape's happy. He's been looking smug all day, as if he were the reason McAllister left in a huff. But I take full responsibility. You warned me about how McAllister might react if he learned the truth, but I didn't listen. I really screwed up, Jan."

Jan chewed the inside of her lip and studied Elise with a concerned look. "You're being pretty hard on yourself. It's not like McAllister's a total innocent in this whole mess. He had plenty to answer for before he even showed up in this little burg."

"Yeah, but he apologized, Jan. He told me he was truly sorry he'd got that unfair settlement for Ted. I think he was even rethinking his whole attitude toward divorcing women in general. I made a lot of headway with the guy, then I blew it."

"He made a lot of headway with you, too, I gather," Jan suggested with a raised brow. "Or did the fact that he was at your house early this morning—*real* early this morning, as if he'd maybe spent the night—mean absolutely nothing?"

Elise took a sip of tea, trying to dispel the bittersweet memories of last night. "Oh, he made headway, all right." She hesitated, then added softly, "I think I'm falling in love with him."

Saying the words out loud and seeing Jan's wide-eyed expression of surprise brought home the hopelessness of the situation. "But now he hates me, Jan. He thinks I'm a liar and a con artist. He'll never forgive me. He told me himself he has a hard time forgiving."

"*You* forgave *him*, didn't you? And for something, I might add, that had a much bigger impact on your life than our tiny little fib had on his."

"The point is, he was always up-front with me, but I sunk to lying. I destroyed his trust in me. He doesn't know what to believe anymore."

"You should have made him listen to you, Elise. You should have been more persistent in trying to explain yourself."

Elise stood up and walked to the sink, dumping her tepid tea down the drain. "Well, hindsight is always twenty-twenty, isn't it? It's too late to do anything about it now."

"Geez, Elise, you've normally got a lot more spunk than this," Jan exclaimed, standing up and putting her hands on her hips. "Don't be a weeny. If you think you're falling in love with him—and who could blame you...the guy's a doll—you'd be crazy to let things end like this."

Elise leaned against the counter and crossed her arms over her chest. "What do you suggest I do?"

"If I were you, I'd go to Salt Lake tomorrow and see him. I'd make him understand that you fibbed about my fictitious divorce, but only about that and nothing else." Jan lifted her chin a notch. "And maybe I'd even tell the guy that I was in love with him! Who knows, maybe he's in love with you, too."

Elise smiled sadly and shook her head. "And the Queen Mum shops at the Gap. I don't think so, Jan. He doesn't strike me as the kind of guy that falls in love at the drop of a hat. Not that I do, either, but something happened to me last night, Jan...." She touched her chest. "Something in my heart..."

Elise shook off the tender feelings that suddenly flooded her and quickly continued to make her excuses. "Besides, he's very wary of commitment. Do I want to get mixed up with a guy who thinks not getting married is the only solution to divorce?"

"He's gun-shy, Elise. And from what you've told me about his brother's marriage and his own marriage, who could blame the guy? The point is, you need to see him again, talk this out and decide if he's worth the trouble. If he can't forgive, if he can't commit, then he isn't worth your time and trouble. But if he *can* forgive, if he *can* commit, then swallowing a little pride by going to see him might just be the smartest thing you've ever done."

Jan was making sense. Elise was getting butterflies in her stomach just thinking about acting on her friend's suggestion.

"I can't go tomorrow. I have to work," she said, thinking out loud.

"See if Dr. Spencer is free to take your afternoon appointments. He has pretty flexible hours since he works mostly in the field, and he certainly owes you one for snowshoeing across a frozen tundra to take care of Pete's mare the other night! Mike can watch the store, and I'll come over and baby-sit the chimp and the pig."

Elise bit her lip and frowned, picturing herself confronting Dylan on his own stomping grounds.

"I don't know where he lives."

"That's why you'd have to go in the afternoon to his office," Jan said, her voice building in enthusiasm. "You know that address."

"Don't I ever," Elise agreed, then began to pace the kitchen floor and wring her hands. Her mind was already racing ahead to what she would wear, what she would say...what *he* would say. Feeling a sudden surge of panic, she turned abruptly and said to Jan, "What if I freeze up? What if I can't tell him why I'm there?"

Jan smiled slyly. "Just tell him he skipped out early and he still owes you two days' work."

Elise smiled back. "That's right. He does." Her smile broadened. "And if he doesn't want to make good on his commitment to the Make a Wish Foundation, I can threaten to sue. I'm sure he wouldn't like the publicity."

"Would you really do that?" Jan asked, surprised.

"No," Elise admitted with a chagrined smile, "but McAllister doesn't know that. I would never drag a worthy charity into a civil dispute. But who knows what he thinks I'm capable of?" She sat down at the table again and looked wistfully at the growing shadows of dusk. "But maybe if I get him down here again, we can come to terms with our disagreements and really get to know each other. You know... develop a little trust."

"That would be nice," Jan agreed, a wistful note creeping into her voice, too. "I'd love to see you just as happy as me and Mike." Then, reverting to the business at hand, she inquired briskly, "So, what will you wear?"

ELISE WORE her best winter white suit. The tailored jacket and long, pleated skirt were feminine and flattering but businesslike and very uptown. With her tall taupe boots and matching wool coat, she knew she wouldn't look conspicuous in the lobby of the offices belonging to Taylor, Trent and McAllister.

But as she stood outside and stared up at the glass-and-steel facade of the Kennicott Building in the center of Salt Lake City's business district, her heart was in her throat. She was nervous and scared, but full of hope and excitement, too. Even if he greeted her with a frown, she told herself, at least she'd see him again. *McAllister,* she breathed to herself. What had begun as a brusque form of address was now an endearment.

Straightening her shoulders, she entered the building, read the directory to find out which floor Dylan's office was on, then entered the elevator and determinedly punched the button to the twentieth floor. As the doors shut and she began to go up, she tried to calm herself by mentally listing all of the good things that had happened that day.

Wasn't it a good sign that she was able to easily arrange for Dr. Spencer to take over her afternoon appointments? she reasoned. Wasn't it fortuitous that she was able to get away earlier than expected and would probably catch Dylan just in time for a noon lunch break? And could there have been a more beautiful, sunnier day to drive up to Salt Lake from Alpine?

By the time she'd marched through the plush green lobby to the receptionist's desk on Dylan's floor, Elise had psyched herself into believing that since things were going so well thus far, they'd certainly continue the same way.

But when she asked the receptionist if Dylan was in, the answer was...*no.*

Elise's disappointment was crushing. It hadn't once occurred to her that Dylan wouldn't go back to work. He'd taken the week off to fulfill his commitment to the Make a Wish Foundation, but he normally had such a busy practice, Elise was sure he'd finish out the week behind his desk catching up on paperwork.

"Is he planning to come in tomorrow?" Elise asked on a desperate note.

The receptionist, an older woman with a kind face, smiled and said, "He'll be in this afternoon. He just left for lunch."

"Oh." Relief flooded through Elise. "I misunderstood you. I thought he hadn't come in at all today."

"He wasn't planning to. He doesn't have any court dates or appointments." The receptionist paused, dipped her head and studied Elise over the top of her reading glasses. "Was Mr. McAllister expecting you?"

"Well, not—"

"Then you're meeting him for lunch?"

"Well, I—"

"You two must have gotten your wires crossed," she said with a friendly smile. "He probably thought he'd arranged to meet you at the restaurant."

Elise saw her chance and took it. She gave an embarrassed laugh. "That's just it. I don't remember what restaurant we agreed on! I was hoping to catch him before he left."

"If you hurry, you might still catch him. He left

just five minutes ago and was planning to walk through the mall to Windows on the Square. Now do you recall?"

"Of course...Windows on the Square. How could I forget?" Elise said, backing to the elevator. "Thank you. Thank you very much!"

Five minutes later Elise was standing at the door to the trendy restaurant with the wide windows that overlooked Salt Lake's historic Temple Square. It was an upscale eatery with snowy tablecloths, flowers, waiters in matching vests and bow ties and a largely professional clientele during lunch hours. She scanned what she could see of the diners, but she didn't see Dylan's dark head anywhere among the seated patrons.

"Good afternoon. Do you have a reservation?"

Elise was being addressed by an elegantly uni-formed host. "I don't have a reservation, I'm—"

"If you're dining alone, I believe I have a small table by the north windows," he offered.

Elise looked behind her and saw at least a dozen people lining up to be seated. If she didn't snatch the opportunity, she might lose the table. She reasoned that she could wait for Dylan as easily inside as out, and she'd be less conspicuous and therefore less nervous.

She smiled at the host. "That would be fine." Then she followed him to an out-of-the-way table just large enough for one...or maybe two if the couple was cozy. Elise's cheeks flamed with heat as she thought about the possibility of sharing the table with Dylan, their knees touching under the tablecloth, his hand reaching for hers....

The host handed her a large fold-out menu and left.

Again she scanned the room, but even with an all-encompassing view of the place, she didn't see Dylan anywhere. She scowled, wondering why she'd arrived before he did when he'd left the office earlier.

Then suddenly she saw him at the desk at the front of the restaurant. Elise's heart crashed against her ribs, and she felt her lips curve into a spontaneous smile. He looked incredible. Like the night at the auction—like the days in court when he represented Ted in the divorce—he was dressed in an exquisitely tailored suit. This one was a deep charcoal gray that he wore with a white shirt and a red tie. The color combinations made his dark good looks all the more striking.

She knew he was mad at her, she knew he might not want to see her, but she was half-way out of her seat and had one arm raised in greeting before she saw...that he wasn't alone.

Elise abruptly sat down and held the menu in front of her face. Her heart pounding with jealousy, disappointment, then a growing anger, she peeked around the menu and stared.

The woman was a blonde...of course. She was tall and slim and looked as if she was in her middle thirties. She wasn't flashy, like his date at Nino's the other night, but she was very nicely dressed in a conservative pantsuit. Dylan cupped her elbow and led her to a table only a few feet away. They sat down, with Dylan taking the chair facing Elise.

"Ma'am, have you decided yet?"

Elise was startled to hear herself addressed by a tall, snooty-looking waiter with a small black mustache and slick dark hair he'd combed over a bald spot from a low part. He wore the usual snappy uniform, but with the addition of a superior smirk.

Still hiding behind the menu, she mumbled, "Um... I'm not sure yet. Could you bring me some water?"

The waiter nodded perfunctorily and left, returning a couple of minutes later with a glass and a pitcher of water.

Elise still held the menu close to her nose, casting surreptitious glances at Dylan as he smiled and conversed with the mystery woman. Elise seethed inside, wondering how he could be so chummy with this blonde after he'd made such tender and passionate love to her less than thirty-six hours ago.

"Ahem!"

Elise jerked when the waiter loudly cleared his throat.

"Do you wish to order now, ma'am?" he asked pointedly, tapping his pen against a small pad of paper.

Elise was in a panic. If she put down the menu, Dylan was certain to see her. Why couldn't she have gotten a friendly, more patient waiter?

"I'm still not sure what I want," she confessed.

The waiter pursed his lips. "We are very busy at this hour, ma'am. Might I recommend today's special of cream of mushroom soup and a caesar salad?"

"Well, okay," Elise agreed, knowing she couldn't stall the waiter forever and afraid she'd attract attention to her little corner of the room if he hovered too long.

"An excellent choice, ma'am," the waiter said in a bored voice, then reached for the menu.

Elise snatched it away and forced a smile. "It's hot in here. Do you mind if I keep the menu to use as a fan?" She averted her face from the room and opened and closed the menu rapidly, creating a breeze.

The waiter's eyebrows shot up. "Actually it's quite cool in here today. Are you feeling *unwell*, ma'am?"

Flustered by the waiter's uncooperative behavior, Elise clicked her tongue and snapped, "I'm feeling *very* well, thank you. But since the sun is shining more on this side of the table, I think I'd like to change seats and sit on the other side."

The waiter blinked but showed no other facial expression. "You wish to face the *wall*, ma'am?"

This time it was Elise's turn to raise her brows. "Is there something wrong with that?"

"Nothing at all, ma'am," the waiter drawled, then he pulled out Elise's chair so she could stand up. Still holding the menu strategically to hide her face, Elise jumped to her feet and scrambled to the seat on the other side as quickly as if she'd been playing musical chairs and the music had suddenly stopped.

Now the waiter was peering at her suspiciously. "Are you more...er...comfortable now, ma'am?" he inquired.

"Much more comfortable, thank you," she primly replied.

He stared at her for a minute, then sniffed and said, "Do you suppose, then, that I might talk you out of keeping the menu?"

Elise laughed nervously and handed him the menu, but when he walked away, she grumbled, "Stuffy old coot. I thought this place was supposed to have quality service with a smile."

But now that she was facing the wall, while Dylan could no longer see her, she likewise couldn't see him. To remedy this, she reached for her purse and pulled out her powder compact, flipped it open and tried to position the tiny mirror so she could watch Dylan in it, while at the same time still appearing inconspicuous.

Twice she caught his reflection—once laughing, once looking sober and absorbed in whatever the woman was saying to him—but Elise's hand started shaking both times, making the mirror jerk and losing her precious view.

While she was ducking and angling and squinting, the waiter showed up again with a basket of rolls and a dish of butter.

"Ma'am, is there something I can help you with?" he asked her with a long-suffering expression on his face.

"No. No, I'm fine," she quickly assured him, snapping shut her compact.

"Are you done powdering your nose?" he inquired.

"Why do you ask?" Elise replied irritably.

"Because a gentleman over there—" the waiter paused and pointed, but Elise didn't dare turn and look. He went on, "—is complaining that the sun is catching in your compact mirror and flashing in his eyes."

"Oh. Well, tell the gentleman I'm sorry and it won't happen again," she said, mortified.

The waiter sniffed again and walked away.

Elise dropped her head into her hands and stared at the tablecloth. She couldn't believe the way she was acting! Dylan walked in with another woman, and she was sick with jealousy and resorting to all sorts of ridiculous postures to spy on them. But since he was with another woman, he obviously wasn't as shook up about their argument as she'd been, nor had he been as bowled over by their lovemaking the other night.

She had to face facts. He just didn't care as much as she did.

Elise made up her mind that she was going to quit making a fool of herself and leave the restaurant while she still had a shred of dignity. She'd weave through the tables and take an indirect route to the door, averting her face and partially covering it by pretending to use a tissue. It would all be wasted effort anyway, because Dylan was probably so enthralled with his lunch date he wouldn't even notice her walking by.

She'd go back to Alpine, and Dylan would never know she'd made a special effort to come to see him or that she was ever in the restaurant in the first place. *Like ships in the night, they'd pass unaware,* she ruminated on a more dramatic note, but was startled once again by the waiter when he crept up on her with her soup and salad.

"Ma'am, here is your—"

But that's as far as he got. Elise's head reared up, and her hand flailed out, overturning the water pitcher. The ice water sprayed into the air, splashing the front of the waiter's pants just as he set the bowl of soup down on the table.

The waiter let out a yowl of surprise, buckled over and dropped the salad upside down on the table.

Lettuce laced with slick dressing bounced and skidded off the table, most of which landed at the waiter's feet as he hopped around in a state of agitation.

The waiter slipped on a chunk of lettuce, fell on his back with a noisy "oomph!" and kicked the table over as his legs shot out from under him.

Elise held her hand over her mouth and, with a look of horror, surveyed the scene of carnage before her. This sort of display was definitely not inconspicuous. As the chink and rattle of breaking dishes and flying silverware gradually subsided, she collected enough presence of mind to stoop and check to see if the waiter was critically injured.

He wasn't...thank goodness. But he was madder than a wet rooster.

"Don't touch me!" he told her, scooting away with a fierce look in his eyes. "I knew you were trouble the minute I walked up to your table!"

"I can't tell you how sorry I am, sir," she tried to apologize, but the waiter had been assisted to his feet and was backing away through the gaping diners.

"Do you always wreak havoc in restaurants?" she heard a familiar voice say with amused sarcasm.

Elise turned and was face-to-face with Dylan Mc-Allister. "Not till I met you," she retorted, glaring at him. "This is all your fault!"

He raised his wicked black brows. "*My* fault? How do you figure?"

"If it weren't for you, I wouldn't even be in Salt Lake!"

She saw a muscle in his jaw ticking away, as steady as a metronome. "So, to use your own line of reasoning," he said succinctly, "you were *spying* on me?"

"Hah!" she exclaimed. "Why would I spy on *you*? I went to your office to talk to you, but when your receptionist told me you were out to lunch, I decided to grab something to eat myself and go back to your office later."

Dylan's eyes narrowed. "You didn't know I was planning to eat here?"

Elise opened her mouth. Her lips had already formed the word *no*, but she suddenly thought better of it. She knew she shouldn't lie to him again, particularly since she was there to convince him that she didn't routinely fudge the truth to get what she wanted.

She sighed. "Yes. *Yes*, she did tell me you were coming here, and I thought maybe we could talk like two civilized people over a pleasant meal." Her eyes flitted accusingly toward his lunch companion—still seated at the table, but looking curiously over her shoulder in their direction—then back to Dylan. "But I should have known you wouldn't be alone."

Kitchen help had been summoned to clean up the mess, and Dylan caught Elise's elbow and steered her out of the way and into a relatively quiet corner. His touch on her arm was thrilling, but Elise kept her expression cool and haughty.

"As you already mentioned, I'm not alone," Dylan repeated, "and I need to get back to my table."

Elise crossed her arms and tapped her toe on the carpet. "So what's keeping you?"

He gave a huff of exasperation. "Do you want to meet me in my office later for this talk you're so eager to have?"

Elise looked daggers at Dylan's date, then turned back to him. She was definitely not going to swallow her pride now and ask Dylan to forgive her for lying. Why humble yourself to a man who didn't care enough about you to suffer for a respectable two to three days after your last argument? she reasoned.

"We don't need to have a long talk about anything," Elise informed him frostily.

"But I thought—"

"The only reason I came up here was to tell you that you still owe me two days' work. I paid a lot to the Make a Wish Foundation, and even though I know it's for charity and I don't begrudge the money, I'm not going to let you weasel out of the deal. Do you understand, McAllister?"

Dylan cocked his head to the side and studied her. His blue eyes blazed with an emotion Elise could only suppose was anger.

"You could have called," he argued.

"And be put off by your secretary?" She humphed. "Not likely!"

By now the restaurant manager was hovering in the background, apparently waiting to talk to Elise to either apologize for the inconveniences she'd suffered or to demand that she pay damages. But Dylan suddenly seemed in no hurry to get back to his date or to distance himself from the embarrassment of Elise's unintentional slapstick routine. He just stood there and looked at her.

As Elise stared back, she felt her anger melting and slipping away like an ice cube on a hot sidewalk. He was standing so close and he smelled so good. She had to exercise extreme self-control not to reach out and touch him. His expression was sober, but his eyes were intensely blue and seemed to penetrate right to her very soul.

"All right, Elise," he said at last in a cool, controlled voice that effectively broke the spell. "I'll be at your house first thing tomorrow morning. We'll have to work off my contract this weekend, because after that I'll be in court again."

In court again, ruining women's lives, Elise thought to herself. And now he had another experience with a devious woman to add to his list of grievances and to justify his prejudices.

But suddenly Elise felt renewed determination. She'd made a mistake, but she wasn't about to make another. And she had two more days to teach Dylan how to play fair. Or if she'd ruined the chance to convert him to her way of thinking, at least she could enjoy the torture of working with him again.

"My first appointment is at eight," she told him in clipped tones. "Try not to be late, McAllister." Then she turned and left before he could answer, ignoring the manager, who finally threw up his hands in defeat and stalked back to the kitchen.

Dylan took a deep breath and returned to his seat.

"Who was that?" Andrea inquired, an amused smile on her lips.

"Her name is Elise Allen," Dylan calmly replied, lifting his cup of coffee to take a sip.

Andrea raised a brow. "Yes, but what is she to you?"

Dylan looked rueful. "What do you mean?"

"You know what I mean. And don't tell me she's a friend or a business acquaintance, because she wouldn't have given me that venomous look just now if you two were just pals."

Dylan sobered and shook his head, sitting back in his chair. "I don't know what she is to me. We've only been involved for a short time...a *very* short time. But I feel like we're joined at the hip. We've been separated for a little over twenty-four hours, and I've been off balance the whole time."

"Is she always so prone to accidents?" Andrea inquired, apparently fascinated by the story.

"She claims she only started making a public spectacle of herself after meeting me."

"All the symptoms are there," Andrea said knowingly. "She's in love with you."

Dylan sat up straighter. "Do you really think so?"

"I'm sure of it."

Dylan's stomach was churning, his heart was racing and his temples were pounding.

"I feel sick," he informed his companion. "Does that mean I'm in love with her, too?"

"Nausea is a common side effect of falling in love," Andrea confirmed. "Don't you remember it from the last time you were in love?"

"I'm not sure I've ever been in love before," Dylan confessed. "And Elise and I haven't exactly had a smooth ride so far. She lied to me, Andrea. And I think she came up here today from Alpine to explain herself and ask me to forgive her."

"Ah. Then she saw you with me and jumped to the wrong conclusion."

"I guess so."

"Well, why didn't you just tell her I was your client, Dylan?"

Dylan chuckled grimly. "Because she wouldn't have believed me."

"Why not? It's the truth."

"Because I don't take female clients as a rule...not when they want me to represent them in divorce court."

Andrea's eyes widened with amazement. "You

mean I'm the first female client you've ever represented in a divorce?"

Dylan shrugged. "You're the first one in five years."

"I guess I called when you were in a good mood," she observed dryly.

"No," Dylan replied thoughtfully, "you caught me right after I decided to permanently change the way I do things...thanks to that beautiful lady vet that just stomped out of here with lettuce in her hair."

Chapter Twelve

Five days ago, when he'd first driven down from Salt Lake to work as Elise's assistant in the clinic, Dylan's attitude had been *Get in, do what you have to do, then get out.* Now he'd changed his tune. He wanted to get in and stay in, but whether or not that meant a permanent commitment was still anybody's guess.

All Dylan knew for sure was that Elise had softened him up enough to help him see the error of his ways...and now he was so soft he melted every time he got near her.

But when he'd found out that Jan's story was designed to make him feel guilty, and that they'd carefully orchestrated the whole scheme so he'd think he'd overheard them while eavesdropping, he was angry, hurt and disappointed. He had begun to think Elise was perfect, and then he was suddenly terribly disillusioned.

Two restless, soul-searching nights later, he realized that whether or not Elise was perfect was not the issue. No one was perfect...least of all himself. And he had no business freezing her out if she wanted to explain herself and apologize. He was sure that's what she'd been in Salt Lake to do, but she'd changed her mind when she'd seen him with "another woman."

He wanted to tell her that he understood and that he forgave her, but his stubborn side was holding him back, waiting for her to make the first move. After all, he reasoned, he'd apologized to her for his mistakes, and now it was her turn. Then they'd be even.

Dylan knew he was using petty, juvenile logic, but he couldn't seem to help himself. Besides, if Elise made the first move, he'd know that it was safe to make the *second* move, etcetera. He was insecure, he admitted to himself, which was a feeling he hadn't experienced in years. He realized then that a person had to truly care in order to be afraid of rejection.

Dylan parked the car out front and glanced up at the gray skies as he strode down the walk to Elise's front door. With any luck at all, there would be another monster storm, stranding him in Alpine at the Allen Asylum for another night. He could only hope....

This time Elise answered the door, but George and Rowena were standing on either side of her. The contrast in greetings he got would have struck him as comical if he'd been relaxed enough to laugh or smile. Rowena was so excited she was shaking from curly tail to blunt snout and grunting to beat the band. He stooped to pet her.

George was clearly disgusted and angry. First he stared at Dylan in disbelief, then he stalked away and sat in the corner under Geraldo's bird cage, his long arms crossed over his Hard Rock Café T-shirt and his bottom lip sticking way out.

Elise's behavior was a mirror of Dylan's. They both stood and stared at each other, feeling awkward and nervous, then simultaneously broke into polite but meaningless conversation.

"It looks like it's going to snow—"

"I hope your drive down was—"

They both abruptly stopped and waited for the other to continue. When the silence stretched endlessly, they started talking again at the same time.

"Did you eat—?"

"I hope you haven't had any trouble with—"

They stopped again and gazed miserably at each other.

"Maybe we should just get to work," Elise suggested with a sigh. "I've already got a full waiting room."

Dylan knew the routine by now. He hung up his coat, watched Elise—dressed in her favorite work outfit of jeans and a soft blue sweatshirt—with longing as he followed her down the narrow hall to the clinic, changed into a lab coat over his practical denim shirt, scrubbed up and put on a pair of rubber gloves.

Then the animal parade began.

The next two hours were agony. Each time he and Elise brushed shoulders or he caught a whiff of her fragrant hair or their gazes caught and locked for an instant, Dylan felt like exploding. But even if there had been an opportunity for private conversation, Dylan still wouldn't have initiated the reconciliation. He wasn't going to tell Elise that Andrea was just a client until Elise told him she was sorry about her scheme with Jan.

Dylan was reinforcing this obstinate train of thought, getting grumpier and grumpier, when a teenage boy stuck his head inside the door to inquire, "Dr. Allen? You got a chimp?"

Elise was examining the ingrown toenail of a Pekingese when this interruption occurred. With a slight frown, she looked up and said, "I'm boarding one for a couple of weeks. Why? Is he bothering you?"

"I don't think he's bothering anyone...yet. I was riding my bike down Main Street just now, and I saw him jumping off your front porch. By the time I got to your house, I couldn't see where he went. Is he allowed outside?"

Elise and Dylan exchanged panicked looks.

"Oh, my gosh. I should have had someone keeping an eye on him, but I forgot. *You* made me forget, McAllister!" Elise accused.

"Now's not the time for placing blame, Doc," Dylan replied, picking up the Pekingese off the examination table and handing it to its owner. "We have a runaway chimp to track down before he gets hurt or in some kind of trouble."

Elise nodded distractedly and turned to the woman holding the Pekingese. "I'm sorry, Mrs. Romney," she said as they rushed out of the room. "I'll be back as soon as I can!"

Sure enough the front door was standing wide open. Rowena was peering out, but she was too domesticated and pampered to have any desire to leave the warmth and security of her home. Besides, she wasn't angry, as George undoubtedly was, that a certain male primate had returned to the tribe to interfere with the womenfolk.

Elise and Dylan paused on the porch and looked left and right, scanning the yard, the trees, the street.

"We don't know the first place to look." Elise sounded miserable. "He could be anywhere."

"He hasn't been gone that long. We'll find him," Dylan tried to reassure her. "Think like an ape," he advised. "Where would you go if you were mad and jealous and wanted to run away from home?"

"This is my fault," Elise announced as they stepped off the porch and headed for the street.

"I thought it was *my* fault," Dylan countered as they waited for a truck to pass. When the driver looked at him oddly, he realized he and Elise were still wearing rubber gloves and lab jackets.

"All I could think about after you showed up this morning was *you,* McAllister," Elise continued, ignoring his interruption. "All I wanted to do was tell you how sorry I was, then I wanted to throw you onto the examining table and make love to you."

"With my bad back, I'd have preferred the sofa again," Dylan drawled, the anxiety crowding his chest moving over to make room for the heady exhilaration Elise's words were engendering. *She cared! She really cared!* He grabbed her hand, and they sprinted across the street together.

"Why are we going this way?" Elise wanted to know.

"Because I saw his distinctive prints in the snow at the curb," Dylan informed her. "Maybe he went to the store to buy a tube of toothpaste for an afternoon snack."

"Or a Dr Pepper," Elise suggested, encouraged. "Yeah, maybe he went to the store to see Jan. I've had him over there a couple of times, and he was mesmerized by all the food."

A bell heralded their arrival as they pushed impatiently through the door and entered the store. Still holding hands, they immediately scanned the area, looking for an ape strolling the aisles or hanging from the rafters with a soda pop can in his free hand.

"Now, there's a picture," Jan observed dryly as she looked them over. "Is this a new fashion statement? Matching jackets is a cute idea, but I think you went a little too far with the gloves."

"George is missing," Elise blurted. "Have you seen him?"

Jan immediately sobered. "Not since yesterday. How long has he been missing?"

"Only a few minutes," Dylan told her. "We thought he might have come over here. We're pretty sure he crossed the street."

Jan pulled on her coat. "I'll help you find him." She flipped over the Open sign to Closed as she left the store.

Outside on the sidewalk, they split up. Jan went north and Dylan and Elise went south.

"Somehow I don't think he's in any of these businesses," Elise said, "or there would be some kind of commotion going on. People aren't going to think it's commonplace for a chimp to walk in off the street."

They went in and out of a few stores and checked in the backyards of a few residences, but still the chimp was nowhere to be found, and it was starting to snow.

"He'll freeze to death. He'll die a slow and agonizing death on some frozen hillside, and it will be all my fault," Elise wailed, rubbing her own arms from the cold.

"You just forgot to have someone watch him while you were taking care of patients, Elise," Dylan said.

"Half the time he's so independent, you don't think about him needing a baby-sitter while you're somewhere in the house with him. You made a mistake. Everyone does now and then. No one's perfect."

Elise searched Dylan's face. "Is there a double meaning in those words?" she wanted to know. "Have you forgiven me for lying to you? You know I only lied the one time," she rushed on. "Every other part of my life you've seen in the past week isn't the least bit fabricated. And the enema really *was* necessary, Dylan."

Dylan grabbed her arms and pulled her close. Nose to nose, he said, "I'd be a jackass if I couldn't forgive you for trying to get through my thick skull with that sob story. I'm a stubborn man, and you thought you had no choice. But promise me, Doc, that we'll always be honest with each other from now on. Do I have your word?"

"You have my word," she promised, a glowing smile transforming her pinched and worried features into something irresistible.

"Can we seal the deal with a kiss?" Dylan suggested, pulling her even closer as they stood in plain sight on Main Street with people and cars passing.

She nodded demurely, and he bent his head and pressed his lips to hers. She melted against him, and her arms slipped around his neck. In the midst of the kiss, with all his concentration focused on Elise, Dylan was undaunted by the catcalls and horns honking, but when he got hit on the back of the head with a hard, cold snowball, he couldn't help but take notice.

Rubbing his scalp, Dylan turned around, ready to shoo away a giggling troop of preadolescent boys, when he saw the real culprit and yelled, "George!"

Yes, it was George, standing in front of Lars's brand-new, just-opened office, screaming ape obscenities and pounding his chest.

"He's got a good arm," Dylan had to admit, still feeling the impact of that well-aimed snowball.

"I don't think he's going to come willingly," Elise whispered, frozen to the spot, probably afraid she'd spook George and send him rushing into the street.

"A tranquilizer gun sounds like a good plan about now," Dylan observed.

"I'm not going to shoot him with a tranquilizer gun, McAllister," Elise said testily. "Not when there are other alternatives."

"I was only kidding," Dylan returned. He paused, then added, "By the way, what are the alternatives?"

"One of us needs to go after him, and it had better be me. He's not a violent chimp—"

"Tell that to my aching head."

"—but he *is* a bit perturbed. Since he sees you as a rival, he might try to conk you with another snowball. You stay here, and I'll advance slowly. Okay?"

Dylan had no choice but to agree. It made sense, and he knew George would never hurt Elise. He was just overexcited by the "jailbreak" and the rush of liberty.

Jan showed up, and soon a small crowd gathered to watch Elise round up her runaway chimp. It was kind of like watching a circus sideshow, admission free.

As Elise got closer, talking soothingly and making promises, George seemed to settle down. Elise had almost talked him into climbing into her arms to be carried home to an ice-cold Dr Pepper and recorded tapes of "Sesame Street," when a passing car honked several times in quick succession. George startled and ran to the door of Lars's office, pushed it open and hurried inside.

Elise rushed in after him, and Dylan rushed in after Elise, leaving Jan behind to police the crowd. With visions of a crazed ape wielding a dentist's drill, Dylan followed Elise as they passed an unmanned receptionist's desk and headed directly for Lars's procedures room.

But just as they reached the door, Lars came out...carrying George.

"Oh, hi," said Lars, smiling broadly, not appearing the least embarrassed about the other night when they'd had to put him to bed dead drunk. "Nice of you guys to come down and see my new office. But I was surprised to see the chimp. I always thought he didn't like me." Lars reached inside his pocket and pulled out a sugar-free lollipop and offered it to George.

Dylan watched with amazement as George took the lollipop and looped his long arm around Lars's thick neck, appearing to consider the hefty dentist his best friend. Dylan figured that George had been so frustrated he'd joined forces with another rival, thereby making it two against one. The dentist and the ape versus the attorney.

It sounded like the makings of a bad joke, something Geraldo could add to his repertoire. *A dentist, an ape and a lawyer were stranded on a desert island....* And you could be sure the punch line would have something to do with the ape's superiority over his human boat mates. In the present case, George was definitely making a monkey out of everyone involved.

"Actually we didn't come to see your office," Elise began. She gave a cursory look around. "Although it *is* very nice, Lars. But George got out of the house, and we tracked him to here." At this point Elise allowed herself a sigh of relief. "It looks like he's finally settled down. If he didn't like you before, he seems to like you now."

They chatted briefly while George smacked away on his lollipop and threw smug smiles in Dylan's direction. Lars apologized again for getting drunk Tuesday night and assured Elise that he'd only been drinking because he was quite nervous about taking her out. He said he rarely drank, and when he did, it went right to his head. Then he thanked Dylan again for saving his life.

Dylan grudgingly admitted to himself that Lars seemed sincere. But he still wouldn't trust him behind the wheel with Elise in the car. Even if he weren't drinking, he'd probably be all over her like a bad case of measles. Besides, Elise was his—

Dylan stopped midthought. Elise was his...*what?* Girlfriend? Lover? *Steady?* He wasn't sure. They hadn't settled anything between them yet or discussed the future. All he really knew for sure was that Elise was *his*.

George knew it, too. That's why he was up in arms and running away like a scorned lover. So why couldn't Lars see the writing on the wall?

"So, since you understand, Elise, and if I promise not to touch another drop of liquor while we're together, is there any reason why we can't go out again?" Lars asked her as they walked to the front door.

Jan stepped inside just in time to hear Lars asking

Elise for another date. There was an awkward silence as Lars waited for an answer. Elise looked at Dylan, seeming to ask with her eyes, *Well, McAllister? Is there any reason why I shouldn't go out with Lars?* Jan stared at Dylan, too, her eyes asking the same question.

But Dylan didn't think it was his call. He figured no woman in her right mind would go out with Lars again after what had happened the other night. And if Elise had the same feelings for him as Dylan had for her, she wouldn't want to go out with anyone else...whether Lars or Kevin Costner were doing the asking. Trouble was, Elise didn't know Dylan's feelings. But he didn't think Lars's dentist's office was the place for what should be a private conversation...particularly since they had a rapt audience.

Finally Elise's gaze dropped from Dylan's face, and she turned to Lars. "To tell you the truth, Lars, I don't think we should go out anymore. As professionals practicing in the same small town, I think it would be best if we stayed friends...and nothing more. I'm flattered, but...well...you understand, don't you?"

Lars looked disappointed, but he smiled resignedly and nodded. "Sure. I understand. As long as I didn't lose you to some jerk like McAllister here," he joked.

They all laughed nervously and self-consciously. Elise quickly took George out of Lars's arms and headed for the door. Goodbyes were quick and determinedly cheerful, as befitted the situation.

Outside, people cheered as Elise emerged with the fugitive chimp. Then the crowd dispersed and moseyed away to have lunch and talk over the fifteen minutes of excitement that had livened up their quiet little town.

"Want lunch from the deli counter?" Jan offered.

"I've still got a couple of patients waiting," Elise declined.

"Then let me take George. I'll feed him and amuse him this afternoon. And don't worry, I won't let him out of my sight. Mike can watch the store. I think you guys need a lunch break without a chimp in your hair, don't you?"

She was also implying that he and Elise needed privacy and time to talk. Dylan couldn't agree more. He telegraphed his thanks to Jan with a warm smile.

Later, after Elise's patients were gone, Dylan found himself alone in the examining room with the best, and the sexiest, vet this side of the Mississippi. They had just cleaned up, shucked their lab jackets and washed their hands. They were leaning against the counters on opposite sides of the room, wiping their hands dry on paper towels, when their eyes simultaneously strayed to the examining table. Her comment earlier about making love on that hard, stainless-steel surface hung tantalizingly in the air.

Dylan knew they needed to talk, but that wasn't exactly what was on his mind at the moment. Nor did he think a discussion was uppermost in Elise's mind, either.

"Race you to the sofa," he suggested in a husky whisper.

"Wouldn't you rather try out the feather bed in my room?" she countered softly.

Dylan's mouth curved in that gorgeous grin of his, and Elise wilted like lettuce in a hot breeze. Maybe she was crazy, but she'd been longing for him all morning. Sure, they needed to talk, and she still felt a little hurt about seeing him on a lunch date with another woman the day after they'd made love, but she felt she could more easily express what she was feeling at the moment by showing instead of telling.

"I don't care where we make love, Elise, as long as we begin in the next ten seconds," Dylan informed her, stepping purposefully forward.

Elise watched him approach. He'd worn a sensible pair of jeans and a denim shirt to work that day, which proved he'd learned something during the week, but his casual clothes only made him look rugged and sexy and touchable. The jeans fit like a glove, his slim hips and trim, muscled thighs outlined by taut denim. His dark, wavy hair had been tousled by the wind when they'd searched outside for George, and he hadn't had time to recomb it. That was fine with Elise, because she couldn't wait to get her fingers in it, anyway.

By the time he reached her, her heart was tap-dancing and her skin was on fire. "We've got about five seconds left, McAllister," she warned him with a coy smile.

He raised a brow. "In that case..." Then he swooped her into his arms.

"Dylan, your back!" she exclaimed on a laugh. "You'll hurt your back!"

"Don't worry, m'dear," he drawled in an unmistakable imitation of Rhett Butler. "I bent my knees. And even if I did strain my back, as long as it holds up for the next hour, frankly, my dear, I don't give a damn!"

Then he carried her through the house, with Rowena scurrying behind, till they reached Elise's bedroom. Dylan pushed open the door with his foot and lowered Elise to the queen-size, old-fashioned bed in the middle of the room.

As she eased into the downy softness of the feather mattress, Elise pulled Dylan down with her. They rolled into each other's arms and gazed at each other, grinning like a couple of crows loose in a cornfield— they just couldn't believe where they were and how good everything looked.

Elise touched his cheek with her forefinger and traced the deep dimple that made an apostrophe at the side of his mouth. "I came to Salt Lake to apologize and explain about—"

He touched her lips and silenced her, saying, "I know. You don't need to do any more explaining. But *I* do."

Suddenly Elise was afraid. She didn't want to hear anything that would make the time she'd spend in his arms bittersweet. She didn't want to hear any disclaimers or modifying statements like, *I care about you and I want to make love to you,* but..." Elise just wanted to lose herself in the moment, to give herself freely and completely to Dylan McAllister and to believe he was giving himself to her with the same freedom.

"I thought you knew when to shut up, McAllister," she said with a smile she hoped hid her fears and insecurities.

He smiled back, but the expression in his sky-blue eyes was deadly serious. "I do. But I have to say one thing before we make love. It's something you need to know."

Elise's eyes fluttered shut as she braced herself to hear something that might have the potential to ruin the mood and, worse still, to break her heart. "I'm listening," she whispered bravely.

"She was my client."

Elise's eyes flew open. She thought she knew what he was talking about, but she couldn't be sure. "You mean—?"

"The woman at the restaurant…the blonde in the pantsuit? She's a client of mine."

Elise's eyes grew wide as the enormity of what he was saying began to sink in. This was much more than reassurance that he wasn't on a date yesterday afternoon. What Dylan was trying to tell her was that he'd…*changed.* He'd changed so much, in fact, he was now taking—

"I'm taking female divorce clients," he confessed, looking sheepish and proud at the same time. "Andrea was the first in five years. Her phone message was on my desk when I arrived at work Friday morning, and because of you, I called her up and made an appointment to discuss her case. She was only free for lunch, and since I was eager to begin, I told her I'd meet her at Windows on the Square. The rest, as they say, is history." He grinned. "You won your crusade, m'dear."

Elise could feel her eyes sting with emotion. "I won something much better than that, Dylan. I won the thrill of being in your arms."

Elise watched as every feature in Dylan's face softened, then took on the intense look of desire. His eyes caught and held her gaze as he moved his hands down her back, pressed her against him and cupped her hips. Then he moved sinuously against her to show her just how much he wanted and needed her.

Elise gasped, and her eyelids drooped as desire and delight swirled through her.

Then his hands were at her waist, unbuttoning the front placket of her jeans. He kissed her as he worked, his lips blazing a trail from her mouth to her ear, down her neck and into the hollow at the base of her throat. Soon he slid his hands inside her jeans and was pulling them down, over her hips and knees. His warm skin against her exposed flesh gave her goose bumps.

Having dispensed with the jeans, he quickly slipped the loose sweatshirt over her head, grabbed her by the waist and lifted her, suckling her nipples through the filmy lace of her bra.

Elise arched her neck and let the waves of pleasure wash over her. Her hands caught in his hair, her fingers sifting through the thick waves.

"Now it's my turn," she warned him breathlessly, pushing him onto his back and straddling his hips.

He leaned back with a look of complete submission, his arms crossed behind his head...but his eyes gleamed with desire barely held in check. Enjoying a sense of power, Elise slowly undid the buttons on his shirt, kissing each exposed inch of flesh as she went along. By the time her chin rested on his belt buckle, he groaned with hunger and she sat up and watched the play of emotions on his beautiful face. She pulled his shirt free, and he lifted his arms, his chest now bare under her seeking hands.

He pulled her down and kissed her, deeply and thoroughly, unclasping her bra and removing it with a smooth deftness that was incredibly sexy. Her breasts ached and throbbed as he cradled and kissed them.

Then he rolled her on her back and took a tender

and passionate inventory of every inch of her with licks and nibbles and slow, sensuous caresses.

In a heady whirl of physical and emotional sensations, they removed the remainder of their clothes and finally lay naked in each other's arms.

It was so good. It was even better than the first time they made love. Elise's only regret was that this passion between them might not be for keeps. Because now, as Dylan positioned himself and entered her warm, weeping center, she knew with her whole heart...that she loved him.

She loved a man who saw the pain and bitterness of divorce on a daily basis...a man who didn't want to deal with it in any way except as someone's attorney...a man who was afraid of making that march down the aisle because half of today's marriages would end in divorce.

How could she ever convince him that they could be the exception to the rule? That they could buck the statistics with love, forgiveness and honesty?

But soon the exquisite tension building in her body blotted out all other thoughts, and she gave herself up to the consuming thrill of being made love to by the man she loved...her ex-husband's divorce lawyer.

Chapter Thirteen

By Sunday morning Dylan was in dire need of a back massage.

"You overdid it," Elise said as she rubbed his lower back with baby oil.

Dylan lay on his stomach with his chin resting on his overlapped hands. He turned his face to the side and smiled. He looked utterly content. His eyes were closed, and the way his black lashes stood out against his tanned skin took Elise's breath away.

"I didn't hear you complaining yesterday afternoon or last night," he teased.

She bent down and kissed his shoulder. "I thought you knew your limits," she teased back.

"Apparently I don't. At least...not with you." Then he rolled onto his back and pulled her against his bare chest. He was lounging on her bed in his boxers, and she was wearing the top of her oversize flannel pajamas and a pair of bikini panties. The Sunday *Salt Lake Tribune* was spread over the tousled bedclothes, and remnants of a French-toast breakfast littered the nightstands.

"Recovery will be slow if you insist on overworking those back muscles," she warned him.

"Then why don't I just lie here and you can do all the work?" he offered, smiling suggestively.

Elise was tempted, but she shook her head and pulled away. "We can't. Jan is bringing George back in half an hour."

"She really is a good friend to keep that hyper little ape for the night," Dylan remarked, sitting up and stretching. "But I guess all good things have to come to an end sooner or later."

Elise couldn't help the panic that gripped her when Dylan repeated that careless cliché. She was afraid he truly believed what he'd just said and expected their relationship to come, like so many others, inevitably to an end. All the love and laughter, all the good times to slip into oblivion and fade away... Maybe not today, or tomorrow, or next week, but eventually.

Eventually.

She stood up and walked to the window, staring out.

Dylan followed. "Hey, why the gloomy face?" he asked her, slipping his arms around her waist from behind and pulling her close. "We can still sneak kisses while George is around. By the way, how long *is* George going to be around?"

Elise leaned into Dylan, feeling a smile curve her lips. She was determined to enjoy Dylan thoroughly while *he* was still around. "His owners get back from England on Tuesday."

"Can't say I'll miss him. He might be kind of fun if he didn't hate me so much."

"He'd get used to you in time," said Elise, turning in his arms and snuggling her head under his chin. "*I* did."

"So you don't hate me anymore?"

Dylan had asked that question before on the night they'd first kissed. She'd held back her answer then, afraid to admit she was far from hating him and had progressed to liking him a whole lot.

Now she didn't dare tell him that she'd actually fallen in love with him…and in just one week! It was a surefire way of scaring off a commitment-shy guy like Dylan. She wasn't ready for the bliss to end yet, but she wasn't sure, either, why he was asking the question and what he truly wanted to hear.

She pulled back and searched his eyes. His expression was guarded and vulnerable at the same time. Maybe he wasn't sure what he wanted to hear, either.

She smiled, trying to control her bottom lip's tendency to quiver. "Of course I don't hate you. How could I make love to a man all night if I hated him?"

He raised a brow. "Then it wasn't 'just sex'?"

"Hardly," she acknowledged, wondering where this was leading.

"I'm glad, because it meant a lot to me, too, Doc," he told her sincerely. Then he kissed her briskly on the nose, gently pushed her away and sat on the edge of the bed to put on his socks. "I've got to go to Salt Lake right away, Elise, and I'd like to get out of here before the chimp shows up."

Elise was taken unaware by Dylan's abrupt announcement. "You have to go to Salt Lake *right away?*" She was afraid to ask why, and she could already feel the pain of separation.

"There's something I have to do."

She could only guess that his urgent business had to do with work. But he apparently didn't intend to give her any details, and she wasn't about to pry. Not knowing where you stood with a person caused all kinds of awkwardness, Elise decided, but she forced a smile and said, "Will you be back before George leaves? Or are you planning to avoid him till he goes back to his owners?"

Dylan threw her a smile as he pulled on his jeans. "I'll be back this evening...if that's okay?"

Happiness welled up in Elise. "Shall I make dinner?"

He slipped his arms into his shirt, and Elise tried not to let her thoughts stray as she watched him button up the front, unfortunately hiding that wonderful chest of his.

"That would be great," he said, rolling up the cuffs. "Unless you want me to pick something up in the city? You don't have to cook all the time, you know. Why don't you take a break?"

"I like to cook," she said. *Especially for you.*

He stepped close and cupped her chin with one hand, kissing her lingeringly on the lips. Her pulse started skittering, and her breath was hard to catch. When he pulled away, he said, "Maybe we'll get lucky and the lights will go out again. You're especially gorgeous in candlelight."

"Candlelight can be arranged, McAllister, without the help of a power outage," she informed him coyly. *Especially if it makes me look that good to you.*

"Perfect," he said with that electrifying smile of his, "because a romantic setting would be very appropriate for tonight."

Elise raised her brows. "Is there something special about tonight?"

"Yeah," he said, tapping her lightly on the nose. "I'm going to be with *you.*"

Ten minutes later Elise watched from the living-room window as Dylan got in his BMW, pulled away from the curb and drove off. She sighed the sigh of a woman in love, then shook her head at her own foolishness.

She couldn't believe it! She was deeply, hopelessly in love with Dylan McAllister! And she didn't have a clue how he felt about her. Well, she had a clue, but she still knew nothing for sure, and it was the not knowing that was making her a little crazy at the moment.

She paced the carpet in front of the fireplace while Rowena watched on the sidelines, the little pig too lazy or too smart to follow what appeared to be rather aimless moving about, and too depressed now that her idol was gone to have much enthusiasm for anything.

"I know just how you feel, Rowena," Elise said to the pouting pig. "I already miss him, too. But this is ridiculous, and I have to snap out of it. I've never been this goofy for a guy!"

So Elise went to work with a vengeance, cleaning up the breakfast dishes and making the bed, only allowing herself the one indulgence of sinking her face into Dylan's pillow and breathing in the smell of his subtle after-shave.

By the time Jan brought George over, with her good-looking husband toting the chimp's pen, Elise was dressed and the house was neat. All telltale remnants of her night of passion had disappeared...except perhaps for the "glow" she knew must be obvious.

"I'd love to stay for a few minutes, Elise," Jan whispered on the way out. "I've got this feeling you need to talk. But this is our only day off, and Mike and I have plans."

Jan was right; Elise would have loved to have a

friend to talk to, but she certainly understood Jan's desire to be with her husband. She smiled and said, "Hey, go have a wonderful day. We'll talk tomorrow."

After Jan left, Elise still felt restless. It was hours before she needed to begin preparations for the evening, and she was dying to talk to someone. She'd tried a couple of times during the week to call Dana but had never been able to reach her. She was probably just as busy as Elise was and had her hands full with the bachelor she'd bought at the auction.

She smiled when she thought about how her best friend would react when she found out Elise had fallen hard for her ex-husband's divorce lawyer. She'd taught him a lesson, but he'd taught her how to fall in love…deeply and forever. No matter how things ended between them, Elise had a rather daunting premonition that she'd always be in love with Dylan McAllister.

She shook her head ruefully, embarrassed to realize that of the two friends, both with bachelors for the week, she was probably the one crazy enough to fall head over heels in love. And she was formerly the levelheaded one.

Elise spent a lot of time playing quiet games with George that day, reading him stories and encouraging a mellow mood. She didn't want him to ruin her evening with Dylan by throwing a jealous fit the minute her date walked in the door. He'd tolerated Dylan pretty well till the night they'd made love, so perhaps Dylan was right about the chimp somehow sensing that his rival had definitely made inroads with their mutual love interest.

Sometimes Elise giggled when she thought about

the fact that she was the object of an ape's affection, but she'd heard of it happening to other chimp caretakers and she knew it was perfectly normal. She just didn't want George's jealousy to throw a wrench in the romance tonight. She couldn't put him to bed before nine without him causing a ruckus, so they'd have to have dinner with the chimp as an extra guest. *And* Rowena. *And* Geraldo. Elise was so glad Dylan was a tolerant man. How many men would carry on a courtship in a zoo?

About four o'clock Dylan called and told her to expect him about six. "Oh, and wear something kinda dressy and sexy, okay?"

There was something in his voice—an undercurrent of suppressed excitement—that intrigued Elise and made her own anticipation to see him that much keener.

She went through her closet and found a slinky little jade green sheath she'd worn last summer to a cocktail party. It was sleeveless, and the hem came to just above her knees, and several people had commented that the dress brought out the color of her eyes.

It was really too light and sheer for winter, but since Elise didn't intend to leave the house, she saw no reason why she shouldn't wear it. It made her feel sexy and attractive, and she had an idea it was exactly the kind of outfit Dylan had in mind. She even wore a pair of green satin pumps that exactly matched the dress.

When the doorbell rang at three minutes to six, Elise was in the kitchen putting the finishing touches on dinner. She turned to George, who was sitting in his high chair, and waggled her finger at him. "That's

McAllister, George, and you'd better behave yourself. Do you understand?"

At the mention of Dylan's name, George dropped the spoon he was using to scoop up his scrambled eggs, crossed his arms and stuck out his bottom lip. Since this was the pose he'd taken just before running away the day before, Elise did not think it boded well for a carefree evening.

Geraldo, too, had heard the dreaded name mentioned and began his litany of "McAllister, McAllister, McAllister's a... *sssssnake!*"

Elise opened the front door with an apology on her lips, but when she saw Dylan standing there in a black tuxedo with a huge bouquet of red roses in one hand and a bottle of wine in the other, she was speechless.

"It's nippy out here, Doc," he informed her with a wry smile. "The wine is supposed to be chilled, but not the roses or the man holding the roses."

"I'm s-sorry," Elise stuttered, stepping aside. "Come in."

Dylan came in, bringing the smells of the fresh outdoors, roses and his tangy after-shave with him.

While Elise shut the door behind him, Dylan raised his chin and sniffed the air. "Mmm. What smells good enough to eat?"

"I think it's you," she suggested.

He turned and smiled down at her. "No, I think it's you." Then he bent and kissed her, making Elise's knees go weak as water. Had it only been a few short hours since she'd last seen him? It felt like a millenium.

When the kiss came to a reluctant and lingering end, Dylan said huskily, "I'll uncork the wine if you'll put the flowers in some water. Deal?"

Elise nodded, then followed Dylan into the kitchen on wobbly legs. She was so giddy for the guy, all he had to do was kiss her and she couldn't walk a straight line! The tuxedo and the roses were a nice touch, too.

"You look beautiful, Elise," Dylan told her as she arranged the flowers in a tall vase.

Elise glanced up, suddenly feeling shy. He'd uncorked the wine and now he was leaning against the counter, his arms crossed over his chest, looking at her—no, *caressing* her—with his eyes. It made her feel warm and wonderful all over.

"You don't look too shabby yourself, McAllister," she returned with a shaky smile. "What's the occasion? You didn't even wear a tux for the bachelor auction."

He pushed off from the counter. "Tonight is a special night, Doc."

Elise's heart went from a thump to a flutter. "Because we're together, right?"

He stood close to her and skimmed his hands up and down her arms. "Right. But there's more to it than that."

"There is? So spill it, McAllister!"

He raised a brow, looking as devilish and sophisticated as Agent 007 himself. "Wait and see. Besides, I'm starved. What have you got to go with the wine, Doc?"

"Now it's your turn to wait and see," Elise informed him. "Entertain the pets while I finish setting the table. Rowena has been trying to get your attention ever since you walked in the door. And George is *dying* to be noticed. He wants you to know how very *pleased* he is to see you!"

Dylan glanced over at George, who was still sitting with his arms stubbornly crossed and his bottom lip thrust out. The sight was admittedly humorous, making Dylan laugh, which made George cross his arms a little tighter and thrust out his lip even farther...if that was possible.

"Just ignore him," Elise advised, so Dylan subdued his laugh to a chuckle and stooped to pet Rowena.

When the food was on the table in the dining room, Elise lit the long, tapered candles that were part of a winter-theme centerpiece, and turned off the lights. "You asked for candlelight, and you got candlelight," she announced.

"Wow," said Dylan, stepping into the room. "You outdid yourself, Doc."

And she had. Elegant china and silverware gleamed on a snowy white tablecloth. Several artistically arranged vegetable dishes and homemade rolls were set out, and there was even a small Cornish hen roasted to a crisp brown for Dylan's nonvegetarian palate to enjoy.

"It's perfect," he praised. "Just perfect." Then he bent to kiss her, but was interrupted by the sound of glass breaking.

"What's that?" he said, his head abruptly rearing up...and away from Elise's waiting lips.

"That's Geraldo," Elise said drily. "Funny how he hasn't done that in ages, but he chooses this moment to demonstrate his unique talent."

And then George decided to make noise. He wasn't getting the hoped-for attention by sulking, so he started banging his spoon on the high chair tray and "hee-heeing" like crazy.

"If we keep him in the chair and give him a Dr Pepper, maybe he'll let us eat dinner in relative peace. For now, I think that would be better than letting him loose," Elise said.

Dylan agreed, and he carried the high chair into the dining room and Elise carried George. Then she tucked him snugly behind the tray and gave him a Dr Pepper. Elise turned off the lights in the kitchen, which put Geraldo to sleep, and Rowena lay down at Dylan's feet after he took his seat at the table.

"Until George returns to his owners, I think this is about the best we're going to get as far as privacy goes," Elise apologized. "I couldn't ask Jan to baby-sit again. This is her only day off, and she wanted to spend it with her husband."

"I'm not complaining," Dylan assured her. "Besides, I'm glad to hear Jan and her husband *want* to be together. It means they have a strong marriage."

They chuckled together. Elise was so relieved that Dylan could tease her about her scheme involving Jan and the fictitious divorce, and that they could both look back on the incident and find it amusing. They'd certainly come a long way since the first day he'd showed up at the clinic to work off his auction pledge. But Elise couldn't resist wondering if this was as far as the relationship would go....

Elise chided herself for getting so serious about Dylan so fast, but she couldn't seem to help herself. She still believed in the fairy tale, and she had the overwhelming feeling that Dylan McAllister was her knight in shining armor...chinks and all.

The only problem was that Dylan didn't believe in fairy tales. He saw unhappy endings on a daily basis. Elise wondered if he could ever believe again in a marriage that went from happy honeymoon to happily ever after.

He was obviously a romantic guy. The fact that he'd dressed up in a tuxedo just to share a quiet dinner and an evening at home with her was proof of that. His intimation that he had something special up his sleeve was probably tickets to the theater or some other plans for an upcoming evening out.

Dylan seemed to enjoy dinner, although he wasn't eating as much as usual. Maybe, like her, he was too wired with desire to have much of an appetite for anything besides a certain someone's lips. But even little love bites seemed out of the question with George keeping a sharp eye on both of them. He'd resorted to mimicking Dylan again, trying to subtly aggravate without being reprimanded for making too much noise and commotion.

Like the good sport he was, Dylan took George's shadow-act in stride and once or twice even did something totally off-the-wall just to watch George's quirky imitation.

"You're so patient, you'd make a great father," Elise said without thinking, then remembered a time when he'd implied that he'd like to have kids but didn't want to have to marry to get them. Suddenly her comment seemed calculated to force their conversation into a serious vein, and she tried to cover her resulting confusion by rushing to clear the dishes.

"Please sit down, Elise," Dylan said, placing his hand over hers. "I'll help you with the dishes later."

"In your tux?" she teased nervously.

"You seem kind of keyed up tonight," he observed kindly. "Am I making you nervous?"

"No," she lied, forcing a laugh.

"Well, I'm nervous as hell," Dylan admitted, surprising Elise with his bluntness. "There's something I want to give you, and it's burning a hole in my pocket."

Elise froze. Had she heard right? Did Dylan say he had something to give her and it was burning a hole in his pocket? And was she nuts to think maybe, *just maybe,* what he had to give her was a...*ring?*

It seemed too good to be true. Fairy tales with happy endings took time. Didn't Sleeping Beauty have to sleep for one hundred years before her prince woke her with a kiss? Dylan McAllister couldn't possibly mean to propose to her after a rocky, one-week romance...could he? It was too soon for him to know he was in love with her...wasn't it? But then, *she* knew, without a doubt, that she was in love with *him.*

"I was going to wait till after George was down for the night, but I'm anxious to see the look on your face."

Bracing herself for the possibility that something really incredible might be about to happen, Elise slowly and carefully sat down again.

"Are you ready?" he asked her.

She swallowed hard. "As I'll ever be."

Dylan smiled and reached into an inside pocket of his tuxedo jacket. What he pulled out was too flat and too wide to be a ring box. But even as disappointment settled around her heart, Elise chided herself for thinking it could have been anything as wonderful as an engagement ring.

"What is it?" Elise wondered aloud, even though she could see it was an envelope.

"Open it," Dylan suggested, handing the envelope

to her with a suddenly serious expression on his handsome face.

But why would he look so serious about ballet tickets or even round-trip air tickets to Hawaii?

Elise opened the business-sized, unmarked envelope and pulled out a folded sheet of paper. She pulled down the top fold and saw the name of her savings and loan at the top.

"What the heck...?" she mumbled.

Then she unfolded the rest of the paper and found that it was a financial statement detailing her latest transactions with the bank. There was last month's loan payment...and then another payment had been made just that day! And the balance of her loan was...*zero!*

Elise stared at Dylan. "I don't understand."

"I paid off your loan," he stated with a shrug.

Elise was flabbergasted...and furious.

"You paid off my loan? Why in the world would you do that?"

Now it was Dylan's turn to look flabbergasted. "I thought it would make you happy," he said.

Elise bit her lip, controlling herself with an effort. George was sitting up straighter, tuned in to the fact that there was tension between the humans. Even Rowena had scrambled to her feet and was watching with a wary eye.

"I'm not like your ex-wife, Dylan McAllister. I expect my debts to be *my* responsibility. I certainly don't expect *you* to pay them off!"

"But I was responsible for this debt, Elise," Dylan objected. "Didn't you go to considerable trouble over the past few days to help me own up to my responsibility and admit that the divorce settlement I got for Ted was unfair?"

Elise's eyes smarted with the beginning of tears. "Yes, but you apologized. And I was satisfied and happy with your apology, Dylan. But now you've just demonstrated that you think of me the same way you think of your ex-wife! You think I care more about the money than the principles involved!"

The raised voices in the dining room woke up Geraldo, and for some reason he launched into his comedy routine. "Aawwk! What looks good on a lawyer?" they heard him squawk. He kept up the babble, and combined with the hoots and squeals George had begun to voice at a crescendo, the racket was getting downright distracting. It definitely wasn't the best background noise when a couple was trying to resolve a difference of opinion!

Dylan rubbed his jaw, obviously greatly perturbed. "How can one little gesture be so misunderstood?"

"This is no *little* gesture, Dylan. This is a *big* gesture. I know you make good money, but you've still got your ex-wife to support. How can you afford this?"

"I have savings."

"You mean you *had* savings. I don't want your hard-earned money. And how did you ever convince the savings and loan to open on a Sunday and allow you—a perfect stranger to me, for all they know—to pay off my loan?"

"I can be pretty persuasive when I want to be—"

"Don't I know it—"

"And when I told them I was planning to marry you, they—"

"What?"

For a moment time seemed to stand still, and a stunned silence filled the room. Sensitive to the moods and actions of the humans, George quit "hooing" and "heeing," and Geraldo quit squawking lawyer jokes. Even Rowena's grunting decreased in volume to the softest of noises. Or maybe they were all still making a racket, but Elise couldn't hear them above the thundering echo of those nine little words...*I told them I was planning to marry you.*

Dylan gave a helpless laugh. His eyes never looked so blue or so full of love as he reached across the table and took hold of Elise's hands. "I certainly didn't plan to propose this way."

Elise had a lump in her throat the size of Memphis, but she managed to squeak out, "To propose?"

"I thought it was too soon, that you'd never believe I could have fallen so completely in love with you in one week. I didn't want to scare you off with an engagement ring, but I had to somehow show you how much I care. I guess paying off the loan was a pretty lame idea, huh?"

"Dylan, I—"

"You're right," he rushed on. "It *was* lame. But when a man is dying to propose marriage and he has to substitute something else, all I could think of was paying off the loan. And now I've got even less to offer you. I've got a good practice, a used BMW and a nice condo in town, but my savings-account balance stands at ten dollars and forty-eight cents!"

"Dylan, I don't care about—"

He shook his head, his eyes gleaming with passion in the candlelight. "I know what you're thinking, Elise. You're wondering what's the use of trying with a man who's already been divorced once...a man who's spent the past several years embroiled in ugly divorce cases...a man who's known for his cynical views on marriage. And who could blame you?"

"But I don't—"

"The thing is, Elise, I don't feel that way anymore. I'm a changed man."

"I know you—"

"And now you're probably thinking, yeah, he's changed but the stats haven't. Two out of three marriages end in divorce. But I'm beginning to believe that while the statistics apply to the general public, there are always exceptions to the rule. And I have this feeling about us, Elise—" he squeezed her hand and leaned closer, his urgency thrilling Elise to her toes "—a good, strong, *warm* feeling. I think we can make it work. I think it can *last*."

He paused then, but Elise was too stunned and happy to try to get a single word in edgewise.

"Elise," he said softly, earnestly. "I love you and I'm asking you to marry me."

George, somehow sensing the ominous significance of all this yammering going on between Elise and the hairless male primate McAllister, dropped his forehead to the high chair tray and was pressing his hands to the back of his skull as if awaiting the final blow.

Rowena, usually so economical in her movements, was nervously twining in and out of the table legs.

Even Geraldo was quietly singing "Camptown Races," as if biding his time, in the other room. All seemed to be waiting for Elise's answer.

She raised a brow. "Is that your closing argument, Counselor McAllister?"

He gave a shy, disarming grin. "Yes. But I could easily think of more arguments to support my case."

"I'm sure you could," she acknowledged, then motioned toward George. "But we don't want to keep the jury up past bedtime."

"I have witnesses, you know," Dylan added irrepressibly. "Even the client you saw me with at Windows on the Square will swear on a stack of Bibles that I'm hopelessly in love with you."

Every time he repeated that lovely phrase *in love with you,* Elise's heart swelled with reciprocal love. But she wasn't done teasing him. Assuming a prim posture, she peered down her nose at him like a schoolmarm.

"Isn't the usual procedure for proposing marriage done with one knee on the ground, McAllister?" she demanded to know.

Delighted by her playfulness, Dylan laughed, then immediately got down on one knee. He spread his arms wide and smiled like a lottery winner. "Like so?"

Elise gave him a royal nod. "Excellent, Counselor," she sniffed. "I have no further questions."

He leaned close, clasping his hands for dramatic effect. "And the verdict is?"

Elise couldn't clown around any longer. She gave Dylan's jacket lapels a yank and pulled him close. He wrapped his arms around her waist, and she wrapped her arms around his neck. They were kissing-close.

"I don't know how it happened so fast, either, Dylan McAllister," Elise whispered. "But I'm in love with you, too. And if you can stand living in a zoo, I'll marry you in a New York minute."

"We don't have to wait till pigs fly, do we?" he whispered back, glancing down at Rowena.

"We'll get her some wings to wear to the wedding," Elise suggested with a soft laugh. "Some of those stiff, frothy things they use for fairy costumes. And George can wear a tux."

"Did you hear that, George?" Dylan couldn't resist throwing over his shoulder at the disgruntled ape. "She said yes. Elise and I are getting married, and you'll be attending the ceremony in your very own monkey suit!"

Not one to take an insult lying down or to lose his best girl to a hairless upstart without a little ranting and raving, George beat his chest and hooted with wild abandon.

Geraldo took his cue by the commotion and squawked another lawyer joke.

Rowena grunted happily and cuddled her snout against Dylan's leg.

Dylan and Elise ignored them all and answered their own call of the wild. They kissed each other with all the steamy heat of the jungle.

FREE VALENTINE'S BROOCH! $9.95 U.S. retail value

This Valentine's Day Harlequin brings you
all the essentials—romance, chocolate
and jewelry—in:

VALENTINE *Delights*

Matchmaking chocolate-shop owner Papa Valentine
dispenses sinful desserts, mouth-watering
chocolates…and advice to the lovelorn, in this
collection of three delightfully romantic stories
by Meryl Sawyer, Kate Hoffmann and Gina Wilkins.

As our special Valentine's Day gift to you, each copy
of *Valentine Delights* will have a beautiful, filigreed,
heart-shaped brooch attached to the cover.

Make this your most delicious Valentine's Day
ever with *Valentine Delights!*

Available in February wherever
Harlequin books are sold.

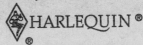

HARLEQUIN ®

Look us up on-line at: http://www.romance.net

VAL97

Weddings by DeWilde

Since the turn of the century the elegant and fashionable
DeWilde stores have helped brides around the world
turn the fantasy of their "Special Day" into reality. But now the
store and three generations of family are torn apart by the
separation of Grace and Jeffrey DeWilde. Family members
face new challenges and loves in this fast-paced, glamorous,
internationally set series. For weddings and romance, glamour
and fun-filled entertainment, enter the world of DeWildes....

Watch for *I DO, AGAIN*, by Jasmine Cresswell
The final installment of Weddings by DeWilde
Coming to you in March, 1997

Grace DeWilde's ambitious cousin, Michael Forrest,
represented everything Julia Dutton emphatically wished to
avoid in a man. Julia had been earmarked "perfect little wife"
material, while Michael's high-voltage sexuality attracted
glamour like moths to a flame. They could barely stand to
be in the same room together. So how was it possible that
one charged evening could make teaching French at the
Kensington Academy for Girls suddenly seem so dismal,
while the chance to assist in developing Michael's new
Berkshire Forrest Hotel loomed as the chance of a lifetime?

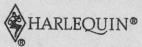

You asked for it....You got it! More MEN!

We're thrilled to bring you another special edition of the wildly popular MORE THAN MEN series.

Like those who have come before him, Mitch Rollins is more than tall, dark and handsome. All of these men have extraordinary powers that make them "more than men." But whether they're able to grant you three wishes or live forever, make no mistake—their greatest, most extraordinary power is that of seduction....

So make a date with Mitch in...

JUST ONE TOUCH
by Mary Anne Wilson

It's a date you'll never forget!

Available in March wherever Harlequin books are sold.

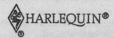

HARLEQUIN®

Don't miss these Harlequin favorites by some of our most distinguished authors!
And now, you can receive a discount by ordering two or more titles!

HT#25645	THREE GROOMS AND A WIFE by JoAnn Ross	$3.25 U.S. $3.75 CAN.	☐
HT#25647	NOT THIS GUY by Glenda Sanders	$3.25 U.S. $3.75 CAN.	☐
HP#11725	THE WRONG KIND OF WIFE by Roberta Leigh	$3.25 U.S. $3.75 CAN.	☐
HP#11755	TIGER EYES by Robyn Donald	$3.25 U.S. $3.75 CAN.	☐
HR#03416	A WIFE IN WAITING by Jessica Steele	$3.25 U.S. $3.75 CAN.	☐
HR#03419	KIT AND THE COWBOY by Rebecca Winters	$3.25 U.S. $3.75 CAN.	☐
HS#70622	KIM & THE COWBOY by Margot Dalton	$3.50 U.S. $3.99 CAN.	☐
HS#70642	MONDAY'S CHILD by Janice Kaiser	$3.75 U.S. $4.25 CAN.	☐
HI#22342	BABY VS. THE BAR by M.J. Rodgers	$3.50 U.S. $3.99 CAN.	☐
HI#22382	SEE ME IN YOUR DREAMS by Patricia Rosemoor	$3.75 U.S. $4.25 CAN.	☐
HAR#16538	KISSED BY THE SEA by Rebecca Flanders	$3.50 U.S. $3.99 CAN.	☐
HAR#16603	MOMMY ON BOARD by Muriel Jensen	$3.50 U.S. $3.99 CAN.	☐
HH#28885	DESERT ROGUE by Erine Yorke	$4.50 U.S. $4.99 CAN.	☐
HH#28911	THE NORMAN'S HEART by Margaret Moore	$4.50 U.S. $4.99 CAN.	☐

(limited quantities available on certain titles)

	AMOUNT	$
DEDUCT:	10% DISCOUNT FOR 2+ BOOKS	$
ADD:	POSTAGE & HANDLING	$
	($1.00 for one book, 50¢ for each additional)	
	APPLICABLE TAXES*	$_____
	TOTAL PAYABLE	$_____
	(check or money order—please do not send cash)	

To order, complete this form and send it, along with a check or money order for the total above, payable to Harlequin Books, to: **In the U.S.:** 3010 Walden Avenue, P.O. Box 9047, Buffalo, NY 14269-9047; **In Canada:** P.O. Box 613, Fort Erie, Ontario, L2A 5X3.

Name: _____

Address: _____ City: _____

State/Prov.: _____ Zip/Postal Code: _____

*New York residents remit applicable sales taxes.
 Canadian residents remit applicable GST and provincial taxes.
 Look us up on-line at: http://www.romance.net

HBACK-JM4